this is
WAR,
baby

K WEBSTER

Books by Author K Webster

THE BREAKING THE RULES SERIES:
Broken (Book 1)
Wrong (Book 2)
Scarred (Book 3)
Mistake (Book 4)
Crushed (Book 5 – a novella)

THE VEGAS ACES SERIES:
Rock Country (Book 1)
Rock Heart (Book 2)
Rock Bottom (Book 3)

THE BECOMING HER SERIES:
Becoming Lady Thomas (Book 1)
Becoming Countess Dumont (Book 2)
Becoming Mrs. Benedict (Book 3)

Alpha & Omega
Omega & Love

STANDALONES
Apartment 2B
Love and Law
Moth to a Flame
Erased
The Road Back to Us
Give Me Yesterday
Running Free
Irrevocably Claimed Anthology with Zeke's Eden
Dirty Ugly Toy

To my hubby.

WAR is worth the PEACE.

Warning:

This is War, Baby is a dark romance. A really dark one. So dark you're going to wish you had a flashlight to see yourself to the end and someone to hold your hand. Human trafficking, dubious consent, and strong sexual themes that could trigger emotional distress are found in this story. This story is NOT for everyone.

It <u>WILL</u> cross lines.

It <u>WILL</u> break the rules.

It <u>WILL</u> make you sick.

And it <u>WILL</u> stress you out.

But…

There is also light.

Once you get past the darkness, you'll find something pure and whole.

Something lovely.

Something happy.

You'll find love.

And it <u>WILL</u> be worth the journey.

"They're in love. Fuck the war."
~Thomas Pynchon, *Gravity's Rainbow*

PART ONE:

Imprisonment

PROLOGUE
Baylee

Three days before...

"L OWER."

His slurp echoes in my bedroom and I tense up. Our eyes meet for a brief second before his tongue starts to lap at me again. My friend Audrey says when a guy eats you out, it's *the most amazing thing on the planet.* Yet as Brandon flicks his tongue everywhere except the part of me that seems on fire with need, I can't help but wonder if she was lying. She's always been one to embellish the truth. And right now, as my body tenses with the urge to explode, I never quite reach the climax I'm after. Audrey most certainly fibbed about this little detail.

Brandon grunts and his gentle thumbs stroke the insides of my thighs as he tastes me. The maneuver itself is sweet and one I have come to expect from my boyfriend of a year and a half. However, just once, I'd like for him to dig his fingers into my legs. To suck my clit that he seems to be dancing around.

1

To force his way into me and break the barrier I'd gladly give to him if he'd take rather than ask.

I chew on my lip and ponder my bizarre thoughts rather than focus on the pleasure that seems to be slipping farther and farther away.

What would Dad do if he were to come in here and find Brandon between my legs? I stifle a giggle. He'd yank him away from me by his hair and drag him out of the house most likely—probably landing a punch or two on his handsome face before he sent him on his way. My amusement dies though when I think about him explaining what happened to *her*.

My mother.

Her pale lips would fall into the slightest of frowns and her blonde brows would pinch together. She'd become shaky and weaker than she already is with worry. That very thought sobers me up completely.

"Mmm," Brandon grunts from below, dragging me back to the task at hand.

I skim my gaze over his spiked brown hair and his bare shoulders. He didn't quite develop into the hot boy he is now until the summer before our senior year. Six months into the school year and I still catch myself grinning. I didn't expect to be in a serious relationship with the best-looking guy in school. But I'm certainly not complaining.

Well…

Maybe I am a little.

He's a great kisser and an attentive boyfriend.

But I crave for him to possess my body in a carnal way that matches the blazing of my heart—to bruise my flesh as his fingers dig into me while he takes me in such a way that suggests his body needs mine for life.

"I love you." His murmured breath against my clit jolts me and I wish he'd do it again. We're both learning here but I hope he learns a little bit faster.

"I love you too. Don't stop."

With newfound fury, he increases the speed at which he circles my sensitive flesh. So close and yet still so far away. I'd like to grab onto that spiky hair and hold him right where I want him. The thought sends a thrill quivering down my spine.

I hear a car door slam and my thoughts immediately go to my dad's best friend, Gabe. He's lived next door to us for nearly ten years now and they've been inseparable ever since. Images of his dark mop of hair that sometimes hides his brown eyes—eyes that seem to always twinkle with delight when he sees me—flood my mind. Lately, I think about him a lot.

Way too much.

When Dad's stressed about Mom's illness, he and Gabe spend hours drinking beer and whispering stuff I'm not privy to hearing. In a way, I'm glad Dad has someone to confide in. I just wish I could curl up between them like I used to before I grew boobs and started wearing makeup. Once I hit puberty, the way I used to climb all over him like he was my favorite tree ended as quickly as it'd started. Gabe now seems agitated every time I'm near him.

His dark eyes will flick over my body briefly, and with a flash of something that makes my belly ache, but he always moves them someplace else and affixes me with his annoyed glare instead. The disdain in his eyes only intensifies if Brandon is around. If looks could kill, I'd fear for Brandon's life.

It was as if he flipped a switch one day and didn't like me anymore.

I may be young but I'm not stupid.

I know, deep down, there's more than what is on the surface with Gabe.

That he wants me.

Brandon hits a spot that has me jolting upright. So close. So damn close. If he'd go back and spend a little more time there, I might find this elusive orgasm. I lean back and rest on my elbows so I can watch him. I'm beginning to lose faith in his abilities once again when something by the open window catches my eye.

A dark shadow.

Brandon swipes his hot tongue back over my clit and I buck as if I'm a live wire jolting with electricity. *More, Brandon. More…*

I close my eyes, hoping to leap over that blissful edge. My brain betrays the one before me though as thoughts of another man flood my mind—a man with messy hair and coffee-colored eyes.

A *man*.

Not a boy like Brandon.

"Oh God," I whimper and bite my lip, attempting to force images of my sexy boyfriend back to the forefront of my mind. "I feel close."

Brandon's tongue goes wild and I squirm against him. I want his tongue to own me. I want him to stick his fingers inside of me and probe where nobody but me has ever been before. I'm ready for so much more than what we've had—for the innocence of our relationship to die a quick death.

A creak of the floorboard in my bedroom has me jerking

4

my eyes open. I expect to see Dad—to meet the furious glare of my father. But I don't.

Instead, it's something a thousand times more terrifying.

And I nearly come despite the alarm that renders me immobile.

I'm a sick girl.

A tall man, dressed completely in black, donning a ski mask holds a finger to his lips as he sneaks up behind Brandon. Terror seizes me and I'm unable to move a muscle. I want to scream. I want to scramble away. I want to know what the hell is going on. But I can't do anything but stare.

His dark eyes through the mask stay on mine as he prowls closer. Of course Brandon chooses that exact moment to hit the right spot. Spots darken my vision and I'm on the cusp of something euphoric.

But my dream is threading with a nightmare.

This darkness fits but it is also wrong and dirty. This can't be real—this can't be happening.

I'm confused, but the moment he grabs on to my boyfriend's hair and yanks him away from me, reality splashes me out of my lusty daze. I find my voice and I scream.

Everything seems to slow down and I'm rooted with my butt on the quilt Nana made for me when I was twelve. Brandon attempts to swing at the man but he's too slow—too young—too innocent.

Crack!

The man's fist connects with Brandon's nose and the sickening crunch has me dry heaving.

"Dad!"

Brandon crumples to the floor as blood gushes from his face. I need to help him. No, I need to get away. Fear releases its clutch on me and I scramble on the bed toward the door. I'm close when a powerful arm hooks around my middle and yanks me back.

His hand slaps over my mouth and my naked body heaves in his clutches. I attempt to wriggle from his unyielding grasp but he's too strong.

"Did you come?" he hisses against my head and frees my mouth.

The room blurs with my tears and I freeze. I know this voice.

"Gabe?"

"It was a yes or no answer, little girl. You have three seconds to answer the fucking question before I slit that pussy's throat."

His threat nauseates me and a sob catches in my throat. *Where's Dad?!*

"Three."

My voice. Why won't it work? Please, God. Help me!

"Two."

No! No! No!

"One. Times up." He reaches behind him and then brings around a huge knife out in front of me. A knife like that would kill Brandon.

"N-N-No!"

A throaty grunt vibrates through my back. If I had to guess, I'd say he is pleased by my answer. And by the way his erection presses into my back, I'd say excited too.

"Good answer," he mutters. "Now, say goodbye to your bedroom and your pussy-ass boyfriend. You'll never see them again."

His hand covers my mouth before I have a chance to belt

out the scream that is now lodged in my throat. Surely this is some sort of joke. A plan for Dad to make sure I don't ever try to sneak around with Brandon under his roof.

Yes, that must be it.

All a game.

"Sorry, sweetheart, but this is going to hurt."

That's the only warning I receive before he cracks me over the head with a blunt object—probably the butt of his knife. Darkness steals over me, and the last thing I catch a glimpse of is Brandon's bloody, unmoving body. *You'll never see them again.* I can't handle the reality of that concept and the thought shoves me into oblivion.

I | Baylee

MY HEAD THROBS.

Thump. Thump. Thump.

Where am I?

What day is it?

I'm aching and disoriented and cold. But that isn't what has me terrified. It isn't that I haven't eaten. Nor is it that I also haven't slept. No. What's terrifying is that I haven't seen anything but complete black in what must be days.

Anger bubbles in my chest at having been stolen by my neighbor. I can't prove it but I know his voice. He took me right from my bedroom. Dad never came. Brandon was badly hurt. And I haven't a clue as to where I am.

I think I hear a thud above me and I try to still my racing heart. Why would Gabe take me to lock me away in some dungeon and let me die? It makes absolutely no sense.

Another thud. Several of them. My heart flares to life and I hope maybe the cops have come for me. That my dad is leading a pack of angry policemen dead set on rescuing me. Seventeen is too young to die. I had plans—plans that involved going to med school. Plans that I'd hoped involved marrying Brandon and having a bunch of babies. We're in love. God, I hope he's okay.

A sharp pain seizes my stomach and I whimper. I want to scream at him to feed me something—*anything*—but I've already tried that. The screams have fallen on deaf ears. Screaming doesn't get me food—screaming gets me a hoarse, dry throat. My cracked lips are the most apparent signs of my dehydration. The throat though, is awful. No matter how many times I attempt to conjure up spit to wet my throat, the most I can come up with is a small, thick ball of phlegm which only serves to nauseate me when I swallow it.

"Help." The croak belongs to me but it's nothing more than a whisper.

I've been all over this space, feeling my way through the dark, but have found nothing to be down here. Not one single damn thing. I've deemed one corner my bathroom. My bodily excretions are what decorate that corner now, not that there's much, since I'm slowly dying from a lack of nutrients.

"Please." This time, my voice is louder but it will never penetrate these concrete walls. Reaching out, I once again finger the walls searching for a way out. How does a room not have windows or doors? How did he get me inside of this tomb?

Something skitters over my hand and I shriek. Must have been a spider. The normal girly-girl I was not long ago would have hidden in the pee corner to escape. This scared prisoner I've become though is hungry. I wonder if I could eat the spider. It would be disgusting but could provide protein.

Or poison.

Once again, I feel defeated. My luck, I'd gobble up that nasty spider only to die from the venom it carries. And then my dad would find my decomposed body hours too late or something.

He'd lose Mom and me both.

A scratchy sob pierces the air and I attempt to drum up tears. Nothing. I cry tearlessly for a minute and then swallow down the emotion. Mom was sick but she seemed hopeful. A liver could come at any time, she'd said. Dad, however, wasn't convinced. He researched. He reached out. He facebooked the world. All in an effort to save the love of his life.

But time is running out.

For the both of us.

I should have told her how much I'd loved her before bed. Instead, I was too worried about hopefully taking that final leap with Brandon that would have sealed our relationship. Sex. I'd made him wait but I was ready. And now...

God, I am so stupid.

I'm not sure exactly how long I've been down here, but it's taking a toll on my sanity. Screamed until I was hoarse and voiceless. Cried until my stomach muscles were sore and aching. Spent unthinkable amounts of time fingering every crack and crevice in the darkness in an effort to find an escape route. Imagined every scenario about Brandon's fate, none of them good. At one point, I even tried to count as high as I possibly could—I was well over six thousand when I got bored and gave up.

I've been here forever.

Hours or days or months—my mind is on a black, endless terrifying reel.

I'm in an eternal, dark hell.

With nobody to talk to.

With no food or water or bathroom.

With nothing but the blackness and insanity slowly seeping through the cracks of my soul to keep me company.

A sliver of blinding light slices across the dusty floor in front of me and I stare at it with squinty eyes in shock.

"Gabe. Please." A tiny whispered plea.

I want to scream and cry and beg.

But I'm cold and tired. I'm disoriented and stressed. I just want to go home.

The slice of light becomes a distinct yellow square suspended about twelve feet above the ground. I blink several times in attempt to shield my sensitive eyes to the bright light. A silhouette—broad shoulders and wild hair—takes up most of the square, protecting me from the offensive light.

"How you doing down there, kiddo? Still alive and kickin'?" His deep voice is a gravelly rumble which used to excite me. Now, it scares the living crap out of me.

"I want to go home," I tell him in a firm tone, despite the wobble in my voice.

He chuckles though it is a humorless sound. Dark, evil, hellish…yes. Out of humor, absolutely not. Who is this man who I've known for the past decade? I've watched him with other women, flirtatious and desirable. I've heard him whisper dirty, sexual promises to girlfriends over the years and would even grow jealous of the attention he showered them with. I mean, I've fantasized about his strong, capable hands roaming all over me as he kissed me for crying out loud. And all this time, beneath the jokes and friendly façade was a demon from hell waiting in the shadows for the perfect opportunity to take what wasn't his.

"Baylee, baby, I told you already," he says in a menacing tone dry of any wit, "you're not going anywhere."

This time, the tears do come. Small, hot tears streak down my cheeks and drip from my jaw. "Why?"

If he doesn't plan on letting me escape, he at least owes me an explanation.

"Are you hungry?"

His blatant disregard for my question irritates me and I hobble over to the light that shines beneath him. My dirty, naked flesh is exposed but I want him to see me. I want him to see the little girl he was supposed to look after. The little girl he took for his own depraved reasons.

"Why are you doing this to me?"

I can't make out his features but I can tell he's annoyed with me. His tell—a frustrated hand running through his messy hair—rats him out. Hair that I know has a few streaks of grey at his temple. Hair that I used to dream about running my own fingers through.

"Sometimes, sweetheart, you have to make sacrifices. You, doll, are a sacrifice. Your part is small, but it is so significant."

His riddles confuse me.

"I want to go home, Gabe. Please, I won't tell anyone. I swear it," I vow. And it's the truth. If he were to let me go, I'd take the secret to my grave. If that meant regaining my freedom, I'd make that promise to him.

"Baylee, you're not going to tell anyone because there won't be anyone to tell. You've been initiated into a new world—a world you're not prepared to handle. Not even close."

I shiver and cross my arms over my chest. It should embarrass me that he sees me naked but I don't care about being modest. I care about getting the heck out of here.

"What do you want from me?" I demand with a nasty bite to my voice. I'm tired of being weak and begging. I want to go home.

"Ahhh, there's the feisty girl I know," he says, almost as if he's relieved. "If I let you out, promise not to run?"

No.

"Yes."

He laughs again and I decide I hate his laugh. "I don't believe you."

I shrug my shoulders and glare at him. "I've never given you any reason not to trust me." Unlike you, you bastard.

He nods finally. "Fine. I'm going to take your word. But what happens if you betray me?"

You've already betrayed me.

"I won't," I lie.

"You're right," he snaps. "You won't. Because if you do, I'll whip your ass with a stick from the yard for every step you manage to take away from me."

The hairs on my arms rise in alarm and my heart takes off like a hundred horses thundering away from me. "I won't run."

"Good. I want to clean you up and feed you. You're mine to take care of for now." He nods and then disappears.

I'm afraid he won't come back but a few moments later, he drops something into my prison. A rope.

"Climb," he instructs, voice cold and uncaring.

I shudder and wobble over to where it hangs before me. Sometimes in PE we climb ropes but not after having been starved for several days. The only reason I'm standing is because I'm running on pure adrenaline at this point. I reach for the thick rope and clutch it. It's rough in my hands and a sad realization comes over me. I'll never be able to climb this thing.

"Climb!"

I jump and reach higher on the rope. My attempt to hoist myself up ends up with me spinning wildly out of control, only managing to further nauseate my empty stomach. Dropping my feet to the dirt, I cry out. "I can't! It's too hard!"

"You have three minutes to get your ass up here or you'll die down there. You'll rot because you were too much of a fucking baby to climb up the damn rope. If you want to survive, Baylee, you're going to have to fight for it. Fucking fight for it!"

Tears blur the horrible world around me but rage blooms inside of me. I grab hold of the rope and try again.

Over and over again.

Sometimes I get a few feet up only to fall and land on my butt on the cold, hard ground. Other times, I slide down the rope and not only rub the skin from my palms but the inside of my thighs as well. It seems like forever but he finally barks out words that send me once again plummeting to my hell.

"Time's up. Nice knowing you, sweetheart. I thought you were stronger but clearly I overestimated your strength."

The door slams down and the light is gone.

My hope—my light in the darkness is vanished.

With a wail of defeat, I curl up on the chilled floor and close my eyes. I hope death is easy on me. I hope he's swift and steals me in my sleep. And I hope Mom finds me soon—wherever we end up on the other side.

Goodbye, world.

Goodbye, Baylee.

Aches. All over. Especially in my head and my belly. Groaning, I crack open my eyes.

Darkness.

Again.

How long was it since he closed me off this time?

Five minutes? Five hours? Five days?

I sit up and something touches my shoulder. A shriek escapes me before I realize it's only the rope. It still hangs from the ceiling. My heart thuds to life as I wonder if without the pressure of his stupid time limit, maybe I could make it.

But I can barely pull my weakened body to a sitting position. How would I ever be able to climb that thing?

I have to, though.

I don't want to die down here.

Standing on shaky legs, I clutch onto the rope. It takes several tries, but I soon figure out that if I twist the rope around my leg as I climb, I can keep myself from sliding back down. My biceps scream in pain and I suck in gasps of air as I slowly inch myself up. When I'm finally near the top, I push the ceiling expecting resistance. But it moves. It moves!

I'm so excited that I nearly lose my grip and crash back onto the dirty cement floor below. At this height, I'd surely break a leg or an arm. Falling is not an option.

I slide an arm through the gap. The room is no longer lit and is dark, but moonlight shines from somewhere which means a window is nearby. Windows mean freedom. With newfound determination, I manage to lift the slat up and get my elbow onto the wood floors around the hole. Now that escape is within reach, I'm no longer weak and I find the strength to get my other elbow up. When I get my knee onto the surface, I nearly cry out in joy.

Almost there.

Now that my eyes have adjusted, I see that I'm in a kitchen. I slowly drag my body out of the hole and across the floor. And once I'm completely out and there are a few feet separating me from the opening, I cry. Silent, all-body wracking sobs.

So close.

A door is nearby and I can escape.

Climbing to my feet, I attempt to keep the shaking in my legs to a minimum. Each step is slow and painful but I'll be free soon. Just a few more. My fingers clutch the cold metal and I twist.

Free.

At last.

I smile for the first time in days.

Until the fire licks at my ass.

One. Two. Three. Four.

I've barely made sense of the pain when the strong arm is back around my waist pinning me against him. Searing hot pain brands my butt cheeks, and my moment of hope is replaced with fear. What is happening?

"I told you. For every step you tried to escape, I'd whip you. And you made it four steps before I caught you. Does it hurt, Baylee?" His masculine scent which used to warm and comfort me—even turned me on, later—infiltrates my pores. Now it only turns my stomach sour.

"Fuck you, Gabe," I snarl.

His hand slides up over my breast and pinches my nipple brutally. "I most certainly intend on fucking you, my brave, sweet girl," he says with a gravelly rumble. "But first, we're going to punish you for that naughty mouth."

I can't do this.

I should have died down there in that hole.

It seems preferable than to be in the steely clutches of this nightmare.

"Time to learn this new world of yours, sweetheart."

A shudder wracks through me as his thumb runs over my nipple, this time almost reverently. My flesh raises at his gentle touch and I nearly vomit.

"I like 'em dirty. And you're as dirty as they come. Soon, you'll be just as dirty on the inside," he murmurs against the shell of my ear, sending goosebumps over my flesh. "You'll like it too. In fact, you'll love it. One day you will thank me."

I will never thank him.

Ever.

II | Gabe

SWEET BAYLEE.

So innocent and pure.

It was almost too late. That fucker had nearly ruined her.

But she's mine to ruin. Every inch of her pale, dirty flesh. All mine. I've waited for so long. So fucking long. And now I have an excuse.

This past summer was the worst. Fucking agony.

Watching her bounce around in her tiny shorts and tight tank tops was painful. So goddamned torturous that I'd nearly yanked her out of that public pool one day and taken her long ago.

But the timing wasn't right.

Things weren't yet in place.

In my world, timing is everything. The early bird may catch the worm. But it's the patient bird who wins the dirt and all the worms in it.

Baylee is the most coveted worm of all.

So alive and free. Sexy yet unknowing of her allure to every man on this earth, aside from her father.

She was meant to be mine.

And she will be.

The girl isn't ready yet, but I will teach her.

Drag her through hell and then hold her on the other side. Nurse her soul back to health and heal all the broken parts of her. I'll be the sun and moon in her world. All thoughts will revert back to me. Always.

The training will be brutal. For her.

For me, it will be decadent perfection.

I will own every inch of her inside and out. I'll fuck her into oblivion. I will be the very thing she craves.

My plan will mean that I will lose her for a bit but when it all settles, I'll claim her again. She'll belong to me and nobody will say a fucking word. Her father will thank me. Her mother will hug me. Her boyfriend will hate me.

And she will love me.

III | Baylee

I KICK MY LEGS OUT IN AN ATTEMPT TO MAKE A CONNECTION with anything that will keep me from going back down into that hole. The house is so sparse though, definitely not the house he owns next door to my own. There's no furniture in the kitchen. Only wood planks stand between me and that black hell.

Gabe is a thousand times stronger than me, especially in my weakened state, and I'm nothing against his grip around me.

"Save your energy, sweetheart. You'll need it."

His warning chills my bones and I fall limp in his arms. At this point, the darkness is preferable to having him touch me and threaten me.

"Good girl."

This is the point where I give up. Whatever will be will be. I'm no match against a forty-one-year-old man. My father was someone I had always counted on to protect me because he was big and strong and fearless. Gabe kind of fell into the same category.

Until he stole me.

Then he became the villain in this story.

If Dad only knew his best friend betrayed him in the worst possible way, he'd kill him with his bare hands. I saw the way Dad pummeled a guy once. He'd gotten several licks in on him before the cops showed up. Some guy rear-ended us and my father exploded in fury. *"You could have killed my wife!"* She was already dying though. My mother and I screeched and cried while my dad punched that poor man relentlessly.

He defended us—*defended her*—with such a furious passion that the world trembled beneath his feet. My dad wasn't someone people messed with. At six foot five, he towered over most men, including Gabe. It wasn't the height that frightened people though. Something in my dad's eyes flickered with a barely contained rage. Even as a child, I sensed that he was brooding about something. That anger ebbed and flowed beneath the surface. Not at me or my mom. Not at Gabe. At the world. The world was always trying to cheat him and take from him. Life was unfair…and Dad hated that fact.

If he knew Gabe had taken me, he'd kill him. No doubt in my mind. Even though Dad loved Gabe like a brother, he didn't look at him like he looked at me.

I'm his only daughter.

His whole world.

The girl who looks like his wife but has his height, although not quite as tall, and his tenacity.

He would rip out Gabe's heart and serve it to me and Mom for supper.

A crazed giggle escapes me and Gabe freezes. "What's so

funny?"

"Nothing," I say and then cackle. "I hope I come back and haunt you until Dad kills you."

His annoyed grunt satisfies me until he speaks. "You passed your first test. You're not going to die now. The worst part is over. It's time to train."

Train?

My mind fades to grey as I ponder what he means. In school, I train for track. I run miles and miles without getting winded. The high jump is my thing. Effortlessly, I flop over that bar as if it's the easiest thing to do in the world. I lift weights and eat right so Coach doesn't give me crap.

That's what training means to me.

But something tells me that Gabe isn't training me to run a marathon. Something tells me he's training me for something dark and sinister.

I'm so lost in my thoughts that I barely register being carried into a bedroom. The walls are made of wood and I realize we're in a log cabin. The floors, the ceiling, the walls, and even the bed are made of the wood that is now permeating my senses.

We're probably deep in the woods.

Nobody will ever hear me scream.

It's me against him.

"Are you sleepy, little one?"

For a moment his voice bears concern, and is familiar. Like the Gabe from before. The man I'd depended on to help me push my car when I'd run out of gas on the way to the mall when Dad was still caught up at work. The man who had playfully threatened my boyfriend not to harm a hair on my head or there'd be hell to pay. The man who had hugged me tight when my dog Molly got run over by a car and passed away.

Exhaustion overwhelms me and I sag in his arms. I'm so tired. So very, very tired.

"We'll talk in the morning," he whispers, almost sweetly, into my ear as he guides me over to the bed. "Over breakfast."

I burst into tears and he calms me with strokes on my grimy skin that should repulse me. But they don't. I want to close my eyes and pretend this didn't happen. I want to pretend he's here to save me.

"I'm scared," I choke out.

He yanks the covers back on the bed in the room and climbs in with me. It's only now that I realize he's wearing jeans but no shirt. My skin reacts and a cold sweat breaks out over me. I'm terrified, and yet, I want him to comfort me. I want him to promise me that this is all a bad dream and I'll wake in the morning in my own bed.

He drags the covers up over us and for the first time in days, I'm warm. Gabe is a monster and yet I'm twisting in his arms to get closer—to get warmer. My arm wraps around his middle and I bury my face into his bare chest.

"Shhh," he murmurs against my hair and then kisses me. "I have you now. You're mine, Baylee. All mine. Rest now and let me watch over you."

His words are enough to calm me and exhaustion steals me away.

After the hell I've endured over the past few days, this is heaven.

The devil is my savior.

Bacon.

My stomach grumbles and I come to. Blinking my eyes slowly, I take in the wooden walls that surround me in this sparse room. Where am I?

I'm in hell. I remember now.

The heavenly scent of breakfast wafting through the cabin, though, is enough to push away my worries and I focus on regaining my energy first. Every muscle in my body screams in agony. I'm not sure if I'll even be able to walk. The thought is alarming.

I have to try though. Maybe we're near people. If I can get out the front door and run to the street, I could flag down a car. Someone could rescue me.

"I told you. For every step you tried to escape, I'd whip you. And you made it four steps before I caught you. Does it hurt, Baylee?"

What if it's a hundred steps to the road before he catches me? I shudder at the idea of him whipping me raw. My backside is still tender from last night. When I go to move my hand to finger the spot—to see if he broke the skin—panic threatens to drown me.

I'm tied up.

I'm tied up.

Holy crap, I'm tied up.

A tug of my legs indicates that my ankles are bound and strung to each post at the end of the bed. My wrists are secured together and rest on my belly under the blanket that's been pulled to my chin. I try to sit up but I have no strength left.

"Help!"

Something clatters in the kitchen. I hear normal sounds that one would expect to hear as someone cooked breakfast. And that is what terrifies me even more. Gabe is carrying on as if this is normal—as if this is okay.

It is absolutely not okay.

"Help!"

Heavy footsteps thunder down the hallway toward me and tears stream out of the corner of my eyes. I'm afraid. I want my dad. I want Brandon. I want someone who could help me.

"Good morning, sweetheart."

If I weren't tied up—if I were here under my own desires—I'd be in awe of the sight. The devil, disguised as an angel, stands in the doorway resembling a combination of both beauty and evil. His dark hair is still wet as if he's recently showered and he's once again shirtless. The man, despite being in his forties, still works out and has an impressive physique. His shoulders are broad and thick while his toned torso tapers down into a narrower waist. Dark jeans hang low on his hips and dark hair disappears into them. If things were different, I'd almost say he was hot.

But I'm his prisoner, not his lover.

So despite his body being hot, it's his eyes that are cold. Coffee-colored eyes are narrowed at me and his chiseled jaw is moving in a furious manner, reminding me of my dad when he gets angry.

"Time for breakfast," he grunts and storms toward me. He's carrying a plate and has a water bottle tucked under his arm. I'm upset and scared, but all I can think about is downing that water.

He sits beside me and I squirm away from him. My bindings don't allow for much wiggle room so the heat of his body envelops me.

"Why are you doing this? Is it sex? You want me for sex?" I demand with tears in my eyes.

He sets the plate down on the bedside table and opens the water bottle. I expect him to unscrew the cap, which he does, and give me a swallow, which he doesn't. Instead, he brings it to his full lips and takes a small sip.

"Mmm, cold."

I sniffle and choke back a sob. He probably wants me to cry and beg. Well, he doesn't deserve that.

"Want a drink, Baylee?"

With a frustrated sigh, I bite my chapped lip and nod. "Please."

He flashes me a pleased grin that roils my stomach. "Good girl."

I'm angry and want to swat the bottle out of his hands, but I'm not stupid. I need to be somewhat compliant if I have any hope of leaving this place. He shoves some pillows behind me to prop me up which makes the blanket slip down to my stomach baring my breasts to him. The man who's always hidden his desire for me, blatantly eyes my breasts before sliding his eyes to mine.

Hunger.

I'm not the only one.

The flash of unbridled lust in his eyes tells me that he has plans for me—plans he's probably wanted to execute for quite some time.

"Drink."

I open my mouth and graciously accept the cold liquid. A tiny moan escapes me as I suck down the water with greed.

"That's enough, Baylee. You'll throw up if you drink too much. Why don't you have a try at eating something?" His saccharine tone sickens me and I glare at him.

"I'm thirsty."

"And you'll get more. You have to slow down though."

With an unconvinced nod, I jerk my gaze over to the plate on the table. A few scrambled eggs, a couple of sliced strawberries, and an unbuttered piece of toast.

"Where's the bacon?" I pout.

He chuckles and I cringe. I hate the sound. *Hate* his laugh. "Oh, baby, you're not getting bacon for a few days. One step at a time here."

"You act like you've done this before." My haughty tone wipes the smile off his face. Good.

"Several times, actually. But never have I enjoyed it so much." He winks and I frown.

Several times? What happened to the rest of the girls?

"Can you untie me?"

His lips draw up into a wolfish grin that frightens me down to the fabric of my being. "Baylee, I would love to untie you. And after training, as long as you're a good girl, not only will I untie you, but I'll let you shower as well. Would you like that?"

The deception in his words is thick.

"I don't believe you."

He shrugs and holds a piece of toast to my lips. "Not like you really have a choice though. If I were you, I'd take a chance and see what happens. Comply and you will be re-

27

warded—that is my promise to you."

I take a bite and chew the dry toast. I'd prefer to suck down that entire bottle of water but I'm trying to behave.

"Good girl."

My belly aches from the food and I squirm in the bed. He's gone from the room and left me here. I wonder if he'll come back and make good on his promise. But with his return will be the training he's referring to. I'm not sure I'm ready for that.

Dishes clang together in the kitchen as he cleans up and I grow annoyed. The dishes can wait. I wish he'd come back, do what he plans on doing, and then let me shower.

What will he do?

The most obvious conclusion would be that he wants to have sex with me. Audrey told me that it hurts the first time but not too bad. Surely I can handle him inside of me. I was prepared to let Brandon make love to me. This is something I can do—something I have to do.

"You ready?" His deep voice from the doorway jerks my attention to him. He stands there holding a large bowl of water with a rag hanging over the side.

I nod and attempt not to shrink away from him when he sits beside me. The bowl gets placed on the bedside table and I strain to watch his every move.

"Are you going to hurt me?" The wobble in my voice gives away my fear and I hate myself for it. "Please don't hurt me."

His smile is gentle, comforting even. "Sweetheart, I'm not

going to hurt you today."

A lump of fear forms in my throat and I desperately try to swallow it down. *I'm not going to hurt you today.* But tomorrow? Or the next? My heart begins galloping at his words.

"Please tell me why you took me, Gabe."

He frowns. "I'll tell you what the plan is. How about that? Will that satisfy your curiosity?"

"Yes."

"I will. Right after training and your shower. I promise."

He soaks the rag in the water and then wrings it out before bringing it over to my dirty body. The rag is warm and I gasp when he begins to sponge bathe me. His movement is reverent, almost fatherly in nature, and bile rises in my throat.

I don't want him to touch me.

Or clean me.

Or even look at me.

He takes his time, washing my breasts first, and then cleans my face, neck, armpits, and stomach. As he gets lower, I attempt to drag my spread legs back together but they're immovable because of the rope.

"I have to wash that bastard from your sweet pussy. This wasn't his to take," he murmurs, an angry glint in his eye.

He pushes the blanket down to my knees and stares between my legs. Then, he draws the rag down and cleans me. All over the outer lips of my sex, he scrubs gently but in a determined fashion. It's not sexual and it doesn't turn me on. In fact, it repulses me. I want him gone from there. The rag is returned to the bowl and he squeezes the water from it once again. This time, when he goes back between my legs, I gasp in horror. He's cleaning my butt—the hole to be exact.

"Stop," I beg.

But he doesn't stop. He carefully cleanses my body one inch at a time. Thankfully, he returns the rag back to the water and disappears with the bowl. A chill from the air skitters over my flesh and goosebumps erupt all over my skin. When his footsteps thud back toward me, I tense up.

"Ready?" he questions from the doorway.

Tears well in my eyes and he blurs before me. I quickly blink them away so I can see him. I don't want him out of my sight.

"Please don't…"

He frowns. "Your pleas will fall on deaf ears. I can gag you, though, if you'd prefer. Up to you. But keep begging and I'll become annoyed. You don't want me annoyed, Baylee. You want to please me. Trust me."

I start to cry but I don't dare utter a word. He seems satisfied and drags the blanket the rest of the way from me, depositing it on the floor behind him.

"You're so perfect," he coos and runs a finger up my shin toward my thigh. "You have much to learn, so we're going to need to get started. Two weeks will come and go pretty quickly."

Two weeks?

And then what?

His finger trails lazily up my inner thigh and I cringe when he drags it along my sex. I can't do this.

"Most men don't like hair there. Soon, I'll reward you with a razor and you can clean this up." He tugs at the hair on my pubic bone and I cry out. "Shhh, remember what I said about the begging. I could gag you with the rag I cleaned your ass with. Would you like that?"

I shake my head in vehemence. "No." *Please don't* is on

30

the tip of my tongue but he'd probably gag me for that.

"Okay then. I can see this will go well." His eyes become predatory as he drags his finger down my slit and pushes between my lips, connecting with my clit. He doesn't move, simply stares at me. "Did Brandon know how to touch you, Baylee? Did he ever bring you to orgasm?"

"N-No."

My chest feels as if it will rip apart and free my exploding heart at any moment.

"That's because he's a boy. You've never had a man with my experience draw pleasure from you."

A wobble from my bottom lip is my only sign of weakness. Of course he sees it and grins.

"See, I could get you off with just this finger," he tells me in a smug tone. "All I'd have to do is press and massage and circle right here." As he says *here*, I grow dizzy when stars dance around me. Despite my feeling afraid and betrayed, my body reacts. It embarrasses me and a shameful crimson heats my skin.

"Your skin is telling me you like this and I'm so glad. I want to prove to you my experience over his. That night, when I came for you, I could see the bored look in your eyes. I can assure you, when I'm between your legs, you'll only be thinking about me."

I swallow and close my eyes. Maybe I can pretend I'm someplace else. For a moment pretend it's Brandon instead, so I can endure the punishment he's about to unleash. The bed squeaks and I ignore it, clenching my eyes tighter.

I can do this.

Think of spiky brown hair.

Think of the sweet smile of my high school boyfriend.

Think about anything other than the—

"Oh!" I screech and yank my eyes open against my will.

Gabe raises a smug brow at me as his thick, wide tongue plows between my lips, dragging pleasure in its wake. His thumbs dig brutally into my thighs and I yelp. I don't want to watch him but I'm snared in his stare.

So hungry.

So primal.

So evil.

One hand leaves my thigh and he pushes a finger into my body. It's uncomfortable but not unpleasant. And with the way he's licking and sucking in all the spots Brandon couldn't find just days ago, I'm starting to lose my hold on sanity. It's hard to be upset and afraid when my body is being overwhelmed with such unimaginable sensations.

Concentrate, Baylee! He's a monster!

My breath stills in my throat as he curves his finger inside of me. He's probing parts of me that haven't been ever touched. It frightens me but my stupid body is rocking against him—betraying me. Again.

His teeth press down on my clit and I shriek in fear. But he doesn't hurt me. It's like he knows exactly what feels good and soon my fight begins to weaken. My thoughts are jumbled. All I can focus on is the way he tastes me. The slurping, ravenous noises that come from him. How his hot breath tickles me. And the way his fingers own the inside of me.

My thoughts dull as sensations take over. I'm no longer able to grasp on to the rational part of my head because all I can think about is the way my body has come alive.

A strange feeling takes hold inside me, an awareness that is as basic and simplistic as male and female, night and day, predator and prey. Yes, I am terrified. But there is also this undercurrent of something else. Something larger. *Lust?* Maybe. I have fantasized about this guy, dreamed about him touching me. I have hungered for his eyes on my naked skin. Imagined his mouth on my breasts. And now, here he is, *touching me.* And it is nothing like I had imagined.

It's too much.

Yet, it's not enough.

There's more, I can feel it.

Another nibble on my clit has me shrieking out in pleasure. This seems to excite him because he growls against my wet body and I shudder in response. My body stretches as he inserts another finger. So full with him. So overwhelmed by him. Even his manly scent has overpowered the earlier bacon aroma and taken root in my lungs.

I'm completely at his mercy.

Cast under his evil spell.

His spit and juices from my body are running down the clean crack of my butt and I want to be embarrassed. I want to squirm away from him. But, right now, I can't. My body is selfish for this moment after so many days of horror. The pleasure is as addicting as the water I greedily consumed.

I need this.

I need this to survive.

"Oh God," I mewl. "Oh God."

And then it happens.

One more hard suck of my clit seems to rip me open. An unearthly moan pours from me as my nerve endings come alive. I can feel them all at once, everywhere, and they seize me. Each and every one of them takes hold of me, clenching in ecstasy. My head throbs in unison with my wild heart and

I nearly black out from desire.

It's overwhelming.

But for some sick reason, my body responds as if it needs this pleasure for nourishment, despite the horrified and disgusted thoughts running through my mind.

As my body shudders, it starts to leave as quickly as it arrived. His tongue still works me but he's slowed as if he knows this orgasm of mine is fleeting and it won't last forever. Tears stream down from eyes as I come to a nauseating realization.

He's going to give me more of these.

And I want them.

I want them so bad.

What the hell kind of person does that make me?

IV | Baylee

H E SITS UP ON HIS KNEES BETWEEN MY LEGS AND SMIRKS. "I knew you'd love that." With his fingers still inside of me, I feel as though I'm his accomplice in an act against myself. For a few brief moments, I joined his side and allowed him to carry out an agenda against me.

"I hated it," I lie. It's not truth either though. I'm conflicted and confused. A war rages inside of me between mind and body.

His face glistens from juices that came from my body and embarrassment once again washes over me.

"Don't lie, sweetheart. I've known you for a long time and can tell when you're doing it. I have plenty more to show you. Some of which you will love—other stuff you won't admit you love. But as long as you're with me, you'll feel only pleasure."

"You're a rapist pig!" I snap. I'm furious with myself for succumbing so easily to him.

He glares at me before launching himself on top of me. I scream and squirm but he crushes me with his weight. His mouth hovers over mine. My scent is all over him and I want to throw up.

"I haven't raped you," he snarls. "When I do take you, you'll beg for it. You'll *want* my thick cock inside of your tight cunt. Do you understand me, sweetheart?"

His erection presses through his jeans against my still wet sex.

"I'll never want you," I hiss and spit at him.

He grunts, makes a crude point of licking the spit from his face, and then begins brutally bucking against me. At first it hurts and I start sobbing again, but soon the build begins to burn in my pelvis. "You think you don't want this, but you do. Look at you. You can barely suppress your need for it."

Thrust. Thrust. Thrust.

I squirm and move but it only intensifies the sensation.

"I could pull out my dick and push it inside you. Is that what you want? To feel me deep inside of you, baby?"

I shake my head but close my eyes when he lowers his mouth onto mine. His kiss is possessive and I'm powerless against it. Poor Brandon kisses me sweetly and his skin is soft. Gabe kisses me with promise. Promise to take and possess. It only serves to madden and conflict me further. My body shouldn't respond so easily. It should recognize the wrongness of his actions and side with my mind.

But it doesn't.

His lips suck on mine. His thick tongue dances with mine. The shadow of dark hair that is growing on his face scratches my skin raw in a delightful way.

I'm going to orgasm again.

I can feel it.

His hardness rubs between the lips of my pussy and I gasp

out in pleasure, acting out against the furious storm brewing in my head. My body wants this. The way he grinds against me is painful yet addicting, like the bliss of heroin surging through your veins after a hit. In your head, you know it's wrong. You know eventually it will kill you. And yet…your body craves it anyway. Against all rational reasoning.

I'm depraved.

"Stop," I breathe.

He deepens the kiss that tastes like me before pulling away. "I'm not going to fuck you right now, but I need to feel you."

His hand slides between us and he fumbles with his jeans. Soon, his erection slides up over my clit and I cry out.

"Oh God!"

A satisfied grunt escapes him before his mouth takes me again. I'm dizzy and lost in him. And the way his smooth, large cock slides against me is the most blissful sensation in the world. I'm wet and I wish—*I actually freaking wish*—he'd push it into me.

He's right.

Gabe won't have to rape me. I'll beg for it. I'm so stupid and—

"Shit!" I curse against his lips. This time, my orgasm seizes me for longer. I flutter my eyes closed and live in the moment. I try my hardest to draw it out for longer. And yet, like before, it's gone within seconds. As I come down from my high, wet heat spurts between us. I startle and my wild eyes meet his hooded ones that no longer seem frightening.

I've satisfied the devil, subdued him into a sleepy state.

"That was so fucking perfect, Baylee," he says, his fingers brushing my lips. "I knew you'd be the right girl for this. Soon, you'll hang on my every word. You'll beg for the orgasms that make you crazy. Your world will revolve only around me."

Terror, the elusive emotion, starts to make a reappearance. Not because I'm afraid of him, but because I think he's right. He knows my body better than I do and he's already proven how he can use it against me.

"I want my shower now." The nasty bite in my voice shocks him—and I don't miss the brief flash of hurt in his eyes—before he climbs off of me.

"Very well. You deserve one after that."

And you deserve to go to hell.

The shower was heaven. I scrubbed his cum from my stomach until I was raw and sore. With the hot shower I was permitted to take alone, I was able to find clarity. To find my way back to reality.

He stole me.

He is a monster.

And I'll do well to remember that.

Once I turn off the water, I peek out of the shower to inspect the window. Maybe I could climb out and run. But then my eyes meet his bored, dark ones and I shudder.

"Thinking of running away?" His gaze travels over to the window. "It would be unwise of you."

I swallow and snatch the towel. Drying off behind the shower curtain, away from his leering eyes, I attempt to compose myself. I need to be smart about this. Once the towel is secured around my body, I tug the curtain away. He's smiling now and I'm once again afraid.

"No."

He frowns but doesn't probe me any further. "Come on, I want to show you something."

I climb out of the shower and follow after him. He hasn't told me to drop the towel and I hold on to it as if it will shield my weak body from his expert touch. We make our way back into the bedroom. The bed has now been made with clean new sheets. A folded blanket sits at the end.

"Sit," he says and points to the bed.

I walk over and drop down to the soft bed. He strides over to a closet and yanks out a box. After he sets it on the floor, he rifles through what looks like photographs and pulls out a few. Once he's done, he makes his way over to me and sits close enough that our thighs touch.

"This is Sandy."

I gape in horror. A woman, probably in her early twenties, stares back at the camera devoid of emotion. She's naked and sprawled out on the bed like I was not even an hour ago. Panic ripples through me but I can't look away. Her hair is dark, a stark contrast to my long blonde locks, and her eyes are green unlike my blue ones. But she's dirty—as if she spent three days in a hole. Like me.

"This is sick, Gabe. You're sick."

He shrugs. "Yeah, I know." The next picture he shows me causes my breath to catch. Her mouth is on his erection. Empty eyes look up at him. It hurts to see this pic. She's gone. Whoever she was before is gone. Is this his plan for me?

"What happened to her?"

He wraps an arm around me and despite the fact that he's the monster, I lean into his comforting hug. "She belongs to another man now to do as he pleases. I sold her."

The world freezes at his words. *I sold her. I sold her. I sold her.*

"I-I-I don't understand."

He chuckles and I squirm away from him. His fingers bite into my bicep while he keeps me against him. "Of course not, sweetheart. Unlike these women, you're innocent."

"Are you going to sell me?"

He sighs and my heart crushes. "Yes, I am."

The reality hits me hard, knocking the air out of me. A wave of nausea clenches the pit of my stomach and pushes bile into my throat. The threat of vomiting is imminent. "B-B-But what about Mom and Dad? Gabe, you can't do this to me!"

The pictures flutter to the floor and he grabs my jaw in a brutal grip. He drags my face to meet his. "You don't have a choice in the matter. We only have two weeks. So if you want to be prepared for that world, I need you to pay attention to your training."

"No, I can't—"

"You'd sell for more being a virgin and all. And believe me, I have thought about it. But I'm greedy, and if anyone takes that from you, it will be me. Besides, I love you too much to send you to the wolves with no armor. I'm going to teach you, Baylee. I'll do fucking awful things to you so that when those monsters get their greedy hands on you, you'll be prepared. When they fuck you and hurt you, you can stare at them like Sandy did. With emotionless eyes. In all honesty here, I'm your savior. You should be thanking me."

Rage explodes from me. His matter of fact stare makes me want to claw his eyeballs out.

"Fuck you, Gabe!"

He shoves me back onto the bed and pins me before I can even think about moving. "Why thank you, sweetheart," he snarls, "I certainly will. I'll fuck every hole in your body until you bleed. And then I'll make you beg me for more. Is that what you want?"

Tears roll down the side of my face and I shake my head.

"Well, too bad. That part, I'm afraid, must occur because if I don't do it, they will. Can you imagine what it would feel like to get raped in the ass by some fat, bastard when you've never even been touched there? He would rip you apart. You would bleed out, baby. I'm going to teach you to enjoy sex— all the dark and dirty parts of it. So when they do take you, you'll like it. Your body will respond and you'll survive."

His words slide over me like oil and I gag. I can't do this. Images of terrifying men hurting me and touching me and fucking me is too much to bear. Gabe's wrong. I won't survive this. I don't belong here. I belong in my own bed worrying over simpler matters like school or my mother's health. Not in the clutches of monsters wondering if I'll live or die.

"I want to go home." My words are nothing but a whisper.

His lips draw up into a wolfish grin and his eyes darken. "You're never going back there, baby. Suck it up and accept your fate."

I will never accept this.

Ever.

"Do I need to tie you up this time?"

The deep voice drags me from my mental vacation. I'd slipped into some hopeless pit of despair—something reminiscent of the hole in his kitchen which now seems oddly safer than this bed.

I can't do this.

I'd rather die.

"Please."

"Please what? Tie you up? Give you more orgasms?"

I shudder at his words. "Let me go."

His harsh laugh startles me. "You're not going anywhere. You will stay with me for two weeks. Then we're going to San Diego where I'll sell you to the highest bidder. The better you behave—*the more you let me prepare you*—the higher the odds are that you'll get sold to someone wealthy. Perhaps someone who will care for you. You'll be… kept. Believe me when I say you don't want to get sold to some of those bottom feeders. They buy a lot which means, their slaves don't last long."

I stare blankly at him. *Slaves.* This is my life now.

"They die, sweetheart. Those bastards hurt and eventually kill them. I'd be fucking furious if they hurt what's mine." His tone is fierce and protective which confuses me.

"Why can't you keep me then?" My question is honest. If I have to be stuck in this world, I'd rather be here with him than some stranger, who could be far more evil than Gabe.

He raises his gaze to meet mine and shrugs. "I need the money," he says in a gruff, dismissive tone. "Ready for more?"

My mind is numb. This isn't reality. This is a nightmare. "Don't hurt me, Gabe."

He flashes me a crooked grin. "Baby, I'm going to hurt you, but you'll like it."

A shiver runs down my spine but I meet his stare with defiance. "Fine. Let's do this. Train me to be a fuck doll."

The scowl on his face is immediate and I realize my words struck a nerve. Good. A realization begins to course through me. He must not want to sell me. He's every bit the greedy bastard he confessed to being, and if he could, he'd keep me. I need to make sure that happens. Maybe if I meant something to him—something more than money—he would change his mind. He would lower his guard for me, and I could attempt escape.

He tugs the towel away from me and proceeds to undress. My eyes skim over his ridged frame and I freeze at seeing his erection. It's huge. His two fingers felt like an invasion—that thing will feel like it's impaling me.

"Did you ever suck Brandon's puny pecker?" he questions in a mocking tone.

I bristle and shake my head. "I relieved him with my hand. And he… he touched me some. We haven't really done much."

"And why do you think that is?"

I don't understand the meaning behind his question. "I don't know. Maybe because I'm seventeen," I sneer.

He laughs—the asshole laughs at me. "Cut the crap, sweetheart. I've been to every single one of your birthday parties since I moved in next door. You'll be eighteen in a couple of months. In the grand scheme of things, that doesn't matter. I want to know why you haven't let pussy boy fuck you yet."

"Because he hasn't tried." My honest words feel like a betrayal to both myself and my sweet boyfriend.

He crawls into the bed beside me and his fingers draw

lazy circles on my stomach. "But you wanted him to?"

I let out a ragged, teary sigh. "Yes."

"Why?"

"What do you mean why?" I demand.

He smiles and the way his eyebrows quirk up, it reminds me of the look he gave me when he was between my legs. It causes my pelvis to ache and I hate myself for it.

"I mean, Baylee, why did you want him to? Was it 'love?'"

"Yes." I swallow but avoid his gaze by staring out the window where the midday sun pours in. "And because I wanted to know what it felt like."

His hand slides up over my breast, along my throat, to where he firmly clutches my jaw and drags my gaze back to him.

"Do you want to know how many times I thought about climbing into your window and fucking you on your bed?" His dark eyes narrow at me and his pupils dilate, as if he's getting off on the simple memory of his fantasy. With a flick of his tongue, he licks his lips and then growls. "Every single night since last summer. You taunted me in those tight clothes you always wore. I'm not fucking stupid, baby. I saw the way you watched me. How you'd bend over and give me a peek at that sweet ass. How you'd bounce around the house in a tight camisole with no bra on, with your tits on full display. You were playing games you had no business playing."

I gape at him. "I didn't ask for this!"

"No, but you wanted it."

"Not like this."

His grin stretches wide and reveals his perfectly white teeth which I'm sure will tear me to pieces one day. "But you admit you wanted me. Well, little girl, you have me. And I'm going to own every part of you until our time together is up."

So smug. So sure.

My instincts tell me to obey, but I want to rattle him and shake the very foundation his world is constructed upon.

"If you talk this much during sex, I'm guessing it will be a total snooze fest," I taunt with a snotty bite in my voice. He takes the bait and snaps at me.

"Playing games will get you hurt."

"So hurt me."

I smile in satisfaction at him. Screw you, asshole.

But my confidence dissipates the moment he slaps me. It was the fleshy part of his palm but it still stings.

"Ouch!"

He roars with laughter. "If that hurt, then we have a lot of work to do. Those men will devour you, baby. They'll tear apart your flesh and bruise every part of you. You have to toughen up if you want to survive."

His mouth lowers to my collarbone and he begins kissing me softly. It almost reminds me of how Brandon would kiss me. I wonder if he's okay. I'm sure half of California is looking for me by this point. Dad will have torn apart our entire neighborhood. And with Gabe missing too, he'll be an instant suspect. I've seen the crime shows Dad watches. It won't take long for the police to assume Gabe took me and then look into his past. They'll search his phone records, discover property he owns or rents. And they will find me.

It's only a matter of time.

His tongue darts over my raised nipple and it hardens at his touch. Then he bites down. Searing pain rips through me, but before I can push him away, his tongue is back to massaging me. My heart rate is thumping along and can't decide if it's from fear or from yearning.

This can't be happening. Not to me.

He's once again doing all the things I seem to be power-less against. His mouth trails down my stomach and I gasp when he dips it into my belly button. My breathing becomes broken, heavy. My fingers crave to sink into his hair. Or rip it out.

"Get on your hands and knees."

I want to cry, I want to scream, I want to do anything but what he demands of me. He rolls away from me and heads back to his closet.

"Now, Baylee."

I scramble to do as I'm told and stare at the headboard. I've stumbled upon some shows on cable late at night. They never show anything but sometimes the man takes the wom-an from behind. In the movies, they seem to enjoy it. I try to convince myself that I can do this.

The bed sinks behind me and his warm hand grips my ass cheek. "This ass is fucking beautiful."

All too soon I realize, this is unlike anything I ever saw on late night television. Something cold and wet drags across my puckered hole. I instinctively buck, fighting the inevita-ble. Jerking my head over my shoulder, I'm horrified to see him teasing me with some metal thing. "What's that?"

He grins and winks. "It's a butt plug. Don't worry, it's small. We'll work up to something larger."

I'm already scrambling away when his fingers dig into my hips and he yanks me back to him. "Don't move, baby, or this *will* hurt." He begins pushing the ice-cold object into me.

"Please no."

"Relax and let me or I'll force it. Fucking understand?"

I whimper and nod. This is not a part of me that is meant to be seen. It's a part of me that *I* have never seen. I realize my fear stems in equal parts from deafening embarrassment at being touched in such a secret place, combined with the pain involved in being penetrated there. Closing my eyes, I attempt to conjure up images of Brandon. But all I can think about is *him*.

Gabe.

His dark, lust-filled eyes devouring me.

His unruly hair when it forms a veil over those evil eyes.

His full lips and hot mouth as it brings me pleasure, just as quickly as it spouts off words that bring me pain.

I jerk harshly and scream in pain at the intrusion, but he holds me steady. It's my inclination to clench in self-preservation but that only seems to make it worse. Eventually, I attempt to relax and it slides in.

It's foreign and unwanted and it doesn't belong there.

"It looks so pretty in your ass. From here on out, you wear this all of the time until you need to shit or when I'm ready to fuck you there."

I shudder and collapse onto the bed in defeat. It doesn't really hurt now but it's uncomfortable.

"Your mom told me you recently had the birth control shot. Is that right?"

I'm horrified at his words. "What? Why would she tell you that?"

"Let's just say I expressed my concern over the probability that Brandon was fucking you. I was making sure she knew the possibility of pregnancy was there. Turns out, she'd already taken care of it."

Technically Dad did. He'd carted me up to the female

doctor and saw to it that I was examined. Of course he waited outside the examination room but afterwards, he informed the doctor of my decision to get the shot. Teens are irresponsible and forget to take pills, he'd told them. Such a personal matter and now Gabe has brought it up so callously. It's humiliating.

"I hate you."

He rolls me over onto my back and the plug jostles me from the inside. "And I love you, baby. Let me show you. Your first time should be perfect."

I start to cry again but his mouth finds my neck and soon he's sucking in that evil, erotic way that he seems to do so well. He kisses away my tears. Gently. His hands roam my body and I don't even try to fight him off. When his hand slips past my pubic bone and connects with my sensitive clit, I buck against him. I must have clenched my ass because an odd sensation throbs from inside of me. It isn't unpleasant either.

"Your first time will hurt but only a little. Then, you'll want me all of the time, Baylee. As much as you want to eat and drink, you'll want me inside your pretty little cunt."

I whimper as he increases the pressure between my legs. He draws me closer and closer with each movement. I hate him. I absolutely hate him. Yet…

"Do you want me inside of you? Do you want to come all over my cock as I stretch you wide?"

His dirty words only seem to make me crazy for just that. Yes.

"No."

"Don't lie, sweetheart."

The pleasure is so close. I want it, just like he said I would.

Before I can stop myself, I beg. "Please."

"Please what?"

"I…" I trail off, unable to find the words.

"You want my thick cock inside of you?" he says. His words taunt me.

An embarrassed mewl croaks from me. "Yes."

The tip of his erection pokes at my opening and I squirm. I should want to push him away and take off running. But I don't. A sick part of me is curious and eager.

"I want your eyes on mine when I take you. Hear me, baby?"

I nod as tears leak out. "Okay."

His mouth seizes mine for a moment and his kiss is ravenous—for one split second, he kisses me like a man would kiss the love of his life. His tongue ventures gently into my mouth. He moans ever so slightly, a sound I've never heard from him before. It's all consuming and it helps me. It helps me cope with the reality of the situation.

I can do this.

"Look at me."

My eyes fly to his and they flicker with excitement. I also don't miss the adoring way he inspects me. That will be his weakness in the end. At least I hope it will be.

"I'm going to make love to you this first time, okay?"

A choked sob escapes me. "Thank you."

He grabs his cock and holds it steady. Our eyes stay glued together as he begins to press inside. At first, it's uncomfortable like when he put his fingers inside of me. But the farther he drives into me, the more painful it becomes. Without warning, he slams fully into me.

White hot pain explodes from within me and I scream.

His mouth covers mine to quiet me but I'm losing my mind. He's too big. It feels like I'm being split open.

"Stop!"

He doesn't stop though and he plows into me over and over again. It feels like he's using that wicked knife of his instead of his cock. I'm cursing his very existence when his hand slides back between us. He continues his relentless pounding but now his fingers are on my clit again.

A few days ago, I was a normal virgin teenager who obsessed over her boyfriend and worried about getting into a good college. Now...

Now I'm some *thing* for this man to use and abuse.

Except now, instead of feeling sorry for myself, I'm gasping as he touches my clit that he's so easily mastered. The way he drove into me hurt at first but now it's dulling to a stinging sensation as another orgasm delightfully teases me.

He brings me to bliss and the only thing that exists is him.

Exactly like he promised.

I'm messed up—just as sick as he is.

"Oh God!"

His low, guttural grunt is the only precursor to his own orgasm. Shortly after, his cock seems to grow impossibly larger as he spurts heat inside of me. The warmth of it seeps out and stings my sore sex.

"I love you, Baylee. Say it back."

A sob catches in my throat as he dips to kiss me. With him still inside of me, it feels like we've somehow become one person. Like I am nothing more than an extension of him now. The thought terrifies me. I don't want to be a part of him.

But now…

Now he's a part of me.

"I love you too, Gabe." The lie on my tongue is just that, a lie. But dread washes over me as I wonder if it will one day become truth.

V | Gabe

SHE'S MORE THAN PERFECT. SHE'S ALL MINE. FOR NOW.

I didn't have to steal her virginity—she begged me to take it. And oh how fucking tight she was. I knew she'd be worth it...worth the wait. It was like we were meant to be. She would have been tight simply from being a virgin, but that coupled with the butt plug secured inside of her, it was like fucking bliss wrapped around my dick.

I can't stop thinking about that first time.

I say first time because I've fucked her over and over again for days now. Each time she gets braver. Says dirty things that still sound innocent coming from her lips. She claws at me and bites back. It's hot as fuck.

And she loves me.

This complicates things but it doesn't change the plan.

The plan is to sell her in less than a week.

I need the money.

But once I get it, I'll get her back. Baylee may be a pawn but eventually I will take back what belongs to me. And she does. Boy fucking does she. Never have I had a woman who complies so easily to my commands. Never have I ever had a woman who comes so easily from my touch.

She's no longer a girl. I stole that innocence away when I broke through her the first time. Now, she's completely woman.

A whimper from the other room startles me from my thoughts. The glow from my laptop is the only thing lighting up the living room. She has nightmares and I'm not delusional to think they aren't about me. Soon enough, she'll get past those. After this is all over, I'm bringing her back here and claiming her as my wife. She'll bear my children and life will go fucking on.

Another whimper.

I read through the e-mail again about the WCT or White Collar Trade location information. A wealthy San Diego real estate agent allows for the WCT to hold their monthly trades under the guise of a business convention. It's a black tie affair and the theme this month is "Innocent Flower." For Sandy and Brianna and Callie and the others, it would have been laughable. Those women were anything but fucking innocent. The dirty things they promised to do would scare the shit out of Baylee.

But my sweet girl, she'll steal the show. I might've stolen her virginity but innocence still radiates from her pores. I'll dress her up in a demure, white gown and affix gardenias to her silky hair.

Purity and sweetness.

Joy.

Secret love.

That flower is perfect and will draw the eyes of the richest men in the room. Most fucks will choose calla lilies or daisies but my Baylee is special and unique.

She whimpers again and I groan. Quickly, I place an order at the flower shop online so I can make sure they'll have what I need before closing my laptop to go to her. In her sleep, she's managed to kick off the covers and her perky tits point up toward the ceiling. I've been gentle with her until now. The occasional bite or bruising have adorned her pure flesh but I haven't hurt her like I promised.

I needed for her to get comfortable with sex first.

And boy is she comfortable. Earlier today, her wild blue eyes found mine and blazed with curiosity when I told her to ride my cock. Despite being unsure, she did. She was quite a vision with her head tossed back in pleasure.

I fell more in love with her in that moment.

But now, as the moon blankets her pale flesh through the window, I crave to prepare her. Those fuckers will hurt her. There's no stopping them. But I can ready her for the pain. And when it's all over, I'll bring her back to me so I can kiss away all of it.

"Baby, wake up," I whisper as I shed my clothes and walk over to her. "It's time to train."

Her eyes flutter open and she gazes at me as if I'm her whole fucking world. It causes an uncharacteristic ache in my chest but I push it away. I want the look gone because I'm about to destroy the pedestal she has built for me.

"Take your butt plug out."

VI | Baylee

I SQUINT AT HIM IN CONFUSION. HE NEVER LETS ME TAKE IT out—when I need to go to the bathroom, he removes it for me. I've grown used to the way it feels inside and I'm almost worried to remove it on my own.

"I'm afraid to do it myself."

My admission seems to excite him. "Pretend you're taking a shit," he sneers.

I gape at him. "What? Why are you being mean?"

His eyes take on that bored stare that infuriates me. The past few days I've stupidly lulled myself into an irrational state of safety. I've allowed myself to slip into his trap and assumed he was really falling for me. Enough so, that he'd forget his whole idea of selling me.

"I'm not being mean. You have more training. Take it out now or I'll dump you back into the cellar."

I study his face for a moment longer and realize he's not kidding. Fear clutches at my heart but I sit up on my knees and spread them apart.

"Good girl. Push it out. Your body will know what to do."

Closing my eyes, I attempt to focus on relaxing and soon, I can sense that it is almost out. As soon as it drops to the bed, I gasp in relief.

He grunts his approval. "You have a three second head start, little girl."

I scrunch my brows together in confusion. "What? But you said—"

"I know what I said. Consider this permission. I'm going to count to three and then I'm coming for you."

We hold each other's stare for half a second longer.

"Run!"

His barked order jerks me to life and I scramble from the bed.

"One!"

I've been outside of the bedroom but never outside of the house. I'm not sure where he wants me to run but I make a beeline for the front door.

"Two!"

Crap! I fumble with the lock and jerk the door open. Tonight, the February air is beyond freezing and my body wants to shut down the moment a cool wind swallows me.

"Three!" he shouts from within the house. "Ready or not, here I come!"

My feet make purchase on the wood porch and I run. The steps, I easily hop down, and then tear off across the grass. Having been fed and hydrated over the past few days, my strength is up. I don't have much time to take in my surroundings but I do notice we're completely surrounded by woods like I'd determined.

I head for the thickest part of the woods hoping I can

lose him in the trees. A normal girl my age might fear being greeted with bears and coyotes. Not me, I fear for what Gabe will do when he catches me.

When.

We both know it's going to happen.

Neither of us are dressed, and running naked through the woods makes no sense, but here we are. Having not run in nearly a week, my chest aches and my calves burn with each long leap toward the trees. I can run through the grass easily, but I know once I hit that brush in the forest, my feet are going to hate me.

Why is he doing this to me?

I'd foolishly allowed myself to get caught up in the way he'd owned my body. Had allowed myself to be possessed by him. In those moments, my body had no longer been made up of skin and bones. I'd no longer held a conscience, the ability to think, tell right from wrong. No. My body had been reduced to a pool of want. It had wanted what it wanted and it didn't care how it got it. That's how good Gabe made it feel. Now, I'm worried there is hell to pay.

A thumping behind me that is quickly closing in lights a fire beneath me. I can't let him catch me. Finding my inner fury, I power through the edge of the trees and ignore the bite of a stick as it stabs my heel.

Don't stop!

I slow, only so I don't break my ankle, and try to dodge a fallen tree and brush.

"Sixty-seven, sixty-eight, sixty-nine, seventy!"

Why is he counting?

The realization literally has me screeching to a halt. *No.*

"Good girl," he snarls before he tackles me into the earth.

Something stabs at my belly and I cry out in pain.

"Y-Y-You told me to run," I stammer as I fight to catch my breath. His naked body presses against mine and he grinds against me.

"I know."

Anger explodes from me. "This isn't fair! Please don't whip me! You told me to run!"

"I also told you not to beg. Such a naughty girl. Let's get your punishment out of the way for disobeying me and then you can reap your reward for listening to me."

He knew I'd fail either way. I was going to receive punishment one way or another.

"I hate you!"

His dark chuckle echoes through the woods followed by the snap of a twig. "Hold still and keep your hands out in front of you. The less you move, the less it'll hurt."

He slides off of me and digs a knee into my back which further causes the stick beneath me to stab me. The skin is broken but it doesn't hurt—not like what he's about to do to me.

Crack!

A howl more carnal than anything crawling in the thickest part of the trees rips from me. Before he can deliver the next blow, I claw at the dirt to no avail in a desperate attempt to get away from the searing pain that surges from where he brutalizes me.

Crack!

The world spins when the next hit is delivered. Licks of fire spread across the flesh of my ass and I'm helpless to douse the pain.

Crack!

The relentless, never-ending swats after that begin to blur into a burning roar of searing agony.

"Stop! Please!" I scream into the woods. There's no moving. He's too strong and in a position where he has an advantage over me, pinning me in place. The next swat is ruthless and my skin feels like it is ripping apart. "Help!" I've never known pain like this. Never dreamed that this level of pain was possible. My hands itch to reach back and rub the sting away, almost involuntarily, but I fight to hold them in place.

"Nobody," he grunts, "can hear you."

Crack! Crack! Crack!

"I'll stop if you beg me to."

Another game. He wants me beg but he's told me before not to. I try to go someplace else in my mind. I remember earlier tonight when he put his tongue not only on me but inside of me. It was slick and firm which drove me crazy. I loved it.

"Beg!"

"No!"

Crack! Crack! Crack!

How many has it been ten? Twenty?

"Your ass is bloody. Beg me to stop!"

"No!"

He grunts and whips me hard until he slows. I may have seventy licks coming my way but I hope and pray he doesn't have the strength to carry them out. Wait him out. Endure the pain and lick your wounds later, Baylee.

Crack!

This hit hurts so much that I black out.

I'm sucked into the cold, dark reprieve and I gladly fall into it.

One comforting person is forefront in my mind.

Brandon. Brandon. Brandon.

"Hey."

I smiled when my boyfriend crawled into my bed and stroked my cheek with a chilled hand.

"You okay?"

Nodding, I fluttered my eyes closed and accepted a soft kiss. "It's not me I'm worried about."

He sighed and pushed a strand of hair out of my eyes. "I know, baby. Is there anything I can do?"

I let out a dark, humorless laugh. "Sure, can you find a liver for my mother?"

"You know I would if I could."

And it's true. If he wouldn't die from it, Brandon's the type of guy who would offer his own if it meant he could save someone.

"Mom is my world. If I lose her..." The words died in my throat and I choked on a sob. "I couldn't handle it."

His lips found mine again and I took comfort in them. He darted his tongue out that tasted of cinnamon gum into my mouth and kissed me with promise.

Promise to be by my side no matter the outcome.

Promise to love me through the good times and the bad.

Promise to hold me when I can't hold it together.

"Baylee..."

"Baylee!"

I'm jerked awake—*away from my safe haven*—and thrust into my painful present. I try to take stock of my injuries but there are too many to count. My mind begs to black out again and return to a comforting memory.

"Fuck," he snarls, his labored breath the only sound

around us. "I can't hit you fifty more times. I don't want to hurt you anymore, baby. I need to be inside of you."

The pain from him pressing into my back is gone as he yanks my legs apart. From behind, he enters my sex and groans. "How are you even wet? You fucking liked it."

His accusation sickens me. I don't know how I could be wet because I hated what he did to me. "I-I-I'm c-cold. It h-h-hurts." The tearstains on my cheeks have chilled and my teeth chatter noisily. There's no way I can take anymore punishment from him. My body is shutting down and I pray for the dark reprieve I was granted only moments ago.

He pulls all the way out and I expect him to slam back into me like he occasionally does.

"This is going to hurt a lot worse."

His cock pushes against my asshole and I wail in agony. With each movement as he breaches the tight ring of muscles, tears stream down my face. He's much too big—far larger than the butt plug. I claw at the earth to try once again to drag myself away from him.

"If you want me to make it feel good then I want you to fucking beg for it. Convince me that you want me balls deep in your tight little ass."

I'm sobbing but I give up on trying to play his insane game better than him. In a game where only he knows the rules, I'm helpless in finding a strategy to win.

"P-P-Please, make it feel good. D-Don't hurt me."

Instead of going slow, he drives deep into me, nearly splitting me in two. Fire rages inside of me as I wonder how I'll ever adjust to his size. My grip on the earth below me weakens as I give up against his brutalization. I can't live like this. I can't take this. I'm crying harder than I ever have in my life. The pain is unbearable. And the fear that more might follow is worse.

"Get ready to come so hard you'll lose your goddamned mind, sweetheart."

I struggle against him but he somehow manages to get his fingers between me and the ground. I'm sobbing in agony when his touch finds my clit.

"Gabe, please!"

The pain, at first, overshadows his attempts to pleasure me. But the bastard soon touches me in an expert way that has me craving for it. Anything to drive away the throbbing in and on my ass. I focus on the way he massages me, becoming almost delirious with the need to come.

My terrified pleas quickly turn into needy moans. I'm freezing and dirty and hurt and yet I'm squirming for that desired orgasm he seems to never fail in giving me. With each swirl of his fingers, he drives me closer to the edge.

"That's it baby," he grunts, "push past the pain. If I gave it to you gentle, you wouldn't be ready for some asshole later. Tonight, I'm that asshole. Find the pleasure, beautiful."

His words coupled with his skillful fingers send me crashing hard.

"Ahh!" I screech as the most intense orgasm to date crushes through me. With him in my ass, I find myself clenching around him with my climax but it thrusts me right into another type of pleasure—one that resonates in another part of my body where he fills me.

My body thrashes with the intensity and doesn't stop. The clitoral and internal vaginal orgasms are intense but this one seems to devour my soul with ecstasy. I hate it but I love it. It's too much and yet blissfully completes me.

"Yes," he groans and empties himself into me. I should be horrified at the feeling of having his cum pour out of my ass and down my thighs but I'm not. I'm cold and numb and quickly coming down from the high he gave me. Pain begins to resurface and I start crying hysterically. He's gentle when he slides out of me and I'm grateful. I should hate him but all I can do is thank him for not hurting me worse.

"Come here, my love. Let's get you back to the house before you freeze."

He scoops my dirty, shuddering body from the ground and pulls me against him. I cry into his neck and snuggle against him for warmth.

"Shhh, baby. I'm going to take care of you now."

I want to scream at him for hurting me but all I can do is pray for warmth and sleep. Soon. The trip back to the house is short and by the time we make it back inside the warm cabin, I'm in shock. I think.

"Can you stand?" His voice is sweet and concerned. It melts me like butter. I cling to his loving nature.

"I don't think so. I can't stop shaking and it hurts."

He sighs and kisses my forehead before setting me on the toilet. The cold lid soothes my sore butt and I try to control my tears. Gabe seems larger than life in this small bathroom. He's every bit a ferocious lion and I'm his caged little bird that he wants to eat. I shiver at the realistic comparison.

The bath begins to fill with hot water. I crave to climb inside and dip below the surface. To hide from the fierce animal that screwed me in the woods as if we were just that—animals.

"Oh, baby, you hurt yourself. You're bleeding."

My tears have stopped falling and my eyes find his. I can't

63

speak so I just stare at him. His brows furrow, almost angrily, as he kneels before me.

"Baylee, I can't lose you now. You're strong and a survivor, remember? I was so proud of you out there. You accepted your punishment like a champ."

I don't bristle. I don't flinch. I don't frown.

I stare.

"Snap out of it, sweetheart. Let's get you bathed and then I'll stitch your wound up. Then I'll hold you in our warm bed, okay?"

Our warm bed.

Seems like heaven.

A small whimper escapes me and my eyes tear up again.

"There she is. Come on beautiful," he says as he helps me to my feet. "I'm going to spoil you."

I want him to fix it.

I want him to stroke my hair until I fall asleep.

I want him to hold me while I dream terrifying dreams of him.

While he's the monster in and out of reality, he's also the slayer of those demons. Somehow, he protects me from himself. It confuses me. I hate him.

No, I don't hate him.

My eyes flick over to the mirror and I gape in shock. The blonde hair I used to straighten and spend hours on before school is now a wild, ratty mess. Dark circles hang below my eyes. Scratches litter my neck and chest from the fall in the woods. Blood trickles from my pouty lips and I frown.

I look terrible.

My eyes raise to the dark ones that seem to stare a hole through me.

"You're the most beautiful thing I've ever seen in my life, Baylee. I want to live inside of you—your body and your mind. You affect some carnal part of myself that I never knew existed. With you," he says and waves his hand in the air, "this is all different. Powerful and meaningful. You're the one."

I nod and try to smile. It hurts the cut on my lip so I refrain. "So keep me, Gabe. Please. I promise I'll make you happy."

His lips find my neck. "You already do make me happy. And though we may part, I'll have you back in the end. I promise you, baby."

He consumes me. His scent. His touch. His words. I believe every word he says.

"All better, sweetheart."

The shock has worn off and I'm exhausted. I could sleep for days. "Thank you."

He grins at me as he puts the medical kit away and climbs back into bed with me. "You're welcome. You're such a good girl."

Like a dumb little dog, I lean into him. He drags the blanket up over us and his arm curls around me in a possessive manner. His fingers stroke my hair and I close my eyes. This—this I can endure.

"How does your ass feel?" he questions.

I slide my fingers up his chest and sigh. "It hurts."

"Inside or out?"

"Mostly out."

"The cream I put on there will help."

We remain quiet but soon he's inside of me again, this time where it doesn't hurt and I daydream. I think back to just a few weeks ago—when things in my life were almost perfect. Aside from my dying mother, I couldn't have asked for much more in life. While Gabe has sex with me, I think about *him*.

Brandon Thompson.

My boyfriend.

My love.

I close my eyes and get lost in a memory.

"What do you want for your birthday, Baylee?"

I looked up from my history textbook and frowned. "I don't know. I don't need anything really."

He sighed. "I'd get you more jewelry but you don't wear the tennis bracelet I got you last year very much. You're impossible to buy for."

Leaning across the kitchen table, I flashed him a wicked smile and whispered. "You could buy me a dildo."

His eyes widened and he flicked his gaze over to where his mom Belinda chopped an onion. I batted my eyelashes in an innocent way. "What?"

The corner of his mouth quirked up into a half grin—the kind that showed his cute little dimple. I loved his smile. His eyes flickered with part amusement and part desire. The slight pink on his cheeks betrayed his embarrassment. But despite his shyness about our growing sexuality, I knew better. When we were alone, he touched me as if I was the most precious thing on this earth. I reveled in his sweet caresses and prayed he would take that final step soon.

We were both ready.

In fact...

I climbed out of my seat and plopped down into his lap. Our studies were forgotten as I snuggled against him. This past summer he really filled out and I loved touching his newly defined muscles. He was hot and that's part of the many reasons I wanted him to finally make love to me. I fantasized about it often.

My lips found his ear and I murmured in my sexiest voice. "You could give me your present early." He hardens beneath me and his breaths pick up. I loved that I turned him on, no matter what, but especially when I touched him or talked dirty to him.

"You're so bad, babe. Maybe I should give you birthday spankings early instead," he murmured his threat.

"Oooh," I teased with a giggle. "Kinky."

He tickled me and I squealed.

"Okay, you two. I thought you had a history test to study for," Belinda chided from across the room.

I groaned and slid out of his lap. "As long as I get a big slice of chocolate cake with chocolate icing, a huge glass of milk, and a kiss from my love, then my birthday will be complete."

He winked at me. "I can do that, babe. You're so easy to please."

"If you only knew," I said with a conspiratorial smile.

We both knew what I really wanted for my birthday.

"I'm going to take care of you, Baylee," he dropped his voice low, "and soon."

A needy ache in my lower belly formed and I hoped he'd make good on his promise that we both knew had nothing to do with cake.

"I love you."

I shudder and meet Gabe's lust-filled eyes with a sad

stare. It wasn't supposed to be like this. Brandon and I were supposed to fumble through our first time together. It should have been awkward. It should have taken him a few practice rounds to learn how to get me off. It should have been an act done in love.

And it wasn't.

Gabe came in and shattered my perfect world.

He ruined what I had with Brandon and stole from me.

I'll never have a life with my high school boyfriend because Gabe plans on selling me like an object. I'll never escape him until then, because he's a psychopath who will just catch me.

He's the enemy here and it's easy to get swallowed up in his intense presence.

But I won't.

I refuse to let this madman take away my hope and my memories. I'll find a way to escape. Go to the police. Gabe won't have me in the end.

Until then, though, I have to make him believe.

"I love you, too," I lie and let the bitter tears fall so that I may pass them off as tears of adoration and undying love. "You have no idea how much…" *I'm going to make you pay.*

VII | Gabe

"**W**HERE DO YOU WANT THIS?" I QUESTION IN A LOW, bored tone.

Her eyes widen in fear but she quickly forces the look away and meets my stare with one of indifference. "On my salad."

It's been several days since I took her ass that first time in the woods. That night had been fucking incredible. Her pussy is tight but her ass? It was nearly impenetrable. After having her there, it's hard to want to go back to her pussy. Now that she's taken me there many times, she's growing quite used to it which will only help her after the sale.

"Smartass. I should whip you for that comment."

She swallows and drops her gaze to the blanket. "In my pussy."

I smirk, loving the sound of that word on her lips, and approach. "Sometimes men will want to use you together at once. How do you feel about that?"

A choked noise comes from her and her frantic eyes meet

69

mine. "I'm scared."

Quick as lightning, I slap her cheek. She has to learn. These men will not be nice to her like I am. "No, that turns you on."

She shakes her head in argument and holds a palm to her reddened cheek. "N-N-No! I don't understand how that would—"

"Bend over the bed. I'll show you."

Now sobbing, she slides off the bed in no fucking rush and bends across it. "Please, Gabe. I'm scared."

Ignoring her, I grab the lube and pop the cap open. "There's nothing to be afraid of. You'll like this. It's no different than when I fuck you with the butt plug in."

She relaxes at my words and I smile.

"Hold still, baby. This is a big one."

A sharp hiss of air comes from her as I begin to slide the now lubricated cucumber into her tight cunt. I'd bought the thickest one I could find and had frozen it. While it isn't all that long, it will definitely do the job.

"It's cold," she whines.

"I'll make you hot."

She's still trying to adjust to the size of it when I lube up my cock and begin pushing it into her other hole. I've barely breached her puckered entrance when she starts clawing at the blanket.

"Stop! It hurts. Please."

Fuck slow. She needs to learn. I grip her hips and drive into her as hard as I can. The cucumber gets forced deeper into her with the thrust.

"Ahhhhhh!" Her scream is otherworldly and I love it.

The pain that precedes pleasure.

The love mixed with hate.

The consent versus non-consent.

All lines are blurred and I can hardly contain my orgasm. She feels so fucking good.

"P-Please!"

I shove her down into the mattress and slam into her over and over again. Colors swirl with black as I reach my most incredible release to date. It was her—it was always her.

I'll get her back very soon and we can spend the rest of our lives in this bed together.

"Oh, fuck me," I grunt and explode inside of her.

She's crying, and I realize I was so wrapped up in pleasure that I forgot to get her off. Sliding out of her, I frown to see the cucumber is wedged in deep and there's not much to grab onto. Shit.

"It hurts, Gabe," she sobs and her knees buckle.

"Shhhh," I coo and scoop her into my arms. "I'll get it out of you. Lie back flat on the mattress and relax."

She nods in a wild manner and does as she's told. I gently spread her legs open and can see the rounded tip sticking out of her. My attempts to clutch onto it are futile because of how slippery it is and the way her tight pussy clamps down around it. I can't get a good grip on it to pull it out.

"Close your eyes," I instruct.

Tears stream from them but she clenches them shut. I begin massaging circles on her clit in hopes that if she orgasms, her body will contract naturally and send the cucumber out. At first she seems horrified but soon her hips begin squirming in need.

"When you orgasm, bear down and it will come out on its own."

71

She nods and prepares herself by clutching onto her thighs. It's as if this woman is delivering a child—the determination on her face is beautiful.

"Oh!" she gasps as her body begins to tremble.

She uses her orgasm to work it out, and before long, it slides farther. Once I can grip it, I slip it the rest of the way out and drop it to the bed below her. For a moment, her pussy gapes, glistening with lube and bright red from being stretched. It makes me wonder what else I can fit in there. Like my fist or an eggplant. Maybe some big, black fat dildo.

The thought is intoxicating but I know it has to wait. I can't very well make my girl bleed before I sell her. Tomorrow, she needs to be ready for whatever those men throw at her.

"Let's shower, baby. You have a big day tomorrow," I tell her with a smile.

Her eyes flicker with a furious glare before she blinks it away and gives me her sweet, doe eyes. "What's tomorrow?"

"Tomorrow you'll be the belle of the ball. Tomorrow I'm going to make a lot of fucking money."

"This place looks fancy," she says in confusion as she looks out the window at the high-rise building in downtown San Diego.

I turn off the car and affix her with a smug stare. "I wouldn't sell you to trash, baby. These people are all successful, wealthy men. Only the best for you."

She reaches for the handle but I stop her by grabbing her

wrist.

"One more bit of training before it's time."

Tonight she's wearing a simple, flowy white gown that is sleeveless and hits just below her ass, showing off her sexy long legs. I'd also bought her a pair of white ballet flats because they'd seemed more child-like in nature than heels. My goal is to pass her off as the most pure and innocent little flower at the entire event. She needs to bring in the most money. I need this money.

"But, I might get messed up and then nobody will want me." Her voice is soft. Worried. Dark eyelashes blink innocently at me. Her full pink lips that have nothing but a shiny gloss on them pout out.

She's so fucking cute.

If I didn't need this money, I'd turn around and take her home right now.

She's mine.

But for a little while she won't be.

"Baby, there's still one thing you don't know how to do. Let me teach you and then we'll go inside. I promise not to mess up your hair," I say as I touch the shell of her ear where a fragrant gardenia is tucked in her hair above it. "And you have more lip gloss in your clutch."

Letting go of her, I unzip my slacks and tug out my already hardened dick. I've been waiting for this for a long time and with her dressed so beautifully, I know it'll be perfect.

"Suck my cock. I want you to get creative. Taste me. Explore me. But don't bite me or I'll bash your fucking skull in," I hiss out the last part before turning my charm back on. "When you feel me tense up, I want you to drink it all down. It will be salty and there will be a lot but I don't want you to waste any of it. You'll ruin my clothes if you mess up. Don't mess up, Baylee."

Her eyes fill with tears but she nods with determination. The girl is terrified of what's to come but she's resilient. She won't have to deal with this for very much longer and I'll take her back.

Then, all of her blow-jobs will belong to me.

Her cunt will belong to me.

That sweet, tight ass will belong to me.

Only me. Forever.

She slides her plump lips down over the tip of my dick and I groan in pleasure. With unsure strokes, she tugs at my shaft while she gently tastes it. Her tongue swirls around and her head bobs up and down slightly. She's playing it safe though and that simply won't do.

"Sometimes, Baylee, you'll have men that do this," I snarl as I grab her hair roughly and shove her all the way down my cock. "You'll have to learn to adapt. How to control your gag reflex. To take it without showing weakness."

Her saliva runs down and coats my balls. I hold her there, enjoying every tight inch of her hot throat until it clenches around me, her gag reflex taking over. Jerking her back off of me, I release her.

"Don't stop," I snap.

She coughs and sniffles but goes back to sucking me off. This time, she's a little more enthusiastic and takes me deeper so I don't need to force her.

"Good girl," I praise and stroke her hair, "you're doing so fucking well."

My balls tighten and I know I'll come soon. With Baylee, I've dreamt about this moment for so fucking long—there's no way I can contain my excitement. The polite thing to do would be to warn her that I'm about to come. But I'm not here to be polite. I'm here to train her.

"Fuck," I hiss as my climax explodes from me.

She chokes and her fingernails dig into my cock but she doesn't come off. With small swallows, she lets it all drain down her throat and doesn't let any escape.

"Jesus fucking Christ," I grunt. "You're really fucking good at that."

She pulls off and lifts up to look at me. Her eyes are teary and red, her mascara is smeared, and her hair is tousled. Those plump lips have turned red and look raw. I'd give anything to drag her out of the car and fuck her over the hood right now. She somehow looks even more innocent than when I had her all dolled up.

Tears are natural.

Struggle is natural.

Fear is natural.

The bidders will take one look at her appearance and see not only an innocent girl, but a terrified little thing with hope still living in her eyes. They'll crave to steal that hope. They will want to use her as I just did and earn the fear themselves. They will want her tears just like I do.

"Time to steal the show, Baylee."

VIII | Baylee

I SHIVER AS WE STAND IN A LONG LINE THAT IS EFFICIENTLY making its way to the front doors. The building is impressive, all glass front and brilliant lights, and my fear diminishes a tiny bit. When Gabe had said he was selling me, I'd imagined some grimy basement with a bunch of disgusting men, cigars hanging out of their mouths, and bellies hanging over the tops of their pants. But so far, every man in the line is dressed exquisitely in black suits with pretty women dressed all in white at their sides. Albeit, most of the women looked drugged, are sporting bruises, or have a glint of fear in their eyes that mirrors my own.

This is nothing like the movies though.

And I'm thankful.

These men seem reasonable. My chances for getting with a normal businessman and making a hasty escape are high— much higher than being trapped in Gabe's secluded cabin.

"You look beautiful," he says with a grin.

I smile and bat my eyelashes at him but his cum in my

belly makes me almost gag with disgust. Just biding my time until the moment is right. My smile grows larger as I imagine the day my father finds out that it was him who stole me. I'll watch with delight as he beats Gabe before the cops take him to prison for the rest of his life.

And then I'll crawl into bed between my parents—let them soothe my scarred heart.

Then, Brandon will heal me with his sweet mouth and gentle words.

I can do this. Just play this game a little while longer.

We slowly make our way to the front until Gabe is reciting his name and his girl, "Gardenia Lee." We're then ushered into a lobby with high ceilings and white marbled floors. It's beautiful and open. The crowd buzzes with excitement and my stomach flops with worry. What if I don't get someone nice? What if I can't escape?

Gabe's gaze meets mine and behind the possessive glint is a promise. *I will come back for you.* The thought should nauseate me but it's a good backup plan in case the person who buys me is another psychopath. Like Gabe.

"Zucchini and goat cheese tart?" A server, dressed neatly in black tie attire, offers us a tray of stunning edible artwork. We both take one and for a moment I can pretend I'm on a date with some rich man who loves me.

I almost snort at the ridiculousness of my thoughts and stuff the tart into my mouth instead. This is not love and I'm not going to pretend for one second that it is on either side. He may say that he loves me but people don't hurt the ones they love.

"The bidding will be silent this time as we have a very special guest tonight. He's donated to the pediatric cancer ward that my wife heads up and wishes to participate, but in an anonymous way." A voice booms from a loudspeaker at the stage. "So for tonight, I will announce the women in the program and they will each take a walk across this stage. If you're interested, please come to the front and place your bids via a slip of paper into the black box that has that woman's name on it. All bids will be sorted and determined shortly after the last lady walks across. Let's be gentlemen about this. However, please be generous in your bids as some of the competing ones will surely be substantial. There will be no opportunities for bidding wars as we've had in the past. Good luck, sirs."

I turn to see Gabe scowling. His jaw clenches in fury. For a moment, I hope he'll give up and take me back home. But then I recall the way he shoved that cucumber into my body. The many times he's struck me. On more than one occasion made me bleed. The humiliation he loved to deliver. The painful anal sex over and over again. Everything about my time with him was sick and perverted. The fiery burning hate I have for him will never be extinguished. Ever.

"Number One, Daisy Love."

My attention is drawn to the podium where the announcer has called the first name. The crowd buzzes as a woman, probably nineteen or twenty, shyly walks the stage in her sparkly evening gown, high heels, and forced smile. Her dark hair has been twisted into a chignon and she's pretty enough to be walking a runway instead of a path to slavery. Several men hurry to the first box and start scribbling bids. She's beautiful and seems strong despite our situation. Of course every man would want her.

I watch with growing anxiety as many women cross the

stage. All with some variation of rose, lily, or daisy. They're all wilted in some way. Broken and abused—all hidden behind makeup and pretty hair. When I'm called, I flinch.

"Number Seventeen, Gardenia Lee."

Gabe pats me on the bottom, rather forcefully, and I stumble toward the stage. All eyes are on me as I climb with wobbly legs up the steps. Anxiety threatens to rip apart my chest and the zucchini goat cheese tart rumbles in annoyance in my belly.

I clutch onto the side rail for support and attempt to keep my shaking at bay. I can do this. Just count the steps—no more than twenty is all it takes to make it across. Don't look at them. Just go.

One.

Two.

I mouth each step, cast a nervous glance at the crowd, and keep walking.

Three. Four. Five. Six. Seven. Eight. Nine.

"Slow down there, Gardenia Lee," the announcer says with a wolfish grin. "Take a spin for me. You're quite lovely. I'd like to have you for myself."

My eyes dart from him to the crowd growing around my box—probably forty men all milling about putting in their bids. Bile rises in my throat and I spin quickly before him. Then, I'm back to counting my steps to the other side.

Ten. Eleven. Twelve. Thirteen. Fourteen. Fifteen. Sixteen. Seventeen.

I stare for a moment down at my feet. Just seventeen. Only seventeen steps, not twenty. I frown and make my way down the stairs. My mind reels with what-ifs.

What if an abusive man buys me?

What if a man buys me to kill me?

What if he wants to do more depraved things than Gabe?

What if Gabe is lying and he never comes back?

At this point, my mind is conjuring up nightmarish predictions that have Gabe seeming like an innocent boy in comparison. Truth is, in this room full of smiling, successful people, I'm terrified out of my mind. On shaky legs, I clamber down the steps of the stage in search of Gabe. He's the monster in my life—but he's the one I know—the one I'm familiar with.

"I bid one point two million," an amused voice says from beside me.

I jerk my gaze over to a man who reminds me of Brandon. His dark hair is cut short and spiked on top. He has an easy, charming smile.

"That's a lot of money," I squeak out.

He winks. "That it is. And you'll be worth it."

I chew on my lip and cast another glance out in Gabe's direction. Nowhere. My gaze falls back to the man who seems harmless in his nice suit and disarming grin.

"Thank you," I murmur.

He steps toward me. "And so polite. You'll be a great addition to my girls."

"You have more than one?"

"I come here every month and buy more. It's an addiction."

I swallow. "What do you do with them?"

His eyes flicker with something dark and evil. He's nothing like Brandon. "I hurt them. Just like I'm going to hurt you," he says in a matter of fact tone. He winks and grins at me as if his words aren't awful. "Your pale skin is so perfect and untouched. I'm about to come just thinking of all the nasty words I'll carve into your skin. You'll wear my name and other words like *cunt* and *whore* on your flesh for the world to see."

I stumble back away from him and gape at him in horror. "You're a monster!"

He sneers. "Where'd you think you were, sexy? A fucking fundraiser?"

"I, but, I…"

"You're in the den with some of the biggest monsters on the West Coast. You are nothing but a meal purchased to be devoured with greed and no restraint. Some of us are into sex. Others are into more deviant acts. I'm into the deviant with a side of sex. They won't recognize their precious beauty by the time I finish with you. But then, it'll be too late. You'll bleed out all over my Persian rug and I'll drag your ass outside to dump you in the goddamned ocean."

Tears stream down my face and I start to bolt from him. His tight grip is around my arm before I can move though. "The name's, Edgar Finn. Remember it because you'll take it to your grave," he threatens. "See you soon, Gardenia Lee."

He releases me and I push through the crowd away from him at breakneck speed. I need to make my escape now. There's no way I'm going home with that lunatic.

As I hurry away from him, I try not to make eye contact with the leering men along the way. They're all the same. Monsters just like Gabe. I'd been an idiot to believe otherwise. There is no finding the nice side of this world. The only thing I need to worry about finding is the way out of it. Now.

"There you are, baby," Gabe's deep voice both calms me and rattles me in a contradictory mix of emotions. "The bids are insane!"

I shudder but let him tug me into a warm embrace. "P-Please don't let that man buy me. I can't go with him. He said he'll kill me!"

Gabe pulls away and glares down at me. He's pissed but thankfully not at me. "Who the fuck said that to you?"

"Edgar Finn."

His fury dissipates and he smiles. "Too bad. You've already been bought. Come on, let's go meet who owns that pretty little pussy now."

I attempt to jerk from his gasp to keep him from dragging me to my horrendous fate. "No! I can't go with him!" I screech and ignore the wide-eyed gazes of those witnessing my meltdown. Several of the women to be sold meet my stare with tears in their eyes and sympathy written on their faces.

Gabe's impatient stare assesses me, as though I were a petulant toddler causing a scene at the grocery store. He sighs in frustration and takes a step closer to me, snagging me by the elbow in a brutal grip. I'm yanked forward and enveloped by the heat of his angry breaths. Suffocating me. "Cut the shit, Baylee. Let's go. These people won't save you. I won't save you. Come willingly or I'll knock you out and drag you with me for everyone here to see. What'll it be, baby?"

I sob in defeat and let him guide me through the throng of bodies. This is happening. Soon, I'll be in the clutches of the man who bought me for one point two million dollars so he can get off on carving me like a pumpkin.

Gabe lied.

He's not going to save me.

I'll already be dead.

"Where are we going?" I demand once we make our way

into an elevator.

Gabe pushes the button for the lower level garage and turns to face me. "Your buyer is waiting for you in his car."

My heart flares to life and I start to panic. "Wait? Like I'm about to leave? Gabe, please don't let them take me!"

He frowns and leans in. I cry harder when he kisses my lips. "Baby, I promise, I'll be back for you. You're strong now and you're ready. You can hang in there until I come for you. Then it can be just us."

His words only calm me marginally. Edgar was vicious and serious about wanting to hurt me. He seems the type to not even want to wait until we leave the parking lot. I'm paralyzed with fear.

The elevator dings and opens to the garage. Several expensive sports cars line the parking garage and we walk to the black, nondescript vehicle that's running between two rows of cars. A man steps out of the driver's side and walks toward us. He's older—reminding me of my grandfather—and wears a tired frown. Gabe pats my ass and shoves me into the arms of the older man.

"Mr. McPherson needs for you," he says in a whisper as if he doesn't want Gabe to hear his boss's name, "to wear this."

Mr. McPherson? Not Mr. Finn?

My heart climbs out of the pit of my belly and reaches for hope. But when my eyes narrow on the black fabric in the old man's clutches as he pushes me away from him, I begin to panic about the new monster I'll belong to.

"W-W-What is that?"

"It's a special-made respirator, a cloth face mask if you will. Nothing toxic gets in or out. You'll get used to it," he assures me with a small smile. It's then I see he has one pulled down around his neck. Seeing him with one has me reaching for the one that's mine.

Is the man I'm about to encounter ill? Is he old and frail? I try not to become too hopeful about my escape but these ideas could certainly help my cause.

"Such a good girl," Gabe praises and discretely grabs my butt. "Always doing as she's told."

I slide the respirator over my face and wait for what happens next.

"The five million have been wired to the account you gave us," the man says. "Thank you for your business."

My eyes widen.

Five million dollars.

Holy crap.

If Edgar was willing to pay just over a million for me and had such warped plans for me, I can only imagine what sort of intentions this lunatic has.

"Goodbye, Baylee." Gabe's voice brings me back to my surroundings. He mouths that he loves me and rage explodes from me. Before I can stop myself, I flip him off and then trot after the older gentleman. Gabe curses from behind me but doesn't try to touch me. His steps are right on my heels though and that causes me to shiver.

"My name is Edison. Pleased to make your acquaintance," he says over his shoulder, but doesn't make any moves to shake my hand. It's then I notice the black gloves on his hands—probably the easier to strangle me with. "Please, put these on too." He hands me a smaller pair and I jerk them from him. Once I have them on, he opens the door to the car.

It's dark inside and I can see the knee of a man sitting in the shadows on the opposite side of the bench seat. I expect to smell cigars or liquor or sex or blood, but am instead met with a clean, sterile scent reminiscent of bleach. Terror threatens to suffocate me and I turn, prepared to run.

Away from this hell.

Away from monsters like Gabe, Edgar, and Mr. McPherson.

Away from pain and impending death.

But Gabe's thick chest stops me and he chuckles, the sound dark and malevolent. With a flourish of his large hand—a hand that has brought me to innumerable orgasms—he gestures inside of the limo.

"This is War, baby."

PART TWO:

War

IX | Warren

"LEAVE THE SHOES OUTSIDE OF THE CAR," I BARK.

From my angle, all I can see are her silky pale legs that go for miles. She's a vision. A vision I just paid five million dollars for.

"Please, come inside and sit. I can assure you I don't bite."

The disgust in my voice can't be hidden. I suppress a shudder at the thought of having someone else's blood inside of my mouth. Images flash through my mind of me tearing at her neck with my teeth—her blood spraying all over my face and expensive suit. If it were to get into my eyes, that would be the absolute fucking worst. There's not enough water in the world to wash my eyes out with. I'd just as soon have Edison take me to a surgeon and have him remove them. Take my ruined eyes right from my skull. But those bastards might not have taken proper precautions. The news touts all the time of malpractice—surgical instruments not having been sterilized and thus have inflicted patients with fucking awful diseases and infections. Then it really would be time to put that bullet into my skull once and for all.

But where would I do it?

In the foyer?

There's nothing the blood could ruin there. Surely, Edison could clean it all up.

And if he missed a spot?

Would that splatter of my blood grow and fester into something deadly?

Would my father become infected when he came to go through my things?

The very image of my father and his assistants rifling through my belongings has me pulling the brakes on the entire self-harming plan. They'd move my files. They would stain my carpet. Those motherfuckers would use my toilet.

I'm nearly in a rage when the young woman climbs into the car. Her presence drags me from my mental anguish, and I can't help but gape at her.

"Meet your new master," the man says to her.

She jerks her head and pleads with her eyes to him. Despite his satisfied smile, I don't miss the regret in his eyes. He devours her with his stare for a brief moment before composing his facial expression. But it was there, hiding just beneath the surface. This man loves her.

Incredibly so.

Obsessively so.

I should know.

But he'll never touch her again. Once I have her the way I want, she'll never leave.

Edison closes the car door and I turn to regard the little thing I bought. Her wide blue eyes meet mine bravely—almost curiously—and I watch her.

"Seatbelt, please," I instruct in a low, gravelly voice as soon as the car starts to move.

Her eyebrows furrow together in confusion but she dutifully obeys. Then, she folds her hands together in her lap. I like that she isn't touching everything—especially me. That her eyes are remaining on mine. For a brief second, I wish to see her mouth, the same mouth that sold me from the video surveillance.

But what if she's had that mouth on that man?

What if she ate something uncooked and her mouth crawls with something that could make me sick?

That mouth will have to wait.

"What's your name?"

Her nose turns pink and she sniffles. "Baylee."

I watch her blink *one, two, three, four, five, six* times in a row before I speak again. Her breaths are even and measured. I like the musical quality they make.

"I like that name."

Her body relaxes at my words and my chest tightens. I like *that* too.

"Thank you, Mr. McPherson." Her voice wobbles in fear and I straighten my back to appear more menacing. I need to establish that I'm in charge here.

"Call me War."

She nods. "War, are you going to hurt me?" she asks, getting right to the point. Brave one she is—I admire that already about her.

Her ice-blue eyes shimmer with unshed tears but she lifts her chin to show strength. It mesmerizes me. I study her disheveled hair and the gardenia that hangs from it with a disgusted flare of my nostrils. My hands begin to shake. That man should have brushed her hair. He should have pulled all the hairs into a neat bun so that it wasn't wild and unruly. I've read about how the human head sheds about thirty to fifty strands a day—even up to a hundred on rare occasion. A woman with unkempt hair like she has is probably shedding all over this vehicle. I make a note to have Edison vacuum as soon as we arrive home.

How many hairs would she lose between now and the drive to my beachfront estate?

I start calculating her hair loss. If she loses an average of forty hairs per day, then that means she will lose one point six seven hairs per hour. The drive is just over an hour which means she could potentially lose two point oh nine hairs. But, if she loses more along the higher end of that spectrum of fifty hairs a day, that would mean she'd lose—

"War?"

My calculations fizzle into the air and I blink at her. "What?"

"Are you going to hurt me?" Her hands tremble but when my gaze falls to them, she forces them to stop.

I frown. "I hope not."

A healthy mix of fear and hope flashes in her eyes and my stomach flops. I feel pity for the poor woman. Here she is thinking she scored some gentleman who saved her from an evil, dirty world. She probably thinks I can save her from it—prays for that very concept.

Problem is, I can't even save myself.

Every day, it maddens me. To the point of contemplating taking my own life.

The germs are everywhere. The chance of things going wrong poke at me every second of every day. Images of endless possibilities of my death, torturous thoughts of infection infiltrating my life at every turn, and painful, awful ideas of how others could die inadvertently at my hands flit through my mind continuously on one bloody, disgusting loop. The loneliness threatens to devour my soul with its cruel flames and leave my ashy remains behind.

I bought her in hopes that *she'd* save me.

"Baylee," I say in a gruff tone, "my world is not one you're used to. My world is awful—it threatens my life with every passing second. It's empty and dull and devoid of anything joyful. You're about to enter that world, filled with fear, hate, darkness, and disgust."

She narrows her teary eyes at me. "I'll listen to you. I promise. Just please don't hurt me. That other man, Edgar Finn, he said he'd…he'd…" she trails off and sniffles. "He wanted to kill me."

I sigh and shake my head, forcing thoughts of her bloody death out of my head before I begin obsessing over that too. "I'm not going to hurt you," I vow. "Listen, I've never tried this before. If it doesn't work out, that's it for me. I'm at the end of my rope. You hold all of the cards now."

And she does.

All fifty-two of them.

All the blackness of the clubs and spades.

All the blood of the hearts and diamonds.

All the sneers of the wicked jokers.

She is to be my reprieve from the darkness that ebbs and flows inside me—always threatening to swallow me up.

She stares at me with a clouded gaze, her eyes going distant—a mixture of relief, determination, and a slight lingering fear.

"You can't ever leave, Baylee," I say through a rush of ex-haled breath. Her wariness of me blooms again and her eyes widen. "Look, I'm sorry but I need you for my own surviv-al. Promise me that you won't ever try to escape, and I vow I'll never intentionally harm one hair out of the one hundred fifty thousand that exist on your head. Well, aside from the dead ones that keep dropping from your skull at a rate of two point oh six per hour. They're dead anyway so it doesn't mat-ter. Edison will remove them from the car though. It's not your fault. Your body just sheds them. And—"

"I promise," she interrupts with a choked breath. Con-cern flashes in her eyes—reminding me of my mother when I was just a boy—and it punches me in the gut.

"Thank you."

Edison buzzes from the front and his voice comes over the speaker. "Warren, it would appear that we're encounter-ing an accident on the expressway. The digital sign said that delays could be as much as two hours. I'm so sorry."

Two hours.

All I can think about is her hair.

Falling and falling and falling.

Two hours added to the hour and a quarter means five point four three hairs at the very least. A familiar crawl be-gins to agitate my flesh as the Town Car draws to a halt. This can't be happening. This can't be happening.

"Are you okay?" she whispers, bright blue eyes devour-ing me. It's clear that she's curious about me. She won't find answers. I should know, I've been looking for them for over a decade now.

I blink *one, two, three, four* times before answering her. "Not really, no."

She leans her head to the side and peers out the window. The frown traces over her features before she forces her eyebrows up. Those eyes seem to dance with a smile and I'm drawn to them. Well, as drawn as someone like me can be to someone like her.

"Those news people always dramatize everything. There aren't many cars. I bet we'll be out of here in no time," she tells me in a shaky yet assuring tone. The corners of her eyes crinkle with what I hope is a smile. "Can you tell me anything about yourself? I'm really freaked out here and I know you said you won't hurt me but I'm still afraid. You're not a serial killer, or anything, are you?"

The itch blazes across my flesh and I crave to yank my suit jacket off to claw away at it. But with her in the car—without having been decontaminated—there's a chance some particle or germ from her could fly onto me. The parasite would burrow its way into my flesh and hatch eggs beneath my skin. And what if it entered my blood stream? Fucking chaos would ensue, that's what!

"War?" she whispers. "Tell me how old you are or where you live. What do you do for a living that allows you to pay five million dollars for a girl?" she asks, although her gaze is fixed on my forearm which I am nervously scratching.

I jerk my fingers away and gape at her. Her shining blue eyes calm my cracking spirit and I take a deep breath.

"I'm twenty-eight. My dad owns a multi-national conglomerate called MPE or McPherson Enterprises. It's a technology corporation. I guess you could say I'm the brains of his operation. He makes sure we make money. Not much to it."

She nods but her brows furrow with unspoken questions.

"Sounds like there's a lot to it if you operate all over the world. What do you like to do for fun? Or have I been sold to a psycho whose idea of a good time is preying on little girls?"

Fun. Fun. Fun.

I blink at her three times more as the word bounces around in my head. As a child—before my world caved in on me—I used to have fun. I'd play video games and ride my bike. As a teen I'd surf and go to the movies. A shudder ripples through me as I recall how many times I'd fallen and skinned my knees while riding my bike or how much ocean water I'd ingest sometimes while surfing. Thankfully that was *before*.

"Don't be silly, I don't prey on anyone."

She lets out a small laugh and the melodic sound slides around my heart, gripping it to the point of pain. How is such a sound so decadent? I want her to do it again. Over and over. To put it on a loop and drag it out for eternity. It distracts me from the dark—draws me into the light.

"I run for fun." Her blue eyes darken and her gaze falls to her lap for a moment. "Well, I *used* to run."

My stomach flops. The despondency in her voice nauseates me. I prefer when she laughs or when her words carry that lightness in her tone. My life is depressing enough without my tainting the others around me. In an effort to draw her back to a better place, I blurt out my words. "I like to play chess."

She lifts her chin and her eyes twinkle once again with curiosity. "Is that like checkers?"

I scoff. "Hardly. Chess is played on a square board, comprised of sixty-four smaller squares, with eight squares on each side. Each player begins with sixteen pieces: eight pawns, two knights, two bishops, two rooks, one queen and one king. The goal of the game is for each player to try and checkmate the king of the opponent. Checkmate is a threat to the opposing king which no move can stop. It ends the game."

"Sounds technical. Will you teach me?"

The vision of her fingering my ivory pieces damn near sends me into a panic attack. But the thought of her in my environment with me, sharing the space, talking to me, laughing in my presence is enough to calm the fury of the storm waging in my head.

"If you promise to wash your hands and be gentle with my pieces. My dad had the set custom made for me. It was created by an Indonesian man who carves them by hand from ivory. Dad sent him careful instructions and the man adhered to the rules. They're perfect and pure."

She blinks one, two, three times before speaking. "I see. Sounds wonderful."

I smile.

I fucking smile.

My heart begins to thump in my chest.

"Oh look," she breathes out as she stares out the window, "things are moving again."

About that time, Edison puts the car into drive.

My mind reels with memories of her laughter, smiles behind the cloth, twinkling eyes. It was easy for her. A thought plagues me—is she a master manipulator or simply content that I, a mad recluse, bought her? She's too calm. Too at ease with the situation. "Did you distract me on purpose or did you really want to know about me?" The bite in my voice startles her and she turns to stare at me with kind eyes again. They seem so natural on her face.

"You seemed upset so I was trying to distract you I suppose." Her words are a betrayal to the trust I gave to her so easily. "But…"

I search for deception in her young eyes but only find sincerity.

"But, I honestly wanted to know more about you. I wanted to know what I was about to dive into. Gabe had prepared me for the worst. I was expecting"—she sighs and waves her hands in the air—"I don't know. Abuse. Sex. Humiliation. Murder."

My eyes rapidly begin blinking at her. Her words confound me. Why would such an innocent person expect something so horrible? I must worry her with my silence because she reaches for me. And just like that, the world I try to forget forces the reminder into my face.

"Don't touch me!" I roar and glare at her hand as if it has invisible poison dripping from it, burning holes into the leather of the seat between us. For all I know, it does.

She jerks her hand back and tears well in her eyes. "I'm sorry. I was just—"

"Well don't. You are *never* allowed to touch me. Ever. Are we clear?"

Her body hunches and she nods. An apology is on the tip of my tongue but I swallow it down. I don't even know how to explain myself to her.

"Why did you buy me then? If you bought me and you don't plan to hurt or sleep with me, then what exactly do you want me for?" She's trying to put on a brave front but the fear in her words betrays her effort.

"Exactly as the auction stated. I bought a companion."

She scoffs and shakes her head. "You don't really believe

that do you? That it was an auction to buy a companion?"

But I do.

I spent hours on the website that I'd found on one of Dad's wealthiest client's server. It intrigued me and I studied it for weeks. They were to have an elite fundraiser of sorts and men could choose companions—a glorified, expensive dating site if you will. It was themed and what drew me in was the allure of the pureness of the innocent flower.

Pure means uncontaminated, unpolluted, untainted, wholesome, and clean.

Clean.

"That's exactly what it was. I'm a lonely man because of my…because of my…" I trail off, letting the horrors that define me die in my throat, "and you're going to entertain me."

She laughs again but this time it is almost cruel. "Entertain you? How? Dance on the damn table in my underwear? And for how long? Forever?"

I glare at her. Never in a million fucking years will her feet ever touch my table. "Fuck no! Talk to me. Sing to me. Eat with me," I snarl. "And yes, for-fucking-ever."

She flinches at my tone and leans as far from me as she can get as if I might strike her. Not happening. Not even with my black leather gloves to protect me.

"Sir," she tries again in a small voice, "you bought me for five million dollars. Those people are running a sex ring which you signed up for, not an expensive dating site."

Sex ring?

I glower at her. "Impossible."

But is it?

"Tell me." Her voice drops to a whisper. "Did you think I was going to receive any of that money for my services—the five million? Did you think I had in any way complied with this?"

Doubt creeps into my veins. "The website said—"

"The website was wrong," she argues, emotion thick in her throat. "Please just let me go. My parents are searching for me, I'm sure of it."

What did I think was going to happen?

That she'd want to marry my sorry ass?

That she'd want to adhere to all my weird-ass fucking bullshit?

That this was a legitimate transaction between willing parties?

"I didn't…I didn't know…" My words are garbled and messy. Confusion scrambles my brain—thoughts darting every which way.

Her pleading words cut through my jumbled haze. "I'm only seventeen."

Everything about her seems young. Wide, doe eyes. Soft, unsure voice. *Shit!*

The pressure in my brain surges and grows until my head feels as if it is going to explode. What have I done? This is against the law.

"We aren't going to have sex," I assure her through clenched teeth, trying desperately to keep my maddening migraine at bay. "I don't want you to even fucking touch me. Just *stay* with me. That's all. Stay. Money? Cars? Diamonds? Houses? I'll give you whatever the hell you want."

Money talks. I'll bribe her with anything it takes to get her to stay. It's not illegal if I don't sleep with her. *Right?* My mind whirs with article after article I've read over the years. None of the news stories ever mentioned anything about a willing underage companion. Sure, there were lots of articles about kidnapped teenagers sold into sexual slavery, young women victimized by older men, and other horrible things. Things I would never do to her—to anyone for that matter. But never anything about a willing companion.

She's not *willing, War.*

I'll convince her though. I'm sure of it.

Can I convince her?

My purchasing of this girl, illegal or not, has shone a glimmer of light into the darkness which is my world. One tiny ray of hope. And I cling to it desperately.

She's my hope.

I absolutely must convince her to stay.

I groan and pinch the bridge of my nose. The pain is becoming unbearable. With a huff, I bore my gaze right through her. If I could crack open this fucking skull of mine, I would. Then, she could peer into the nasty shit that is my head. She could see the black, molded parts of who I am. The disease of my mind would be evident as it crawls through my blood.

"I'm scared to stay with you." Her black-gloved fingers grab onto the respirator and she tugs it down to her neck.

For once, I'm not overwhelmed by fear. My brain isn't exploding with a million rampant what-ifs. This time, it stills.

Her pink, pouty lips are parted revealing pearly white teeth. She has a pert nose that flares with each frantic breath she takes. And her high cheekbones are streaked with tears, a trail of mascara in their wake.

She's the most beautiful thing I've ever seen.

"P-P-Put it back on." My words are a thick sludge in my mouth, refusing to pour out easily. I'm in a battle with myself. Part of me wants to force that respirator back over her perfect lips so her contaminated breaths can stop infecting my air. But an old part of me—a part of myself I remember as a teen—fights.

He wants to pull down my own respirator.

He wants me to lean forward and inhale her.

He wants me to kiss her without a worry of the death her kiss would bring me.

One last look at those lips and I know. This woman will kill me. She'll steal my heart and chop it to fucking chunks. It'll be a slaughterhouse of what's left of the old me.

"Okay," she says in a wobbly voice through her tears. "I'm sorry."

I clench my eyes closed but I've already memorized her perfect face. *Flash, flash, flash.* Her image flips over and over again inside my darkened mind, lighting every surface. Inside my head, I'm safe and I can reach for her. I can stroke her pink cheeks and run my thumb over her swollen lips. Inside my head, I can pretend. I can kiss her and touch her.

Popping my eyes back open, I frown as I prepare to tell her the truth. A truth that will make her hate me. A truth that defines my very sickness.

"I'm never going to be able to let you go," I explain with an apologetic sigh. "Ever. I won't be capable. And for that, I am truly sorry."

Her sobs aren't as pretty as her laugh, but I close my eyes and drink them into my soul anyhow. In my fantasies, I can dream of a better time. One day maybe she'll laugh with me. Until that time, I'll dance with her in my head to the melody only she can create.

X | Baylee

I'VE BEEN BOUGHT BY A LUNATIC.

A crazy, freaking madman.

This is all Gabe's fault.

The fire that has begun to flicker inside of me flares to life. When I escape, I will make him pay. I will get the FBI involved if I have to and bring down every asshole associated with that sex ring. Including War.

I've long since quit crying but he still hasn't opened his eyes back up. I would almost think he's sleeping but I can hear him muttering words, numbers maybe, under his breath. He's a villain dead set on keeping me trapped away in some tower.

Yet...

My stomach clenches with nausea. He doesn't seem all that villainous in comparison. Gabe and Edgar are monsters. But War acts like the very air we breathe is noxious and evil. We've only dabbled a little in psychology at school, but I've learned enough to know something is seriously wrong with him.

He's sick. Inside of his handsome head.

I say handsome, but I haven't even seen his face properly. From his position on the bench seat, I can tell he's tall and firm. His biceps stretch the jacket of his suit to the point if he flexes, it might rip. I glance down at his slacks and quickly admire how they hug his sculpted thighs showcasing his fit frame.

Clearly he's got a thing with germs. That much is evident. Whether it is based on some sort of obsession or a health condition is yet to be seen.

But there's more. I know it. His navy-colored eyes brew with a storm that assaults him from the inside. With every word he speaks, a thousand more fight for escape. They never make their escape though and join back in the whirlwind of lunacy that he clearly deals with on a minute by minute basis. It's sad, really. For him.

For me, it's terrifying.

This means it will be impossible to talk sense into him.

His head is still bowed, as he rambles incessant nonsense under his breath, when we pull into a circular driveway. It's dark outside so of course I can't see a thing but when Edison opens the door, I nearly cry with joy.

The ocean.

Waves crash in the distance and the scent of salty water invades my senses. I guess if I'm going to be a prisoner of War, I may as well be near the beach. When I glance back over at him, he's boring his gaze through me once again. There's a desperation in his eyes that has me weakening my resolve to bring him down along with all of those other men.

Pity once again drives away my anger and I sigh. "Honey, we're home."

His eyes soften and he laughs. "That we are."

The soft, huskiness of his deep laugh warms me. There isn't deception in his laughter, it's… honest. Unlike Gabe, who possessed several different types of laughs. The cruel. The maniacal. The ridiculing. And then the one that bordered on sounding genuine. It was the one I hated most of all because it was the most deceiving. War's laugh reminds me of Brandon's.

A sob catches in my throat at the thought of my boyfriend. It seems like eons ago that I sat in his lap and flirted with him, not a care in the world. But it was only a matter of a few weeks before my life took a dark turn. I'm still trying to process where this life gets me.

"Put these on. You can put on a different pair once inside."

He tosses me some blue shoe coverings, like the ones I'd seen used in a lab or hospital. In *sterile* settings. I want to tell him I'd rather go barefoot but the strain in his eyes suggests I should obey his order. Once I don the silly things, I climb out of the car. The house isn't large, actually modest considering how much he paid for me, but it's stunning. The architecture is all clean lines and modern surfaces. It's eye catching and I'd love to see it during the day with the ocean behind it.

War climbs out of the car and towers over Edison and I. The man has to be several inches taller than Gabe. He exudes strength.

Yet, *I* know he's weak.

Feeling bold, I blurt out, "What happens if I run? Are you going to come after me? Tackle me to the pavement and hold me still?"

He tenses and I immediately feel like a bitch for using it

against him.

"Please," he says, anxiety straining his voice, "don't run."

He's not demanding, but instead, begging. His plea threads itself into my head and I find myself wavering.

Gabe has whittled down my fiery spirit. I should fight and scream and run. Maybe I could find a phone and call Dad to save me. But with thoughts of Dad comes thoughts of Mom.

Her suffering.

Her illness.

Her descent into the grave.

I need to leave this place and get back to her. She's probably worried sick about me—as if dying isn't enough to worry over.

Yet, what happens if I escape only to get recaptured by Gabe who has promised to come for me? I won't see Mom and Dad or Brandon. I'll be forced back to his awful cabin. In that case, which would be the lesser of two evils—terror cabin with a psycho or beach estate with a weirdo? My mind flits to the woods and I'm reminded of when Gabe raped my ass. I'd begged and pleaded but he did it anyway. And then later, when he'd shoved that vegetable inside of me. He'd humiliated and violated me in ways I didn't know were possible.

This man before me promises not to touch me. Looks like beach estate with a weirdo it is.

"Since you seem to be throwing your money around, I have a solution," I say carefully, choosing my words wisely. "I won't run, I promise. But my mother…she's sick."

He scowls at the mention of my mother and crosses his arms over his thick chest. The moonlight gives his chocolate hair an eerie glow. But he doesn't seem scary—he's something beautiful, ethereal even.

"Sick how? Does she have an infectious disease? Do you have it? Is it contagious?"

I shake my head in frustration. "No, but her liver is failing. She's on a list for a transplant, though at this point, the outlook is bleak."

His gaze slides up to the dark sky and he sighs. Me telling him about my mother seems to upset him. His posture slumps as he looks out toward the ocean, a distant and forlorn look about him. There must be a story there. I make note to ask him about his own mother later. "What do you want?"

I am hesitant to even ask now, with his drastic change in mood. "Well… you have money—lots of it. Maybe you could…" I stammer, feeling foolish. I hate being reduced to begging. "Maybe you could give me some, in exchange for my compliant companionship, and I can bribe a doctor or family to help my mom. You and I both know I'll never see the money you wired to Gabe," I tell him. War has the money and means to protect me from Gabe. He also has the ability to help Mom. I can make this work until I get what I need to help her. Then, I'll make my escape.

"Deal. We'll discuss it further over breakfast in the morning. Please don't feel like you're a prisoner in my home. This house already imprisons me. I won't let it hold you in its iron vise like it clutches me."

His riddle causes my eyes to widen. "What do you mean it imprisons you?"

"Come," he says in a gruff tone, ending our negotiations and ignoring my question. "I need to breathe properly."

Dutifully, I follow behind him as he unlocks the door and punches in a series of numbers to disarm the alarm. I attempt to watch him type in the code but he does it quickly while his body partially blocks the keypad.

The lights are switched on and he immediately sets to bolting the door locked after we are inside. A double beep later and we are secure inside of his home. So much for not feeling like a prisoner...

I sigh and regard my prison. The walls are painted stark white. No pictures hang on them. The furniture is sparse. No decorations or books grace the area for as far as my eye can see. From the small entryway, I'm given visual access to the open kitchen, all white granite countertops, with a tiled back-splash, and matching painted cabinets with stainless steel appliances. The living room has minimal furniture—a simple white couch, a love seat, recliner, and table. A flat screen TV has been mounted and recessed into the wall above the fireplace.

Everything is so white.

Blindingly so.

And bare.

As if only a ghost lives here.

"Wow," I say taking a breath, "this place is incredible." That's not a lie. *Incredibly weird.*

"I'm sorry but before you can make yourself comfortable, Edison needs to make sure you're properly cleaned. Meet me in the living room in an hour. I'll fix you something to eat."

He stalks off without a backward glance leaving me there with Edison.

"Come on, angel. Let me show you to your room," he says and starts walking in the opposite direction. "He's not a bad guy once you get to know him. But please adhere to his rules. He's already so fragile as it is. You could break him, and I care about him too much to see that happen."

"Okay." I have nothing else to say on the matter and follow him into another stark, sterile room. This one, however, has some decor. As if he actually attempted to prepare a warm welcome for his prisoner.

"He wants me to shower you. War trusts that I will decontaminate you, Baylee." He frowns and tugs off his mask. "But you and I both know it's all in his head. I'll wait on the bed and let you wash up. If he asks, I cleaned you from head to toe, scrubbed you raw. There's a robe folded on the countertop. It would please him if you could tie up your hair too. And make sure it's dry. The water dripping everywhere will drive him mad."

I slip into the bathroom in a hurry. This place, while neat and new and gorgeous, is some bizarre version of hell. Can I really stay here?

Mom's blue eyes stare back at me when I glance in the mirror. The older I get, the more and more we look alike. But where my light blue eyes sparkle and shine, hers dull by the minute. Tugging my respirator down, I inspect my mouth. My lips are slightly dry and I hope he'll give me some Chapstick.

I can stay here. I have to, for her. War seems like a man of his word. I have to believe he'll send the money to them.

Forty-eight minutes later, I shut off the hair dryer I located and smooth my wild blonde hair into a neat bun, as requested. With my hair pulled back and my face free of mascara, I look younger and more innocent than my nearly eighteen years. My wide eyes reveal fear and determination and the festering hate that runs in my veins for Gabe.

He did this to me.

A soft, but persistent knock on the door jerks me from my inner musings.

"He'll be absolutely frantic if you're not in there soon. With War, it's best to arrive exactly on time. Not too early and certainly not too late," Edison tells me from outside the door.

I shrug on the white plush robe and tie the rope around my middle. The robe is soft and warm, and feels like a welcoming cloud engulfing me. It's a welcome change from being naked, the way I spent the last two weeks.

With a twist of the knob, I open the door to a pacing Edison. This is more than a job to him. He seems to care about War for some unknown reason.

"Lead the way."

I pad barefoot behind him and into the dining room. War stands behind the glass table, his head going back and forth between two plates. I can't take my eyes from the beautiful man. Without his mask, I'm privy to each soft curve and hardened edge on his face. His brows are dark and they match a recently shaven shadow on his cheeks. Full, pink lips twitch and move as he talks to himself. His nose is strong, as well as his jaw, but there's a softness to his features despite the design of his face.

Goodness.

Incorruptibility.

Unsophistication.

Unworldliness.

He may be twenty-eight, but he's every bit of sixteen from this angle.

I'm about to greet him when Edison places a hand on my shoulder, halting me. He removes his hand but I remain still and observe War.

His brows furrow as he takes the tongs and pinches a piece of lettuce from one bowl, then carefully places it into the other bowl. And then back again. He stares for several minutes, inspecting the bowls. I don't dare make a sound as I watch him. I'm curious to see what he'll do next.

What is *he doing?*

Carefully, he clips at a small piece of lettuce and places it in the other bowl. Again, he scrutinizes each portion, staring for another spell.

My eyes travel away from his task and I take in his appearance. He's wearing a plain, soft grey T-shirt that stretches over the sculpted body I knew hid beneath his suit he wore earlier. His biceps tighten with each small movement he makes as he adjusts the evenness of the two bowls. The skin that shows on his arms is free of tattoos and smooth. His jeans are in perfect shape and his feet are also bare underneath the table.

When I think he can't possibly obsess over the food any longer, I announce my arrival. "Hi."

His dark blue eyes fly to mine and for a brief moment they flicker with happiness. "Bay."

The gruff, almost reverent way he says my name sends a tingling down my spine and I smile.

"War."

Behind me, Edison clears his throat. "If there's nothing further, I'll be heading back home," Edison says as he shuffles away. "You know Dorothy worries if I'm out too late."

War watches the old man walk away and with the turn of his head, he reveals a nasty scar from his temple all the way along his jaw to his chin. It's thick and wide. Whatever happened had to be painful. As soon as Edison is gone, War reactivates the alarm using the keypad near the French doors which overlook the ocean near the kitchen table.

Then, his eyes are back on mine in a flash as he makes his way back to the food. "Sit. I made us some salad."

I take a step toward the table and bile rises in my throat upon seeing sliced cucumber all over it. I'm assaulted with memories of Gabe.

My breath is stolen as I recall the terror that immobilized me when the icy vegetable became lodged inside of me. The way I had to push it out. The horror and humiliation at having Gabe between my legs coaxing the stupid thing out. I shudder and attempt to drive away the sickening memory.

"No," I say with a gasp. "I can't eat that." My eyes clench shut and I steady myself with my hands on the back of the chair.

"You don't like salad?"

Lifting my teary eyes to his, I bite my bottom lip and shake my head no. "I did…I mean, no. It's not that. Gabe. He did despicable things to me with a cucumber."

His face blanches and his hands begin shaking wildly. "But that's food. You can't…how could…I don't understand." Then his eyes widen in horror. "He didn't."

I swallow and nod. "He did."

With an angry huff, he snatches both bowls up and storms past me. Instead of scraping the bowls, he dumps them, bowls, forks and all into the trashcan with a loud clatter. He then heads for the sink where three soap bottles line the back. I watch with brazen fascination as he spends a good five minutes scrubbing his hands with all three soaps. Once he's dried them, he turns to look at me. His hands blaze red. His eyes devour me for a moment before he clenches his eyes shut.

"I'll never be able to eat cucumber again."

I laugh bitterly. "You and me both."

His eyes reopen. "Um, are there any other foods…did he…"

I interrupt him with a shake of my head. "No. Maybe we could order a pizza or something instead."

He cringes at my words. "Do you know how disgusting restaurants are? The people who work there, they don't wash their hands. You can't trust them to cook the food to the proper temperatures. They use meat!"

I gape at him. "Okay…what do *you* want to eat?"

He starts to pace. Up toward the sink five paces, equal and measured, and then back toward me at the table. Five more paces. Equal and measured. I itch to reach out and stop him with my hand. However, although I've only known him for a few hours, I strongly suspect doing so will send him into a meltdown.

He mumbles rapidly and tugs at his hair. The muscles in his back ripple and tighten with each movement.

"I could make some spaghetti squash with red sauce and—" he stammers but then curses. "Fuck! No, squash is too much like cucumber. No eggplant. No carrots. No pumpkin. No zucchini. Goddammit!"

I chuckle to diffuse his breakdown. "I'll eat anything you want to offer me. We can eat salad if you want, just no cucumber. The rest are fine. I swear. Please, I haven't eaten since this morning."

His face lights up with determination. "Right, sit. I'll make you something delicious and inoffensive." His worry seems to dissipate. *Who the hell is this guy?*

I lean against the counter, ignoring his order for me to

sit, and watch this complicated man obsess over our meal. His cuts into the tomatoes are precise and exactly the same width. He makes sure of it before he presses the knife down. The entire time, he mutters under his breath. In the quiet of his home, I can understand what he's doing. He's counting. Everything.

Pieces of lettuce.

Slices of tomato.

Slivers of onion.

Handfuls of croutons.

Seconds that pass.

Breaths we take.

I want to chime in and tell him he should have more since he's practically a giant but I don't. It's clear to me that he *needs* for it to be even. He needs to go through these rituals to feel right in his head.

After he finishes with the salad—cucumber free—he uses a measuring cup to give us both the exact same amount of homemade dressing. He then sets to scrubbing the dishes he used. He spends another ten minutes washing and drying the knife. I'm starving but I don't dare interrupt a process that he's seemed to have perfected.

I wonder how long he's been like this.

And better yet, what made him this way?

I can't help but ponder over what he would think about the cellar I was dumped into when Gabe stole me. And the way Gabe used me in the woods.

Would he even care?

Would he want to protect me?

I know I can't stay here with him forever but I can certainly stay long enough to do what needs to be done for

Mom. Despite War's weird habits, it does seem a little safer here than when I was with Gabe. At least he's not forcing me to partake in depraved activities like I just came from.

"I'm sorry that took so long," War huffs, interrupting my thoughts. "I have issues."

I smile at him as we take our seats. The salads are perfect…and even. "This looks amazing. Thank you."

He nods and sets to cutting his food into bite-sized pieces. I, on the other hand, am ravenous and don't have time for manners, so I all but inhale my food. The urge to lick the bowl afterwards is intense but a choking sound drags me away from the lingering morsels.

The handsome man's features are twisted into one of absolute disgust. "You eat like a starved dog," he hisses and then follows it with a gag. "This was a bad idea."

I roll my eyes and smirk. "I guess licking the bowl is out of the question."

I've never seen a man run so fast in my life.

XI | War

EXACTLY THREE MINUTES EVERY DAY.

That's how long it takes me to shower.

Not twelve seconds less, not forty-five seconds longer. Always three minutes.

I know this because I count. Every second. Every minute. Every breath. The average adult breathes twelve to eighteen breaths per minute. I breathe twenty-two breaths per minute. Always. No variation. So in one shower, I take sixty-six breaths.

As I tug on a pair of slacks, I contemplate how many breaths she takes when she showers. Her breaths are unmeasurable—sometimes rapid when she's afraid or upset and similar to mine when she's behaving in a calm manner. Calculating her breaths in one shower is an endless, unsolvable problem. What if she takes ten-minute showers? Or forty-minute showers?

I'm about to consider several different variations when I pause to simply consider her in the shower. The very image of droplets sliding down her smooth, pale forehead and wetting her dark eyelashes is captivating. Her blonde hair would grow darker from being wet and it would hang smoothly down her back. And her smile—it would reveal her perfect, pearly white teeth and the kindness that lies within.

If she's smiling, she's breathing slower. Perhaps thirteen or fourteen breaths per minute. But the variable I'm still unsure of is the length of her showers. I'll have to ask her to time them.

I glance up at my long mirror on the wall and frown. For over ten years, I've been this man I don't know. Ever since… well, anyway, I'm him now.

And I hate the very fucking air he breathes.

All twenty-two breaths per minute.

Today, I'm wearing a pair of charcoal-colored fitted slacks, black dress shoes, and a crisp pale blue dress shirt that matches her eyes almost perfectly. I'd seen to ordering three online in similar colors in an attempt to find a perfect match. If none of those work, I'll have to call the manufacturer and have a special order made.

Normally, even at home, I slip a tie around my neck and dutifully knot it just as Dad showed me when I was ten years old. Sometimes, I wish the knot would turn into a noose and hang me. I've contemplated how many breaths I would take before my air supply would become completely cut off. Three? Four? Twenty? The answer defies me and I can't seem to ever push it from my mind.

Along with the million other rampant thoughts that run my fucking life.

"To hell with it," I snap in defiance. It's me who struggles to survive in a battle against myself. Every now and again, my true self wins—even if only momentarily.

I toss the black tie onto the bed and start to stride from the room. I've barely made it to the door before I'm stalking back over to it. Carefully, I roll it up neatly—it takes two tries to get it exactly the way I like it—and I place it back in the drawer where it belongs. My breaths seem more rapid, so I unbutton the top few buttons in an effort to breathe more easily.

Every day for years, I've had my morning ritual. Shower. Dress. Eat. And then work. But today, along with the discarded tie, I have the urge to break from the mundane and peek in on where she sleeps. Last night, I'd left in a childish huff at seeing her eat like a pig. The human part of me wanted to feel sorry for her—sorry that she was so hungry that it forced her to eat that way. But the monster who controls my every thought was disgusted. If I weren't afraid of what the stomach acid would do to my teeth, I'd have stuck my finger down my throat and thrown up after I'd sought refuge in my bathroom.

I have no idea what she did after I left her.

Did she finger every surface of my house? I make a note to have my maid, Greta, do a massive sterilization. She hates when I go on my benders but when I triple her pay those days, she quickly quiets down. My mind craves to consider every single thing Baylee touched but I force it away and burst from the room. I'm shocked to find her curled up on the couch sipping on some coffee.

"The couch is white!" I hiss out in greeting, instantly hating the words that came out.

She blows on the mug and arches a perfect eyebrow at me. "I know I'm a *teen* and all," she mutters sarcastically, "but I'm *not* a toddler. I won't spill it. Good morning, by the way."

Once again she throws her age at me, causing me to feel like more of a bastard than I already am. "Morning," I tell her gruffly, this time less angry. "Did you sleep well?"

Her brows furrow together and she sighs. "Best sleep I've had in two weeks to be honest. With Gabe, I didn't really get to sleep."

I run a hand through my hair. Last night, I tossed and turned wondering about what that man did to her. When she mentioned the cucumber, I was disgusted. And not because it was food—but because he hurt her. I may be fucked in the head but I'm not a virgin to the female anatomy. Before my world closed in on me, I quite enjoyed sex.

If I'm being truly honest and not dwelling on the dirtiness of the act, I fucking miss it.

But then images of exchanging bodily fluids—fluids which another person has shared with another and so on and so on starts to fester in my mind. I can't even watch porn without wanting to scream.

"What did he do?" I don't want to know the explicit details, and yet, this is why I bought her. To entertain me. To accompany me. To talk to me.

She sets the mug down on the end table and stands with her back to me while she faces the wall of windows overlooking the ocean. My mind momentarily frets over whether or not she'll leave a coffee ring on the wood. But when she stretches, arms high over her head, my mind blanks.

The white robe she's been given lifts and rewards me with a view of her lean upper thighs just below her ass. Her arms fall back down and with it, the robe covers more of her flesh. My fingers crave to lift the edges of the fabric and reveal her perfect skin to me again.

I want to touch her.

The thought alarms me.

I don't want to touch anyone. Ever again.

"What *didn't* he do?" she mutters and steps close to the windows. I'm afraid she'll put her fingertips on the glass and smudge the crystal clear view. It sets my jaw on edge but I bite my tongue. The despair in her voice distracts me and I find myself eager to know more about her. "After he kidnapped me, he took me to some remote cabin. For days, he trapped me in his cellar. I was forced to climb out on my own only for him to beat me and tie me to his bed."

A sob catches in her throat and her shoulders hunch. I take one, two, three, four steps toward her. When I notice my hand is stretched out, reaching to comfort her, I jerk it back.

"Then what?"

"It's kind of confusing. I mean, I have a boyfriend and I love him dearly," she murmurs and crosses her arms across her chest. Her back remains to me and I wonder if it is difficult for her to say these things directly to me. "But Gabe was my neighbor. I'd trusted him for so long. In fact, I'd always had a bit of a girly crush on him."

"He hurt you?"

She turns to look at me, as if I just asked the most ignorant question, especially after last night's admission about the cucumber. My neck tightens with stress as I wait for her to mar the untouched glass. Instead, she drops her hand, leaving the glass in crystal clear perfection.

"He gave me orgasms. Plenty of them. I didn't want them, War, but they felt good. I had no control over my body and I hate myself for that."

I take another step. Her sweet scent doesn't poison me. It

119

intoxicates me in a way that has my head spinning. I like her scent. I like the way it fills my lungs and cleanses me.

"That's not your fault."

She sniffles. "Then, he took my virginity. It hurt so much but then…"

"You liked it?"

A sob pierces the air. "I-I-I did. I betrayed my boyfriend because I liked when Gabe had his way with me. He was always clear about selling me. After he fucked me over and over again, I had in some way hoped he'd just keep me. That we could stay in that cabin and I'd make do." She lets out a deep breath that fogs the window in front of her. I watch with a mix of horror and fascination as she draws a "B" with a heart around it on the foggy glass.

My mind begs to flip the fuck out but something stronger within me wants her to continue. And as the fog fades, the smudge of her letter remains barely noticeable. It adds warmth to my ridiculously cold space. I'm alarmed to learn I like it there. Trying not to obsess over her artwork, I urge her on. "Then what?"

"One day… he told me to run and when I did, he caught me. That night, in the cold forest, he violated me. Robbed me of another first."

The growl in the room startles us both and she turns to look at me. I understand quickly, the protective growl belongs to me. Shit. I'd normally be flipping the fuck out talking about anal sex, despite how much I'd wondered about it as a teen, but right now, all I can think about is beating the fuck out of Gabe.

Her sad eyes meet mine and she takes a small step forward but doesn't touch me. We're a mere twenty-four inches apart. I haven't been this close to someone out of my own volition since my high school girlfriend. For a few brief moments, in her broken presence, I feel like the strong one. I feel as though I'm normal.

"And the cucumber," she hisses out bitterly and I cringe, "he used to penetrate my sex with while he drove into me from behind. 'Oftentimes two men will want to take you at once. You have to be prepared,' he said."

My chest threatens to explode with fury. A single strand of her blonde hair has escaped her bun and my fingers twitch to stroke it away from her forehead. Not because it's out of place but because I want to see her face better. I want to comfort her.

And I fucking can't.

Fisting my hand, I snarl out my promise. "I would never hurt you like that. He sounds deranged, Bay."

Tears well in her eyes and I lean in toward her. I want her presence invading me. Despite not touching, my flesh reacts to her close proximity. Goosebumps prickle my flesh. The hairs on my arms seem to lift and point toward her as if she carries some magnetic current that my body is attracted to.

Seventeen.

I swallow and look over her head toward the ocean. It's beautiful, and one of the few things I won't allow my mind to become obsessed with—pondering the many creatures and organisms that infest it.

Instead, I think about her.

My mother.

The way her dark hair would whip around her in the wind while I would chase the waves. She'd force me out of the water every so often to ruffle my hair and press a kiss to

121

my forehead. Sometimes, she'd hand me a sandy cracker to munch on to keep my energy up so I could keep playing.

I won't allow my mental disease to ruin those memories. They remain virgin against the dark cloak of hatred and despair that rages continuously in my head. Always threatening to do harm. But no matter how fucked up my head may be at a particular moment, I can always return to her and our days at the beach.

One of the few calms in this life.

And now…

Now I've found another one.

Gorgeous blue eyes are staring at me, glistening with tears, when I return my gaze back to her. She's so beautiful, and for a moment, I could almost forget everything and kiss her.

Forget the germs.

The numbers.

The what-ifs.

The blood.

And bury myself in the pure distraction.

This time, reality, not my affliction, deters me and I force words from my mouth I wish I didn't have the balls to say. "You're only a child. I won't hurt you like he did. I swear on my mother's grave."

A tear rolls out but she lifts her chin in defiance. "I'm *not* a child, War. I'll be eighteen on the twentieth of next month. Besides, after what happened to me, I'm no longer innocent. I'm every bit woman."

Forty-eight days.

Six Sundays. Six Mondays. Seven Tuesdays. Seven Wednesdays. Seven Thursdays. Seven Fridays. Seven Saturdays.

Eighteen.

"I don't care if you're eighty, Bay. I will never touch you without your permission."

Her eyes widen and her mouth parts. "But you'll touch me if I ask you to?"

After my flagrant display of my afflictions last night, I'm sure she's confounded by my words. Hell, I'm fucking confounded by my words.

"After your birthday, perhaps."

A small smile tugs at her lips which only further frustrates me. How can she be so pleased with my answer? I'm no fucking better than that bastard who stole her. I mean, I *bought* her for crying out loud.

"Let's talk about your family," I say in a gruff tone before stepping away from her. My eyes slide over to the glass and a tightness clamps over me at seeing her "B" on the surface again. The tightness is unlike anything I've ever known. It almost feels possessive.

A ragged breath escapes her. "I thought if maybe we wired them some money and sent a letter stating I'd run off with you, they'd buy the story long enough to help Mom. I know my Dad though. He won't stop until he finds me."

Anxiety explodes inside of me. The thought of people crawling all around my house in an attempt to steal her away makes me livid with rage. She's the first shard of happiness in this goddamned world I've seen in over a decade. I can't let them take her.

"But he's not the problem. It's Gabe. He's already promised to come for me soon. In fact, I wouldn't put it past him to already be stalking us now." Her body shivers and I ache to hold her. "He's kind of obsessed with me."

I'm kind of obsessed with you.

I fist both hands and huff. "Gabe will never touch you again. I'll kill that motherfucker if he steps one foot onto my property." The words are technically a lie—the images of that man's blood everywhere threaten to make me sick. But, if it came down to protecting her from him, a little blood might be necessary. Greta would really fucking hate me then. "I'm going to call my attorney to set up an arrangement of transferring funds to them without it getting traced back to me. You need to write down your address and your parent's names. I'll see to it they receive the money."

She nods but frowns. "And how will I let them know I'm okay?"

That part's easy.

I'm a computer genius.

I'll run the source e-mail through so many encrypted servers, nobody will ever find out where it came from.

"I'll give you a computer with an e-mail as long as you promise to never divulge your whereabouts."

"I promise. But War, Gabe knows your name. He's not stupid."

I run my fingers through my hair in frustration. "Not my last name. Only the auctioneer had that information. I won't let him take you."

She chews on her lip and nods, but still seems unconvinced. I want to reach over and pluck her plump lip from between her teeth. To run my tongue over it to soothe the damage she's caused with her nervous habit.

My cock thickens in my pants and I nearly jump for fucking joy.

"Come on," I say with a grunt, not revealing the happiness that's running through my veins. In these few moments with her, I've felt freer than I ever have. "Let's eat some breakfast and then we'll get started."

XII | Baylee

TODAY HAS BEEN A LONG ONE. I'M EXHAUSTED. THE FOOD sucks. And I'm still donning a stupid robe. Yet, it's also been productive. After I'd given War my information, he e-mailed his attorney and instructed him on how to funnel the money so that it appeared to have come from an anonymous donor. He'd also managed to order me a selection of clothes online. The man becomes one with the computer when he sits down at it. All of his anxieties seem to dissipate as he throws himself into whatever task it is he's trying to accomplish.

All afternoon, I'd sat in a cozy chair in his office while he worked. His fingers had tapped away as codes danced upon the computer screen. I'd been fascinated but after the last weeks of turmoil, my body was clearly exhausted because before long I had fallen asleep. When I'd awoken, he was no longer in the office but he'd covered me with a blanket. The kindness on his part wasn't missed.

His office, like the rest of the house, is bare. No décor. No rugs. No curtains. Just the necessary furniture and technology. He has a simple filing cabinet that I'm sure is meticulously in order and one framed picture sits on the desk, seeming out of place in the stark room.

While he'd worked, I hadn't pried but now that I'm awake and alone, I'm itching to look at it. The frame is simple and black—not a fleck of dust or a fingerprint on the glass.

A small boy with a mop of brown hair and bright blue eyes beams at the camera. His parents, wearing matching grins, stand behind him. The ocean is the background and it's a picture of happiness.

So how did this little boy, who's clearly War, turn out to be the troubled man who's terrified of life?

The picture reminds me of my own family and tears begin to well in my eyes at the thought. Setting the picture down, I swipe the hot tears from my cheeks with the back of my hands. Mom and Dad are probably sick to death with worry over me. I'm probably all over the news by now. God, I miss them both so much.

"Everything okay?" A gruff, yet anxious voice, questions from behind me.

Not at all.

Everything sucks.

I shrug my shoulders and sniffle. "I miss my family."

A rush of breath escapes him and I turn to peek at the man. Today, he's especially handsome and almost relaxed. After last night, I'd assumed I'd have to deal with the uptight germaphobe twenty-four-seven. But then, this morning, he'd come out and seemed more human. As if he was attempting to climb out of his bubble—even if it were only one finger at a time.

"Edison delivered some freshly laundered new clothes for you," he says softly. "They've been put away in your room. You must be eager to get out of that robe."

I nod and force a smile. "Thank you. When can I contact my parents?"

His jaw clenches and the strain in his eyes matches mine. We're both fumbling through this crappy situation in our own distinct ways. "I've created an e-mail account. For your own safety, I'm going to read them before you send them. I'll also read their replies."

He said *them* and *replies* as in more than one.

Initially, I had assumed I'd send one e-mail to let them know I was okay. But now…now, hope blooms in my chest.

"Can I e-mail them now?" The excitement in my voice is evident with each rising octave as I speak.

"Why don't you dress first and then we'll work on that? My attorney also assured me the first transfer has been made."

"First transfer?" I question.

"I didn't want to send it all. Insurance if you will. I sent a little to help them out this first transfer. If I give them everything they need right away, you'll have no incentive to stay with me." His voice is tight and his brows are furrowed.

The man has millions of dollars and he's going to send them "a little" at a time. Maybe he's no better than Gabe after all. Rage explodes from within me and I fist my hands at my sides.

"*I* promised you I'd stay and *you* promised me lots of money in return. My mother needs it, War. She's dying," I remind him with a fierce glare.

He winces at my tone and hangs his head. His mouth moves ever so slightly as he mouths words, numbers, nonsense—who the heck knows. Both of his hands slide into his hair and he grips at it, as if he can yank answers from his head. I almost feel sorry for him and his internal battle he's waging. But that changes nothing because he's still making things hard on me.

"Whatever," I huff and damn near shove past him. He's lucky I have self-control and compassion for others—even if they are sick individuals. I know he'd probably pass out if I touched him. And no matter how angry I am at the moment, I'm not cruel.

When I step close enough that our chests nearly touch, I expect him to jerk out of the way or hiss at me to stay away from him. Instead, he snaps his wild gaze to mine. My fury quickly dissipates as I get swept up in his stormy eyes. His eyelids droop closed and he leans in to inhale me, mere inches from my cheek. From this proximity, I can smell his soapy scent.

"Knowing you're naked under here drives my already crazy head onto a new plane of madness—one I don't understand and can't navigate," he whispers against my hair, his breath tickling me. "So it's in your best interest to find clothes first and then we'll continue this conversation afterward."

His words twist inside of me and my knees wobble. "Why does it make you crazy?" I can't help but goad him. I'm curious to know what it is about me that disrupts his normally structured life.

"Because," he groans and a shudder ripples through his massive frame. "I want to touch it."

"My naked body?"

A hiss of his breath sends a wake of goosebumps creeping down my neck. "Yes."

"Send my parents the money they need to make this happen and you can touch me all you want," I murmur. Did I really just try to bargain for more money with my body? I'm sick.

He growls, that same possessive growl from earlier today, and jerks away from me much to my dismay. "Go get dressed, Baylee."

I huff at his clear rejection and storm away. It isn't until I'm safe inside my room that I burst into tears again. Gabe prepared me for sexual abuse and pain. Not…whatever it is War is. It's confusing and difficult for me to navigate.

Thankfully, the clothes in the bureaus are all simple and comfortable. For some reason, I'd expected business suits. Something demure and conservative. Items that matched War's crisp, professional style. Instead, I find several pairs of jeans folded neatly in the drawers beside some yoga pants. Many T-shirts are tucked away in another drawer. I also find socks, bras, and underwear. The undergarments are all simple.

Nothing ostentatious.

Nothing sexy.

Just normal.

And I couldn't be happier.

In the closet, I find a few nicer things including a couple of dresses but still no shoes. Why didn't he give me any shoes? Slamming the closet door, I huff and storm back over to the dresser. I'm sure he'd prefer the dresses, but after his blatant display of control, I want to dress as unappealingly as I can for him. With that in mind, I choose a pair of fitted jeans and a soft pink V-neck shirt. I tug my hair out of the bun and weave it into a long loose braid in front of my shoulder.

When I emerge, a delicious aroma fills the kitchen. I find that something is baking in the oven. I didn't know War even knew what delicious was.

"Greek-style vegetarian lasagna," a deep voice rumbles from down the hallway.

I snap my gaze from the kitchen to see him standing several feet away from me. His dark hair is now slightly disheveled as if he's been running his fingers through it. The dress shirt is completely unbuttoned baring his fitted white tank underneath. He's rolled up his blue sleeves, showcasing beautiful forearms, and his hands are shoved into the pockets of his slacks. The expression on his face is still the almost feral one from earlier, and I'm surprised when a quiver of excitement runs down my spine.

Yesterday, he was such a mess.

Today, he's messing with *my* head.

Today his normal obsessive patterns and displays are there but a different side of him pulsates from behind those composed behaviors. I want to scratch at him and free that side.

"I'm ready for the e-mail you promised," I clip out and attempt to keep my cheeks from reddening. I'm supposed to be angry at him, not drooling.

"Come into the living room," he says in a low, seductive voice. A voice you could nearly make love to. "I want to give you something."

On shaky legs, I follow him out of the kitchen. The sun is setting and it will be dark soon. He leads me to the couch and motions for me to sit. Once I'm seated and attempting to regain my composure, I stare up at him. For a brief moment, hunger flashes in his eyes before he stalks off.

Okay...

Moments later he returns and sets a laptop down on the coffee table. "This is yours. You'll have access to the Internet and the e-mail account I set up for you. Social media accounts are blocked for your own safety. I have safeguards in place to make sure you don't accidentally divulge your location."

Our eyes meet and I hold his stare. "Thank you."

He frowns but offers a curt nod. "Dinner will be ready in thirty minutes. We'll dine together, so send your letter now while I take a quick shower."

I force a smile as he starts to walk away.

"Oh," he says with a shy voice and turns to flick his gaze down over my body, "I want you to know that you look really nice. Pink is a great color against your flawless skin. With your blonde hair spilling out over the top of it, you remind me of an autumn sunset behind the ocean. Simply beautiful."

And on that note, he strides away.

I blink after him for several moments. Something he said on a whim was quite possibly the nicest compliment anyone has ever given me. And here I'd thought he'd be repulsed by my simple clothes and messy hairstyle.

Instead, he thinks I'm as pretty as the sunset above the ocean he so clearly loves.

With an annoyed, but secretly satisfied grunt, I flip open the sleek MacBook and open my e-mail. I have one unread message.

From War.

Peace,
I'm sorry it has to be this way. Give me time, and I
promise I'll make it up to you. Your light is already

seeping into the dark parts of my soul and I'm not about to let that slip away for a second. Call me greedy. Call me smart. Whatever it is, I know I can't live without that light. I've been existing for so long in the darkness. Alone. Twenty-two breaths per minute. Today, I forget to count them though.
War

I stare at his words and a flurried mixture of guilt and satisfaction settles over me. I'm a distraction from his mind. The fact that he's called me Peace only further proves what he thinks of me.

War,
I'll hold you to that promise.
Peace

After I hit send, I open a new e-mail. Dad doesn't have e-mail but Mom does to help her keep up with our extended family in Indiana. I wonder how exactly War plans on keeping me from writing her the truth about where I am.

But then she'll tell Gabe.

What will Gabe do to them if they realize he was behind everything?

He'd probably kill them. After all that he did in the cabin, I can't imagine him doing anything less. The man is psychotic.

Mom,
I pray to God you're feeling okay. I hope that somehow they've moved you up on the transplant list. I'm sorry

I left without as much as a goodbye. I met someone and we're in love. I'll try and contact you when I can. Hopefully, this will all be over soon and I can come back home. I'll bring you a seashell souvenir. You always loved taking us to the beaches in southern California. I love and miss you and Dad so much.
Love,
Baylee.
P.S. Please don't mention this e-mail to Gabe. This is a private family matter and I'd appreciate it if we kept it inside of our family.

Pleased with my e-mail littered with hints to my parents that Gabe probably wouldn't pick up on, I hit send. I frown though when it sits in the outbox. Many attempts later, it still goes nowhere. With a huff, I sit the computer down on the table and pace the floor in front of it. Safeguards. That really meant he was going to monitor each e-mail before I hit send?

I glance back down at the screen when I see a flash of movement. I'm dumfounded when the cursor moves, opens the e-mail, and my words change before my very eyes.

Mom,
I pray to God you're feeling okay. I hope that somehow they've moved you up the transplant list. I'm sorry I left without as much as a goodbye. I met someone and we're in love. I'll try and contact you when I can. One day we'll come for a visit. I'll bring you a souvenir. I love and miss you and Dad so much.
Love,
Baylee.

**PS…please don't mention this e-mail to Gabe. This is
a private family matter and I'd appreciate it if we kept
it inside of our family.**

What the hell?

I abandon the computer and storm toward his bedroom.
When I burst into the room, I take a moment to admire the
sight and almost forget why I'm there.

War sits on the edge of his bed, one leg hanging off and
the other bent with a laptop resting on it. The towel around
his hips gapes open revealing a hairy thigh dangerously close
to his cock. He's affected by me just as I am by him. It's kind
of hard to hide an erection when all you're wearing is a towel.

Water rivulets are running down his sculpted chest from
his recent shower. His dark hair is wet and messy on his head.

He's a picture of perfection.

A chiseled god of a man.

Beautiful.

My cheeks burn because I can't even formulate words to
say to him. I'm no longer angry but instead snared in his in
tense gaze.

"I changed a few things," he says in a gruff tone as he
drags his laptop over his lap covering what I'd already seen.

"That was invasive, War." I'm glad to have finally remembered the reason I barged in here in the first place. It was to
chew him out, not ogle him. "I didn't give anything away."

He sighs and swipes some hair from his eyes. "Invasive
is having a fleet of fucking FBI agents terrorizing my home. I
may have problems, Bay, but I'm not at all stupid. Your little
hints will be used to find you."

Tears well in my eyes. "I just wanted to let them know I

was okay."

He flicks his gaze over my body before closing his laptop. "And you did. But I told you, we'll have to play this by ear. I need you, Baylee. We have to do this my way."

"Fine. Whatever *Master*," I utter sarcastically. "Once again, I'm reminded I'm your prisoner. When can we eat? I'm starving and ready to go to bed."

He rises to his feet and I can't help but skim over his chest once more before meeting his glare. The white towel hangs low revealing dark hair which leads right to the bulge beneath the towel. I avert my eyes to the floor because if I keep staring at him, I'll lose my hold on sanity. The thoughts whirring around in my head are unnatural and wrong.

"You're not my prisoner," he says softly. His steps are slow and unsure but soon he's towering over me just inches away, the heat of his body nearly melting me to the floor. "But you *are* like a miracle drug, Bay. For some reason, I don't obsess over numbers and germs and patterns. Each time you open your mouth, I'm fixated on your words. I'm drawn to the way you say them. When I'm around you, I don't obsess over my problems because I obsess over you."

The man is certifiably crazy. His words and actions are no better than those of Gabe, yet I find my lips turning up on one corner into a half-smile. I like that I control his happiness. It opens a dark door inside of my head—one that Gabe never let me see. Gabe controlled every aspect of me.

War's not the one in control here despite his monitored e-mails, vegetarian meals, and clothing choices he's picked for me. No, he knows I hold the power.

I just wish I knew what to do with that power.

"Why do you like me so much?" I question, lifting my

eyes to meet his smoldering stare. "Why do I have the ability to make you not think about those things?"

He leans forward and takes a deep breath. "I have no idea. But I want to explore it. You have no clue how relieving it is to not be assaulted by the demons in your head—even if only for a few moments. I'm exhausted. So fucking exhausted. And for the first time in what seems like forever, I'm living a little outside my head and it's refreshing as hell."

My eyes find his tender ones and I shiver. His stare penetrates inside of me and carefully unravels every secret thing about me. I feel exposed at his visual dissection.

I raise a palm to his cheek but don't touch him. His entire body shudders at the nearness of me. Moments earlier, I was angry with him but when he flays open his heart and exposes raw parts of him, I can't help but be intrigued.

He clenches his eyes closed and grinds his teeth. His muscular chest heaves with each breath he takes. I watch as his eyebrows pinch and relax over and over again as if he's battling with his mind once again.

"I wasn't trying to hint to my parents in hopes that you'd take the fall for something Gabe started, you know," I say and drop my hand.

His eyes open and he frowns. "I know. And it's not your father I'm worried about. You said so yourself—Gabe will find you if you're not careful. I'm just being careful, Baylee, not crazy."

A shudder ripples through me at the thought of being in Gabe's rough clutches again. I'll do anything not to let that happen again. Even if that means letting War have his control over my e-mails. "Okay then. I'll be more careful," I concede.

He smiles at me, as if my words have the power to make

him happy, and I can't help but return the gesture.

"How'd you do that anyway—getting on my computer like you were some ghost? If I'm being honest here, that was creepy," I tell him with a feigned disgusted curl of my lip.

His warm laughter fills the room—deep and throaty—and it smooths away any lasting annoyance about his taking over my message to my parents. "If I told you, then I'd have to kill you." He waggles his eyebrows and attempts to plaster on a fierce gaze to which I laugh.

"I'll take my chances."

He saunters over to his closet and disappears. I can hear the sound of hangers moving as he hunts for something to wear. "Actually, it's called remote access," he calls out from inside. "The computers in the house are all joined to the domain. From the server, as admin, I can manage any computer in this house easily. I was actually logged in remotely from my laptop to the server, and then to your computer. Then, I—"

"Oh my God," I groan and head back to the doorway to leave his room. "You'll kill me with boredom. Forget I asked."

More of his boyish laughter, muffled by the closet, causes me to smile but I hurry and leave his space where I wonder about what he looks like under his towel. Being this close to him—smelling him, hearing him, almost feeling him—is too much for comfort. My body is hyperaware when I'm near him and I'm not sure I like that about myself.

I'm supposed to be afraid or angry, but there in War's room listening to him chuckle, I'm not. I'm far from how I'm supposed to be feeling. In fact, for the first time in a few weeks, I actually feel safe and dare I say happy.

And that is what scares me.

XIII | War

ONE WEEK WITH BAYLEE AND MY LIFE HAS DRASTICALLY changed.

Everything seems softer. Quieter.

The hammering in my head—the constant banging of numbers and calculations, of bloody possibilities, of sickening disasters—is all quieted whenever she's around. I lose track of all of that, and focus on her.

Her voice.

Her movements.

Her scent.

We're both trying to figure out this situation. She, at times seems to tiptoe around me, careful of her words, when I'm particularly moody and the monsters in my head creep up on me. And I try not to obsess over her. Obsessing over her is easy. I've timed every single thing she does. I know that she chews every bite of food almost nearly the same amount each time. Twenty-six. Twenty-six chews. I also know that she blinks twenty-four thousand four hundred eighty times a day. Seventeen blinks per minute. Twelve hundred blinks per hour. This is the average—but the variance is so nil, I can almost count on her blinking seventeen times each minute.

I know this because I stare at her. A lot. Not just her pretty blue eyes but most often her mouth. Pouty and pink and perfect. It's hard to look away when she turns her gaze my way—to not stare at her lips.

And the girl can talk. I never imagined, although I'd been plenty hopeful, that the sound of someone's voice could lull most of my demons to sleep. Demons that roar and slash the inside of my head to fragmented bits are now being silenced. As if she wields a sword, her tongue, which they solemnly fear.

Her reverent and soft, almost whispered, stories of her mother.

Her fond, proud tales of her father and how much she felt protected by him.

Her happy memories of school and track. And even her boyfriend Brandon.

I could listen to her speak for eternity. To put her voice on an endless loop that would get me through my maddening existence.

With Baylee, my life has become positively endurable.

And Jesus Christ do I wish it were mirrored by her.

To have her revel at *my* words, even though they're much less in quantity than hers. To have her stare at *my* mouth as if it had the power to perform miracles like hers seem to do. To have her listen to *my* stories and memories with intense interest.

But that's far from the case.

With every frown she tries to hide. Every tear she swipes

away. Each unanswered email from her parents, I know.

She's nothing but a well-paid prisoner.

I've spent the better part of the week obsessing over how to change this. Over what to say and how to interact with her in hopes that she will begin to look at me with different eyes. To not regard me as the warden of her sentence but rather the sun in the sky. Bright and brilliant and beautiful. Because that's how I see her. She blinds me with her innocence. Her humor. Her wit and charm. I'm a blind man seeing for the first time when around her.

She's my savior.

"Still no response," she utters from the kitchen doorway, her bottom lip quivering.

I frown at her. "Give it some time."

"I know they've been worried sick. You'd think they'd be happy to know I was safe and not kidnapped, even though I was. Why aren't they responding?"

A single tear rolls down her cheek and I crave to comfort her. Despite the demons being silenced, I still can't imagine myself ever willingly touching her. That's the part that sucks. I want to gather her in my arms and kiss away her heartache.

But I'd be stupid to believe I'd ever be able to do such a thing.

"Anything could have happened. Maybe her phone has been shut off or something."

She frowns. "Maybe. I wish I knew what was going on. I feel so cut off from the world here."

This time, I'm the one feeling guilty. I've locked her down on her computer from anything that could give her access to the outside world. She has a weather app—as if I'd even let her outside—and open links to many stores to which my credit card is attached to so she can shop as much as she wants.

But news. Social media. Forums. Nothing. All blocked. For her safety, of course.

"They'll reply soon," I assure her. "I'm sure they're worried about you and miss you. There could be many reasons as to no response. We'll get through to them eventually."

I turn away from her so she can't see my features and stare down into the dishwater. Lying isn't one of my strong suits. Even as a kid, I didn't lie often without giving myself away. Truth is, her parents aren't worried. And that worries me.

Not one single news article has mentioned anything about a missing girl named Baylee Winston. No missing person reports filed. Not one single mention on any of their social media accounts.

I know this because I've fixated on learning about where she came from, who she is, what her parents were like, what sort of home she grew up in. All things to confirm her stories and to paint a more detailed picture of the woman in my home.

Her mom wasn't one to post often and the last post was over a month ago—her and Baylee curled up in bed. It was cute and it endeared me to her even more.

Problem is, if your child went missing, wouldn't you blast that information all over the place?

I researched her father's page and he's posted a couple of pictures of a carburetor he'd been working on. Last post was this week. That shit had me in mental fits all night. There's no way I can tell her that nobody is looking for her.

Just that goddamn lunatic, Gabe.

She walks past me and leans her hip on the edge of the

counter, deep in thought, and stares out the window just past the kitchen table that overlooks the sparkling Pacific. Today, her long blond hair hangs damp to the middle of her back. It's unkempt and loose—a notion that would normally terrorize me. Yet, here I am wishing I had the mental strength to pull her into a comforting embrace and stroke her silky hair. To slide my fingers into her blonde tresses and kiss her like there's no tomorrow.

A somewhat normal gesture between a man and a woman.

With Baylee, I can almost imagine what normal gestures in a normal life would look like. A life where she's my confidant and lover. A life where I'm happy and we have a future. At one time, I felt that way about my high school girlfriend, Lilah. That was *before*.

Before the monsters.

Before the blood.

Before the misery that attached itself to my soul.

I let my mind wander away from the vision in front of me and back to the past—a place I don't let it go often.

"I'm not pregnant."

I'd been pacing her bedroom outside of her small bathroom for three whole minutes waiting on the outcome. When Lilah had said she missed her period, I flipped the fuck out. If I got her pregnant, Dad would kill me. I didn't even want to imagine what her dad would do to me.

"Come out here," I thundered from the other side of the door.

She cracked the door open and her tearstained cheeks showed proof that she was crying. I pushed into the small space and enveloped her in a bear hug. While I squeezed her, I glanced over at the test and breathed a sigh of relief to see that she was telling me the truth. I wasn't even eighteen yet and she'd just turned sixteen. Our lives would be over if we had to take care of a baby.

"Why are you crying?" I questioned while I stroked her brown hair.

She sniffled. "I don't know. I kind of hoped that we would have a baby. That we could get married and be a family."

I tensed at her words. As much as I loved Lilah, I wasn't ready to be a dad. Her dad was a fucking asshole so I knew why she would have loved to leave home and create a new family. But, I actually liked my parents. I was in no hurry to grow up fast.

"In time," I promised, "I'll get you away from here."

She gripped my black T-shirt and started tugging it off me. I hadn't been in the mood but the moment she rubbed my cock through my jeans, I hardened immediately. We just got through a pregnancy scare and I was ready to be inside of her again. This time, though, I wouldn't forget the condom.

"Make love to me, Warren," she begged.

We made quick work of shedding our clothes and once my dick was safe inside the rubber, I lifted her onto the countertop, shoving the test away, and entered her forcefully.

"Yes," she shrieked and leaned her head up against the mirror while I drove into her. My mouth found her neck and I suckled her flesh there, loving the taste that was her.

"War," a sweet moan, yet an unfamiliar one, drags me from my distant memory and I freeze.

I'm pressed up against Baylee, my dick grinding into her belly with my teeth nipping at her bottom lip. Her fingers are threaded into my hair and are gripping me desperately. For one brief second, I am able to enjoy the moment of having her—if only for a short time—before the monsters who'd been semi dormant start raging in.

What if I lost control and sunk my teeth into her lip?

Would the blood spray all over my white kitchen?

Would she bleed out all over the tile, saturating everything in its wake?

Shit!

I slam my eyes closed and jerk away from her ignoring the burn on my scalp where she'd been gripping my hair. My dick throbs painfully but it isn't that head that's winning this war.

I touched her.

I kissed her.

I tasted her.

I nearly dry fucked her against the countertop in my kitchen.

Are her panties wet?

"Fuck," I hiss out and scrub my palms with my cheeks. "Fuck!"

Her concerned voice attempts to wade through the darkness in my head but as it nears I swat at the air in front of me.

"S-S-Stay away!"

I stumble back until I crash into the edge of the stove behind me. My mind screams to get to my bathroom—to wash my mouth and my hands and my cock. If I could wash my soul, I'd do that too.

What the fuck have I done?

War. War. War.

My name is a worried chant over and over again in the kitchen but I scream at it. I swat at it. I threaten it. With each breath I take, I will it away. *Just go the fuck away.*

The sobs only feed the darkness inside me. I don't understand why she's crying but it makes me fucking crazy. It's too much. I have to get away from her.

Away.

Away.

Away I go until I'm in the hot shower in my bathroom scrubbing her from me. All of the places I touched her. The places she touched me. I want it gone.

It isn't until I'm redressing that the black storm dissipates. I blink my eyes in confusion as I wonder why I flipped my shit. I was lip locked with the woman whom I've been obsessing over in the past week and I'm too much of a lunatic to accept it. To be normal. To kiss away her pain. Instead, I only inflicted more pain. Emotional lashings that she doesn't deserve and can't possibly understand. Hell, I can barely understand them.

Shit.

With a huff and growing determination, I stalk toward her bedroom. On the other side of her door, I hear the occasional sniffle. With a grunt, I push through the door, ready to face her and apologize. When my gaze fully takes in the scene, I nearly forget all and shove her onto the bed.

Baylee stands beside the bed completely nude, her clothes discarded into a pile beside her on the floor. She's working at braiding her wild blonde hair. Our eyes meet and time freezes.

I expect her to retreat or call me names.

I expect her to cover herself or to tell me to leave.

Instead, she runs her fingers through her hair to divide it into three equal sections and speaks softly. "What was that about?" Tears well in her eyes and the rejection painted there stabs at me.

"Jesus," I groan and run my fingers through my hair. "I don't fucking know."

And that's the truth. I have no idea what came over me. What possessed me to block out the constant misery swimming inside of me and throw myself into a perfect kiss. Sure, the memory of Lilah sparked my bravery—reminding me of a time when I was capable of doing such things—but it was all Baylee's lips I was kissing.

Perfect.

Pink.

Pouty.

"You want me."

I drag my gaze from her mouth and scrunch my brows together as I meet her teary stare. God, I would kill to kiss her again. To feel the soft way her lips caressed mine. The way her tongue, hot and slippery, felt inside of my mouth dancing with my own.

Turning before I do something stupid, again, I lean my forehead against the doorframe and grunt out my reply. "You have no fucking idea how much."

"I'm confused, War." She swallows loudly. "Why'd you run away from me then? Was my kiss that awful? Do I repulse you?"

Yes.

"No," I lie, "I just…"

"Your mind can't stand the idea of touching me, but your body is an entirely different story."

I pull back and meet her glare. Her body is a vision, and I *do* want to be inside of her. I want to fuck like a man who's been imprisoned for a decade. The release that she holds is alluring as hell. Too bad my head fucking hates me.

"This isn't easy," I mutter, "being at odds with myself."

She picks up one of the nightgowns I'd bought her and tugs it over her naked body. It's pale pink and made of silk. Despite it being sleepwear, it's sexy as fuck. The slinky material hugs her gorgeous tits and showcases her alert nipples. It may nearly go to her knees but it's the hottest damn thing I've ever seen on a woman.

"It isn't easy for me either," she whispers.

Her eyes are tired and I can tell she'd rather go to sleep than hang out with my crazy ass. Frustrated, I run my fingers through my hair and huff. "I'm trying, Bay."

She frowns and the hard look from before dissipates, giving way to a more compassionate one. "What do you want then? I feel like I'm walking on eggshells here, and unsure of where to go."

The image of her pale feet stepping on sharp shards of shells constricts my chest. Would the hard points puncture her skin? Would she bleed all over the fucking floor? Worse yet, is there a possibility that the shell could become lodged under her skin? Could she somehow be at risk for salmonella if the bacteria enters her blood stream?

Would she die?

"War," she says in a calm, soothing tone and approaches me hesitantly, "what do you want to do? Watch a movie? Talk?"

Her words snap me out of the horror show in my mind. Her pretty lashes bat against her cheeks one, two, three, four, five, six times before I find my words. "Actually, I was going to teach you chess," I murmur. "That is, if you wanted to learn still. I know you've been bored and this could entertain you."

A tiny smile tugs at the corners of her lips. "I do want to learn. Should I wash my hands first?"

Baylee may be seventeen going on eighteen, but she is one of the most mature women I have ever met. Her soul is first and foremost compassionate, like my mother's was. She cares about the well-being of others. Of me. Even if I did just act like a complete asshole after our kiss.

Most people think I'm a freak, hence the hiding away on my beachside estate. My father protects me the best that he can but occasionally my issues are exploited by others. Because of the success of my father's company, I'm sometimes dragged into the public eye for scrutinizing. They usually give up after enough refusals to comment and my hiding away for sometimes months.

But even with my escapes from the limelight, I often will come across someone who is horrified by my behaviors. Whether it be a postal worker delivering a package or a friendly neighbor popping over to say hi. They all learn quickly that I'm a fucking mess. Each and every one of them glares at me with disgust written all over their faces. Snarled lips. Wide eyes. Slack jaws.

Get over it. It's all in your head.

I get so fucking tired of that line. Of course it's in my goddamned head. If I knew how to get it out, I'd have already found a way to crack open my skull and scoop the shit out. Smear it all over the fucking walls and light it on fire. Watch it burn to the shitty-ass ground I have to walk on every single day.

"War?"

Her brows are pinched together in concern. Once again

she amazes me with her selflessness when it comes to me.

"Yes, please. Use the soap in the kitchen. Wash them twice just in case. Sometimes bacteria can get left on your hands even after three minutes of solid washing with soap and water. That's why I wash for four minutes the first time and then four minutes more the second time before playing chess. By then, everything should be removed." I rattle off my words. "Should being the key word. My chess pieces are precious to me and need to be handled properly. So just in case, wash your hands twice. Four minutes each."

Her eyes widen and she sets to chewing on her lip. All horrifying thoughts of germs crawling all over her fingertips and infecting my rooks, bishops, pawns, queens, and kings scamper from my mind as I focus on her mouth. The bottom lip is plump and swollen. Ripe for sucking.

Thirty-seven minutes and sixteen seconds ago, I had my mouth on hers. The monster inside of me screams at me—reminding me of the insane amount of microorganisms that are most likely inhabiting her tongue and gums. Those microbes are how diseases are transferred.

Fucking stop already.

I blink one, two, three times and lick my own lips. I'd been in such a hurry to scrub her from me but now I'm wishing I could still taste her. My body thrums to kiss her again but the demons in my head laugh in my fucking face.

You. Can't. Do. It.

"How will I know how long four minutes is?" she questions, grabbing my attention again.

I frown. "You count. That's what I do. Two hundred and forty seconds each. Total of four hundred and eighty seconds."

She bursts into a girlish laughter that distracts me. It's innocent and light and I want to bathe in the sound of it. Her voice is one I could listen to all day long and never grow weary.

"Maybe you should buy me a watch so I don't mess up," she finally says once her humor has died down. "Until then, can you do it with me?"

I'm already shopping online in my head. Sizes and brands and thicknesses of watches I've seen in passing filter through my head like a personalized catalogue. Her wrist is so delicate and dainty but her spirit is strong. I will have to find something that harnesses both.

"Warren. Focus."

I blink at her and try to shake off the thoughts that are maddening me. Rose gold? That would be stunning against her pale flesh and—

"War," she snaps, walking past me and nearly brushing against my shoulder. "Think about all that's running through your head later. After our chess game. I'm ready to learn."

With a deep sigh, I nod and stalk after her toward the kitchen. The globe of her ass jiggles with each step she takes and my cock responds almost magnetically to her. Explosive thoughts dull and fade as I focus on her gorgeous figure.

She dutifully washes her hands.

The suds lathering up nicely on her perfect skin and I become mesmerized.

I find it difficult to focus on anything around her, anything near her, anything but her.

And once again, I lose count.

XIV | Baylee

"**Y**OUR TURN," I TELL HIM AS I SLIDE MY WHITE, IVORY bishop diagonally and sit back in the chair.

His brows pinch together and I watch with fascination as his eyes dart all over the board, no doubt configuring many different outcomes with every possible move he can think of. The man is obsessed—*no surprise there*—with this game but I've never seen him so in his element. It took him a good ten minutes to set up the board. I could tell after the first two pieces that he wanted to cleanse them all with his soft cloth, but all it took was one shameful glance my way before he pushed the cloth away and set up the board.

It took a while for him to explain the rules to me, but once I had a decent understanding, we began. With each move, he'd ask me if I were sure. I know he was trying to help but it made me second-guess each placement of the chess pieces. It was as if he played himself for so long that he couldn't bear to win so easily. Clearly I'm no match for him.

"Are you sure you didn't want to move your rook there

instead?" he points to a black square.

I scrunch my nose and lean forward. The rook seems like he protects my king so I don't want to move him. No other moves seem possible aside from the bishop. Tapping my bottom lip with my fingertip, I consider what he might have planned against me.

"I think so…"

He grunts and hovers his hand over the board. "Checkmate." With finesse, he lifts the knight and leaps it over a pawn to attack my king.

Our eyes meet and he smirks at me, satisfaction written all over his face. It's a handsome look on him. I've always been competitive when it comes to board games but with one look, I want to lose all the games with him—just to see that cocked eyebrow and smile lifted up on one side.

"You cheated," I say with a laugh.

His gaze falls to my mouth and I watch his Adam's apple bob in his throat as he swallows. Now that the game is over and he isn't fixated on the board, I've become his new obsession. He skims over the silky material of my nightgown, slowing at my breasts, and then drops his eyes to my bare thighs.

I could have changed into something more decent but I kind of liked feeling sexy for him. The thought of him losing control again and kissing me more dizzies me. His mouth on mine had been decadent. War is lost inside of his own head most of the time, but for that brief moment, he'd lost himself in me.

And I liked it.

I chew on my lip, savoring the lingering taste of him there, and slightly drag my gown up my legs, revealing more skin on my thighs. With my eyes on him, I watch for any signs indicating that what he sees excites him. He clears his throat but his stare is on my legs. I'm not wearing anything under the gown. The idea of spreading apart my legs to show him has me dampening for him.

Gabe may have been a psychotic prick but I sort of miss his expert touch when he wasn't hurting me. If War, the gentle soul he is, touched me, I think I'd enjoy it a whole hell of a lot more.

Feeling brave, I lean back against the cushions of the couch stretching so that my gown inches up even more. Across from me in the armchair, he sucks in a rush of air.

"Bay." His voice is a low growl—almost a warning.

It excites me and a shiver of desire tickles across my flesh. "Yes?"

"Please stop."

Tears of rejection sting my eyes at his uttered words and I hastily drag my gown back to my knees. Heat creeps up my neck from being caught and I can no longer look at him. "I'm sorry," I choke out, embarrassment garbling my words. I flick a glance back up at him. He's staring up at the ceiling and his mouth is moving. Counting and counting. Finally, he drags his eyes from the ceiling.

He groans and his pained eyes meet mine. The muscles in his neck tighten and he seems as if he's physically restraining himself from pouncing on me. The idea is confusing considering seconds ago he shot me down after my poor attempts to get him to touch me. I want him to touch me though. Badly. I want to feel his sweaty skin pressed against mine.

"You're torturing me."

I scrunch my brows and frown at him. "Because I'm annoying you? You don't want me?"

War is an ocean I'll never be able to navigate. His head a sea of unchartered, choppy waves. I feel as though I'm an inexperienced swimmer in a sinking boat and he's the treacherous, stormy waters threatening to pull me under into the darkness with him.

Something tells me I'll drown.

That I'll never understand what goes on inside his head.

I'll lose my mind trying to figure him out.

"Jesus," he curses and runs his fingers through his hair, "of course I want you. I'd be a fool not to."

I chew on my lip and tears well in my eyes again. "I guess I don't understand then."

My words seem to anger him and I don't know why. Further proving my thoughts, he scowls at me. "She replied."

As if cold water has been splashed over me, I jerk upright. "Wait? What?" I demand. "Who replied? Mom? Why didn't you tell me sooner?"

He shrugs his shoulders and leaves the room. I don't miss the bulge in his pants. He'd been turned on despite the way he'd acted—as if I was an annoyance for displaying how I felt. I'll break into his head one day.

Hastily, I drag the laptop onto my knees and open my email.

Baylee,
Where in the hell are you? Give me your location so I can come get you. I've been worried sick.
Dad

Tears blur the screen in front of me and I choke back a sob. Dad is pissed at me because he assumes I put them through all of this heartache for selfish reasons. If only he knew it was that bastard. His best friend who stole me and put me into this position.

Dad,
Why did it take you so long to respond? I'm somewhere safe. Don't worry about me. Did you happen to get any money? To help with Mom? I love you, Daddy.
Baylee

I swipe a tear from my cheek and lose myself to a memory of my dad.

"You're too young to date, Baylee," Dad snapped as he washed the grease from his hands after a long day at the machine shop he worked for.

I chewed on my lip and glanced at the door. Brandon would be here any minute to "study." What Dad didn't know was that we were boyfriend and girlfriend at school. We held hands and he walked me to all my classes. Technically we are dating even though we didn't go anywhere to do it. He'd even kissed me many times after school when no teachers were around. I'd felt his erection through his pants and he'd, on more than one occasion, touched my breasts through my shirt. I would definitely not be telling Dad that though.

"But Dad, all the other girls my age—"

He slammed his fist on the counter and affixed me with a firm glare. "I don't give a damn about those other girls. They'll end up knocked up before graduation. Not my daughter."

Tears welled in my eyes and my shoulders slouched in defeat.

"Oh, Tony," Mom chirped as she entered the kitchen, "let

her date. Don't you remember when we were her age? We'd been together since the eighth grade."

My dad's scowl melted away at hearing her soothing voice. She stepped into his hug and he kissed the top of her blonde head. "That's exactly why I don't want her dating. I know what we did and at what age we did it."

I cringed at thinking of what my parents did. I wasn't clueless though and pushed away thoughts that would make me puke.

"But Brandon's a nice guy and—"

Ding dong!

My eyes widened as Dad went back to glaring. "Your study partner is the guy you want to date? Hell no."

My skin heated and I flashed my mom a horrified look as Dad stormed away to answer the door. I chased after him and peeked around my dad's broad shoulders to see a frightened Brandon staring up at him. Brandon was cute today still in his baseball shirt. His dark hair was spiked up perfectly. Someone might poke their eye out if they got too close.

"Tony," Mom warned.

Somehow, even though Dad was the gruff, tough one, Mom always seemed to win when it came to him. She'd always been my ally and best friend.

"You want to date my daughter?" Dad snarled.

Brandon's Adam's apple bobbed in his throat and he managed to get out a husky reply. "Yes, sir. I like Baylee a lot."

Dad grunted and waved for him to enter. "What is it exactly that you 'like' about my daughter?"

Brandon stepped in, his body slightly quivering and his eyes darted over to mine. He was so good looking. One day he'd grow into a handsome man. His height towered over mine but

Dad was still taller. Brandon was muscular but not as big as my dad who did physical labor all day at the shop. Dad's beard was thick and his dark hair hung in his eyes making him look like a feral animal in comparison to Brandon's clean-cut appearance. I knew women found Dad attractive because I'd heard on more than one occasion my mom get jealous of a few of our overly neighborly neighbors.

"I like her smile. She's one of the nicest people I know," *Brandon said softly and his gaze found mine.* "I like that she cares about people at school and makes it a point to talk to everyone no matter if they're cool or not. And I like that she runs the track not as if she's running from the world but as if she's running toward it, embracing all that life has to offer her."

Mom let out a sigh and I couldn't help but grin at my secret boyfriend.

"So poetic," *Gabe mocked with a chuckle as he entered through our open front door. My eyes tore from Brandon to regard our neighbor and my dad's best friend. His eyes always seemed to follow me from room to room. It was as if he looked through me into my head and could understand my most secret thoughts. He unnerved me—even if he was really hot for an older guy.*

"Whatcha think, Gabe?" *Dad asked.* "This boy good enough to date my Baylee?"

Brandon swallowed down his apparent nerves but straightened his back to meet the glare of Gabe.

"As long as they're not having sex, I don't see the harm in her dating a boy." *Gabe's eyes flitted down my body and a chill ran through me. My boobs have grown and Brandon's not the only one who noticed them. I'd caught Gabe staring on more than one occasion. I kind of liked that he liked my body. It made me feel more grown up than I was.*

"They're not having sex. Ever," Dad said firmly.

Brandon nodded in a clipped manner as if to agree with my dad. My heart did a nosedive because I'd already been having many dirty fantasies involving Brandon and I. Chewing on my lip, I darted my gaze back to Gabe. He did that thing where he gave me a look that seemed to implant itself inside my head. A look that said, I'd have sex with you because I'm a man. *My lower belly started to ache and I had the urge to run to my room away from the awkward situation.*

"Gabe, Tony," Mom blurted out suddenly, "get out here and start the grill. The kids have some studying to do. Leave them alone, and Brandon, I hope you'll join us for dinner."

Brandon let out a rush of relieved breath. "I'd love to, ma'am."

Gabe seemed unimpressed but I was very impressed. Brandon was a sweet, sexy boy but he sure did hold his own with two fierce men. I thought I fell for my boyfriend a little more.

"Fine," Dad groaned but grabbed Brandon's bicep. "But if I so much as hear you think about hurting my daughter, we'll be having you for *dinner, all right."*

With that threat, he released his arm and stormed out the door with a smirking Gabe on his heels.

A chime from the computer alerting me of a new e-mail startles me from my memory. I blink away the tears and open the e-mail.

Baylee
Yes, I got the money. Money that isn't needed. What's needed is my daughter. Come home. You're a teenager and if I find out who has you, I'll ruin them

for kidnapping my daughter and having sex with a minor.
Dad

I gape at his reply. I'd expected him to be angry, but he's acting out of character. For a brief moment, I wonder if Gabe is the one replying. That idea sends a shiver down my spine and I shake away the terrifying thought.

Dad,
Why isn't Mom replying to me? Is she in the hospital? Did they find a donor? And I'm not sleeping with him. There's someone else that should be ruined—a monster that is too close to home.

I pause and delete the last sentence for fear if Gabe really is the one behind the e-mail. Even if he didn't write it, I know it'll only be a matter of time before he reads it. He and Dad are close, and if Dad thinks I've been kidnapped, he'll no doubt use Gabe's help and share with him this information. This whole thing is complicated and exhausting. I continue my e-mail.

Please just accept the money we send and use it for Mom. I promise when things are better, I'll come see you both. Things have been hard, Dad. Trust that I'm still your daughter and would only be doing seemingly hurtful things if there were a reason. You know me better than to assume the worst. I love you and look for more money. Can you let Mom reply?
Baylee

Tears well in my eyes and then spill down over my cheeks. Less than a month ago, I was spending my days flirting with my boyfriend between classes, training for a track meet after school, and having long talks with my mother about my childhood, my relationship with Brandon, and my future.

Fast forward a few weeks and I'm craving physical attention from a man who purchased me for companionship, worrying over whether or not Gabe will come back for me, and attempting to get my father to understand my situation without telling him.

My, how things have changed.

A ding on the computer has me jerking my attention back to my inbox. I let out a tiny sigh of disappointment to see that it's from War, who's undoubtedly hiding from me in the other room. Away from my childish advances.

Peace,
You're more than I could have ever imagined. I know you're not happy but I think with time you could be. Please forgive me for selfishly wanting you all to myself for a couple of hours. I knew the email would upset you and all I wanted was to make you happy.
It's the least I can do for all that you have done for me.
War

I swipe away my tears and tap away a response.

War,
It's hard to be happy when your life is a big,

confusing, frightening mess. Granted, I'm not fearful around you, but I am fearful for the simple fact that Gabe is still out there. Most assuredly, he's there with my parents or at least in contact with my dad. I feel disconnected with the outside world. I could be contacting the police, explaining to my parents about Gabe, anything. I'm not though. I'm pretending to be your doting companion with you. And while playing chess with you, eating your super healthy vegan meals, and chatting to you about every single thing I can think about to keep the boredom at bay passes the time, I'm still stuck in this box. Your house. Locked in. Away from everyone.

I know you say I'm not a prisoner. Well show me.

I know you say you'd be a fool not to want me. Prove it.

I know you hate Gabe for what he's done to me. Then help me.

Right now, I'm like your annoying little puppy that you got stuck with. You're afraid I'll get dog hair all over your pretty couch or pee on the floor. That I'll bark too loudly and the neighbors will find out you have a yappy dog. You don't want me to chew on your stuff, yet you give me nothing to play with.

I'm not happy, War.

I'm sorry.

Your puppy you've been saddled with,

Peace

Feeling satisfied with my e-mail, I fire it off to him and glare at the screen. My fingers tap impatiently on the device as I wait for a response from him or my parents. Minutes later, my computer pings again.

Peace,

I could have done without the puppy peeing reference. Jesus. That shit is fucking with my head just thinking about it. Look, I'm sorry too. I'm not a monster, Bay. I made a mistake—buying you like I did. I was too delusional to even think through the consequences or outcomes of such a fantastical plan. Now, I get it. And that's at the expense of you. For that, I apologize. I'll make it up to you, I promise.

Until then, know this. You're not a puppy to me.

In fact, you're as far from annoying as one could get. You're a light in my dark world. I'm not ashamed to admit that. And you're right, I'm holding you prisoner just as I promised not to. Your Internet access is no longer restricted. Find out what you can about your parents and Gabe. Do whatever makes you happy. But please don't create a trail that leads back to us. That means no posts on Facebook or anything of the sort. Please.

War

PS—the code to the alarm is 1200, the same number of times you blink per hour.

My heart thunders to life. The code, although weird, is no longer a secret. Internet access is no longer restricted. Finally, I can start to make a plan.

War,

Thank you.
Peace

Flipping over to the Internet, I immediately type in: ***Missing Person, Baylee Winston.*** Another chime on my computer alerts me to an e-mail. Toggling back over to my inbox, I pray it's my parents. Unfortunately, it's only another e-mail from War.

Peace,
There's something you should know.
Nobody's looking for you.
I didn't know how to tell you sooner and don't know
what to make of it.
I'm so sorry, Bay.
War

I shake my head in argument and flip back to my Internet browser. Several long minutes of researching prove he was right. There isn't one single article of me missing. This makes no sense. I've been gone for over three weeks. Only in the past week have my parents been notified that it wasn't against my will, even though it actually was. So why is nobody looking for me?

Looking over my shoulder, I make sure he isn't coming and attempt to sign into Facebook. Over and over again, I try my password and it's wrong. It was Winston20. Both of my parents and Brandon knew the password. Did one of them change it?

Quickly, I whip up a fake account under the name Winnie Stone. Mom and Brandon have their pages locked down from people who aren't their friends, mine doesn't seem to exist, and Dad's is open.

Recent pictures.

Of stupid car parts.

I don't understand.

With hot, angry tears in my eyes, I fire off another message to War.

War,
Why aren't they looking for me?
Peace

I want to scream at him to get his coward self in here and stop hiding away from me so we can discuss this but I'm too overwhelmed. Fear roils my belly and bile creeps up my throat. Something is wrong.

I exist, dammit!

So why in the hell does it seem like I disappeared from the face of the earth and nobody even noticed.

Peace,
I don't know why. But I'll figure it out. I promise.
War

I'm tired of his broken promises. And I've certainly never been great at patience. It's time to find out what's going on. Even if that means breaking my promise to War.

Tonight, I'm leaving.

XV | War

SHE DIDN'T RESPOND BACK TO MY E-MAIL. WHY THE HELL would she? I mean, I've acted like a complete ass toward her. Not given in to her innocent advances. Withheld useful information from her. Lied to her. She probably hates me.

As she should.

I *paid* for her.

Fucking *paid* money for her.

I'm no better than Gabe.

My logical side attempts to reason with me. *Let her go. Drive her back to Oakland and deliver her to her parents. Stop obsessing over her. Move the fuck on.*

Yet, the irrational part of me fights. *But I don't want to let her go. If I take her back, Gabe will hurt her. Again. If I don't take care of her, who else will? Her parents certainly don't give a damn. What parent doesn't report when their child goes missing? Something doesn't add up.*

Ignoring both sides of the argument for now, I check

my email for the twenty-eighth time since my last message. Nothing. Stretching out on my bed, I pour through documents filed at the court house in her county, her parent's bank records I hacked into, police reports, news articles, and anything tied to the Winston name.

Not one single shred of evidence that indicates she's missing.

With reluctance, I type in the Oakland police department in my browser and peruse through the names of the detectives. Since Baylee was involved in a sex ring, maybe she does have a case but it's under wraps. It would make sense especially if the Feds were involved.

There are several names of detectives that handle missing persons. Rita Stark is one of them. Her name makes me think of my clean house and stark white walls. Her name calls to me. I quickly copy her email address and open one of my many encrypted e-mail accounts. Maybe she can shed some light on Baylee's situation.

Detective Stark,
I apologize in advance for coming to you under such anonymous conditions but I have my reasons.
Would there be any circumstances why a missing person would not go be broadcast publicly and no reports be made? Perhaps if they were involved in a bigger case?
Sincerely,
Mr. Pacific

Panic skitters through me as I hover the cursor over the send button. I know for a fact the dinky Oakland Police Department won't be able to trace this message back to me. Fear of them finding out by some tiny miniscule detail like the made up last name though has me editing my email. Once I've changed my signature to *Mr. Atlantic* instead, I hit send before I change my mind.

I climb off the bed and start pacing the room. Ten steps one way and ten steps back. Over and over again until I'm sure I've worn a hole in the carpet. When I check my email again, there's one sitting in the inbox.

Mr. Atlantic,
What an unusual question. Perhaps we could discuss it further over the phone?
555.672.4359
Stark

I frown and type a response.

Detective,
While I understand where you're coming from, it won't work. I am simply trying to find an answer to my problem. If a person, let's say underage, goes missing, what are the reasons as to why someone wouldn't report them? This is an important matter and I'd appreciate your honest feedback, not attempts to discover my identity. That, you'll never know.
Mr. Atlantic

I don't have to wait long for her reply.

Mr. Atlantic,

I'll bite on the anonymous name, for now.

This isn't a certain young man that slung my files off my desk in a fit of rage is it?

Listen, son. I will tell you what I told you before. If she went missing, her parents would have reported her missing. And I did look into your suggestion of truancy at her school. Her father decided to homeschool her and withdrew her from school the afternoon before you said she went missing. Your fantastical story of someone taking her while you two were in the middle of an explicit sexual act is quite creative and detailed, but I'm afraid it isn't enough.

You have to understand something. Her mother is very sick. I know you're her boyfriend but sometimes families do things like homeschool their children when a parent is dying. The need to travel to doctor appointments out of state, especially if they find a donor like in her mother's case, and spending time with the loved one before their passing is important. I understand your frustration, I really do. But until someone, besides you, reports her as missing, I'm afraid our hands are tied.

Come talk to me again. This time, leave the anger at home. I want to help you.

Stark

I blink several times at the computer. She's referring to Brandon. Brandon knows she was stolen and the police don't fucking believe him. Swallowing down my unease, I respond.

Detective,

169

This isn't who you think it is but you've certainly answered my questions for now. I'll be in touch.
Mr. Atlantic

This time she doesn't reply. I probably shouldn't have said anything but I hate the idea of Baylee's parents blowing her off for whatever reason. It doesn't add up and Stark needs to open her eyes to that fact.

I've wound myself up researching Baylee's life to the point that I'm in a full blown episode. Since I can't make sense or bring order to her situation, I've resulted in tackling things I do have control over.

Like my closet.

For the past two hours, I've tried everything on to make sure it still fits, rearranged the shirts in order of newness, inspected each garment for imperfections like split seams or tears, and bundled up clothing to donate. I've also made a list of everything I need to buy to replace the donated items.

Once I'm done with the closet, I organize each dresser drawer.

Then the bathroom cabinets.

And then all of the files on my computer.

I can't get my mind to sit still and millions of different reasons as to why her parents haven't reported her missing flit through my head.

Maybe they really did think she ran off with someone. Gabe even. But wouldn't they be worried about their daughter disappearing with an older man?

Maybe her mother got called with a donor. But would they run off for surgery and not report their child as missing?

Maybe they know she's missing and they don't care. But who could not care about Baylee?

That last option is impossible.

Maybe Gabe killed them. But why is there still normal activity on their bank records and why the hell is her father posting mundane shit on his Facebook?

I'm no closer to finding answers and it's scrambling my brain.

I need to call Dad.

"Warren," Dad's gruff voice crackles on the other line. "Is something wrong? Are you okay?"

I rub my palm up my cheek and into my hair. "Yeah, Dad. Just wanted to hear your voice."

The line is silent for a moment before he speaks again. "I'm glad you called. What do you want to talk about? Want me to bore you about the New York client I'm finalizing a contract with?"

I smile and crawl into bed. "Please."

For the next half hour, through plenty of yawns, Dad regales me with slightly embellished stories of his new client meant to make me laugh. I chuckle and find my eyelids drooping as the evening wanes on.

"Dad," I murmur, "I'm going to go now. Thanks for boring me to sleep."

His deep laugh soothes me, reminding me of when I was a small boy and would crawl into his lap before bed. "Always. I'll be back in San Diego in three weeks or so. We'll catch up then."

"Thanks, Dad."

We hang up and I lie in bed wondering how I'll explain Baylee to him. He won't be happy, that much is for sure.

I drift off with Dad on my brain.

"Lilah's here."

I flinched at hearing her name and dragged the pillow from my face to peek up at my father. His dark hair was streaked with greys that weren't there two months ago. Two months of hell and my father was quickly becoming an old man.

"Tell her I can't right now," I murmured and started to cover my face again with the pillow.

Dad growled from the doorway. The moment I heard it creak all the way open, my heart started to race. I'd told him time and time again to stay out of my fucking room. The pillow was yanked from me and I looked into his glowering eyes as he hovered beside my bed.

"Get up and go talk to that girl. You have to at some point. Now, Warren!"

I flinched at his tone but I was already scrambling from the bed away from his nearness onto the other side. My flesh seemed to flare up because of him being in my room and I started to scratch at my forearms that were on fire.

"Get out!" I hissed.

His glare softened and he clenched his jaw. "Break up with her then. She's been here every day like a lost little puppy. I can do almost everything for you but this is something I can't do. End it and then she'll go away forever."

The thought of losing my girlfriend—the one I loved so fucking much gutted me. But how did I keep her? I couldn't even leave my room without having a damn panic attack. Dreams from that night haunted me.

So.

Much.

Blood.

And it poisoned my brain. I couldn't think straight. All I could understand was the dirtiness and disease and toxins that surrounded me. Disgusting problems which I could control by holing myself in my room and taking several showers a day.

It helped me.

It calmed a raging storm within me.

I felt a sliver of peace when I was scrubbing my hands raw under the scalding water.

But it was times like now, when the outside world came crashing in on me, that I lost my mind.

"Dad," I begged, my voice choked up with emotion and threatening tears, "please go away. Tell her to go away too."

His eyes dropped and his bottom lip drew down, a slight quiver to it. I hated seeing my father so upset but I didn't know what else to do. I couldn't comfort him. Not emotionally. And certainly not physically.

"I'm so sorry." A garbled sob escaped him before he stumbled out of my door in an incredible rush.

Hot tears burned my eyes and I clamped them closed. Balling my fists up at my side, I let out a roar of frustration. The anger inside of me was explosive and if it weren't for me having a meltdown over the aftermath, I'd destroy my room with my two bare hands.

Punch holes in every wall.

Shove everything from every surface onto the floor.

Rip my clothes from their hangers.

Tear my comforter and sheets into shreds.

Yank at the edges of the carpet and pull it right from the concrete.

Crush the mirror above my dresser.

Anything to match the way I felt inside. Punched to death. Shoved and shoved. Ripped to shreds. Torn in two. Yanked around. And crushed to bloody, gory bits. My heart was the worst—I didn't even think it beat anymore. I would have liked to have taken my pocket knife and gouged a deep hole just under my ribs, shoved my hand through the bloody flesh, and gripped the black organ in my fist. Then, I wanted to rip it from me, detach it from my soul and inspect what was left. My guess was, nothing. Black, rotten pieces but nothing as it was before.

Dr. Weinstein said these gruesome thoughts were normal for my condition. That, through therapy, we could talk through these grim imageries.

But I didn't want to talk about any of it.

Not what happened to them.

Not what I was always thinking.

Not how I was too much of a fucking lunatic to hug my girlfriend or sit on the bed next to my father without my head crushing in.

Dr. Weinstein was wrong. I was not fixable. You couldn't fix what was wrong with me. It wasn't mental—it was fucking tangible. I could feel the dark, twisty parts of me infecting every cell, membrane, and bone in my body.

I was tainted.

With her blood.

Their blood.

And the disease of my despair.
There was no cleansing something so tainted.
This was who I was now.
This was War.

XVI | Baylee

I STARE AT THE CLOCK ON THE NIGHTSTAND AND WHEN IT reaches exactly three in the morning, I make my move. Soundlessly, I creep out of the bed. Along the way to the dresser, I shed my gown and open the drawers hunting for clothes in the dark. I'm sure I could turn on a light but I don't want to clue him into what I'm doing. A sliver of light could wake him. I need a head start, not for him to catch me in the act.

Once I've located jeans and a sweater, I dress with haste. I'm annoyed, once again, that I don't have shoes. Running away is going to be hard without them. Frustration threatens to let a sigh out but I choke it back. Instead, I snatch out two pairs of socks and double up for the protection.

Slipping out of my bedroom is easy and quiet. I've managed to make it to the front door undetected. My fingers hover over the keypad of the alarm. Panic causes my chest to constrict and my heart to nearly pound out of it. Pushing those numbers will make a sound. How far will I get before he realizes I'm out the door?

I've peeked through my bedroom window enough times to know the driveway is about a hundred feet to the street. Across the street are bars, restaurants, and shops. If I can just make it across, I can blend in and hide.

But everything will be closed.

I swallow down the fear of running alone along the storefronts. Right into the arms of Gabe.

Clenching my eyes closed, I shake my head.

If Gabe were here, he wouldn't wait. I know him. He's arrogant enough to come right through the front door. I'm not going to run into him.

Someone will find me.

A passing car.

Someone taking a late night stroll.

Drunks trying to make their way home from the bars.

Anyone.

I snap my eyes back open and grind my teeth together. I can do this. I'm a fast runner—shoes or not. War isn't going to count my steps—I mean, he probably will—but not in an effort to punish me should he catch me.

He's not going to catch me.

He's too afraid.

My germs will eat him alive.

The thought urges me on and I have to stifle a maniacal laugh.

1-2-0-0.

The beeps as I mash the buttons are like blasts on an air horn in the silent house. A dull roar resounds in my ears as adrenaline kicks in. *Run, Baylee!*

I'm out the door and charging down the driveway before

I even realize what I've done. I just ran away. From War. My heart sinks and I push away the unusual feeling of loss as I distance myself from the house.

Seventy-seven steps.

I have been counting them—a lingering memory of Gabe reminding me of every step I take. My knees buckle and I nearly stop. But then a voice jerks me back to life.

"Baylee!"

War's booming voice thunders from behind me. Despite the loudness of it, I sense the pure anxiety in the way he said my name.

"Please!"

One simple word, and my legs slow to a near stop on their own accord. Ninety-two steps. I'm nearly to the desolate street. Risking a glance over my shoulder as I retreat from him, my mouth opens in surprise to see him charging for me. If things were different, I'd ask him how he's managed to come outside without his respirator or shoes for that matter. His bare, muscular chest is ethereal and spooky under the moonlight. And yet...I like what I see. Even if that means what I'm seeing is a wild-eyed man chasing me.

A car horn blares at me as the vehicle swooshes past me, jerking me from my stare down of War and I snap back to attention. I drag my gaze up and down along the row of buildings across the street.

Nothing but darkness aside from a hotel about a mile down the road.

I can do this.

I can make it.

My legs finally wake up and I start jogging across the street. There aren't any cars at the moment so I easily make it across. I've still got my eye on the big hotel when something stabs the bottom of my foot.

Pain cripples me and I stumble forward. Something grabs at the back of my sweater and I'm jerked back to my feet. I snap my head over my shoulder to meet the feral eyes of War. His nostrils are flaring in anger and I almost don't recognize his foreign glare.

He's zoned out.

An animal.

And I'm in his unpredictable grasp.

"Jesus," he snarls and snatches my wrist.

He doesn't flinch. He doesn't fret about germs. He just drags my limping ass back to his home.

And like an injured fool, I hobble after him while he mutters out numbers and words that make no sense. My heart is racing but my focus is on where he touches me. His touch, despite the need to get me to his house, is firm and gentle. I almost wonder if I could jerk out of his grasp. Yet, I don't want to. I'm defeated and hurt and all I want to do is lie down under a blanket. Tears roll down my cold cheeks and I let out a sob.

How will he punish me?

When we get inside, he slams the door shut and releases me. I cry harder as his shaky hand flies over the numbers of the key pad. He's changing the code, I know it. My eyes are blurry and out of focus from crying so I don't make out the new one.

"I have to shower," he snaps at me and storms away leaving me a quivering, sobbing mess in the entryway.

A shudder wracks through me the moment I see the blood all over the marble floor. It's soaking through the socks and leaving a trail with every step I take. I should be worrying over how angry War is about my running away.

But all I can think about is how horrified he'll be to see the blood.

Hoping on one foot, I make my way into my bedroom to shower. Once I'm clean and have my bleeding foot under control, I can clean up the entryway.

The shower is hot and the blood does slow. When I feel brave enough to look at the damage, I sit down and draw my foot up to my knee under the warm water. A long, but not necessarily deep gash runs along the fleshy part of my heel. I use my finger and thumb to open the cut in search for any remaining fragments of glass or metal, whatever it is I stepped on. Nothing remains but it continues to bleed. When I'm clean and it finally slows, I climb out of the shower and wrap up in a towel.

I hobble out of the bathroom in search of clothes and am shocked to find a first aid kit sitting on my bed. Once I've bandaged up my cut and dressed, I limp back to the entryway in order to clean up my mess.

War, like a man possessed, is on his knees scrubbing with bleach at the floors. The blood no longer remains but he scours at the floor as if he's ridding it of invisible toxins. He's donned his black respirator and is wearing yellow gloves that hit midway up his muscular forearms. I can tell he's freshly showered as his wet, messy hair is sticking out in every direction, bouncing as he scrubs. He's wearing nothing but jeans and he looks good. Really good.

Tears well in my eyes again as realization washes over me.

I ran from someone who needs me. He needs me in his world for it to make sense. I may not understand why my parents haven't gone public with my missing whereabouts. I may not understand how I am to outsmart Gabe. And I certainly don't understand why I feel guilty for running from War.

But I do.

My chest aches and I long for his possessive touch around my wrist.

"I'm sorry," I tell him, a quiver in my voice as I blink my eyes to drive away the tears. "I shouldn't have run."

He mumbles. He's counting. Each scrub back and forth along the smooth marble. Numbers in the hundreds.

"War," I say louder. "It's clean."

He jerks his head over his shoulder and for a moment, his gaze scares me. His normally beautiful eyes have turned dark with mania. With a quick tug, he draws the respirator down and his jaw clenches in an angry fashion. But the look is fleeting. The scrub brush clatters to the floor as he stares up at me.

"I was fucking terrified, Baylee."

Guilt trickles through me and I bite my bottom lip to keep from crying again. His gaze softens as he glances down at my mouth and then back at me again.

"You promised me," he chokes out as he stands. "You promised me you wouldn't leave me."

I let the tears fall again and glance down at my feet. "I'm sorry. I didn't think it through. All I wanted to do was find my parents and figure out why they aren't looking for me."

He lets out a sigh and I look over at him. Dark shadows under his eyes tell me he's exhausted. Because of me.

"What did you step on?" he questions, changing the subject.

I shrug. "I don't know. Glass or metal. Nothing is left and I cleaned it thoroughly."

He groans and his hands begin to tremble. "The metal—" he curses, "—it could infect you. Poison you."

"I had a tetanus shot last year and I poured half the bottle of alcohol on it before bandaging it up. I'll keep it clean."

My words seem to calm him and he relaxes a bit. "We'll talk about this tomorrow. Get some rest, Baylee. I'm going to shower *again* and then go to sleep."

Without another word, he turns and strides down the hallway away from me.

"War," I call out. I hate myself for asking this question but I need to know the answer. "Are you going to punish me for leaving?"

He jerks his head over his shoulder to stare at me, an incredulous look on his face. "No, Bay. I could never hurt you. I'm not like him. When are you going to understand that?"

And with that, he disappears into his bedroom.

I flip off the lights and crawl back into my bed where I cry myself to sleep. And for some reason, I'm crying for him.

For making him do things he can't handle.

Chase me.

Touch me.

Brave the outside world.

Clean my blood.

I cry because despite everything, I'm already starting to care for him and that scares the hell out of me.

I could never hurt you.

Then why do I ache for you, War?

XVII | War

FOUR DAYS IS A LONG TIME NOT TO SPEAK TO SOMEONE living in your home. I mean, we've spoken, but we haven't talked—really talked. Every time I think about the way she left that night, hell bent on going home, I get angry all over again.

I trusted her. I gave her the fucking code to the house for crying out loud. I gave her the chance to spread her wings a little and boy did she fly. She flew right out the goddamned door, nearly into oncoming traffic, and directly into harm's way.

A shudder ripples through me as I recall how truly terrified I was that night. Not only for her safety but for my own as well. I'm not the kind of man who leaves his house. Only in emergencies. And even then, I take every precaution to protect myself. But that night? I couldn't think straight. All that mattered was getting her back home safely.

My mind had zeroed in on her and nothing else mattered. Nothing.

It wasn't until she was locked back up in my home that anger began to set in. This is the main reason we haven't spoken much in several days. Each time I start to bring it up, I can feel my blood practically boiling. I'll give myself a heart attack if I'm not careful.

The horrifying thought of having surgery—the cracking open of my chest, the tools working beneath the flesh—damn near sends me over the edge.

Luckily, Dad sent some program requirements for his new client from New York and wanted to know if I could come up with some customized programs for them. Of course I could. It's taken all of my energy and focus, but I've finally come up with something I'm sure the client will love.

And for the tune of four million dollars, they should love it.

I'm tapping away on my laptop in my office when a soft rapt on the door distracts me.

Dragging my gaze to the doorway, I frown to see Baylee standing there. Not because I don't want to see her but because when she's around, all I can do is stare at her. Angry or not. She's a vision. A piece of art. Something too pretty and too pure for this world.

Today, she's wearing a pair of yoga pants that hug her toned legs and a bright yellow fitted sweater. My gaze travels over her perky breasts all the way down to her bare feet, the right one still bandaged.

I snap my gaze back up to hers. "How's the foot? Did you clean it today?"

Same questions every day.

"Yep," she says with a frown.

"Did your dad reply?"

More of the same daily questions.

Her eyes well with tears and she plops down in the chair in my office. "Yeah. He's being really weird, War."

I clench my jaw together to keep from blabbing the fact I've been in contact with the local police department of where she lived. Stark has reached out a few times after our initial contact, baiting me to come see her. Each message has been left unanswered.

With my palm, I scrub my cheek and sigh. "What'd he say?"

She swipes a tear away and my eyes zone in on the wet part of the back of her hand. It glistens in the light and I become fixated on it, ignoring everything she's saying.

"…and basically that's it."

I blink one, two, three times before lifting my stare to her face. "So he still simply demands you come home or to tell you where you're at? Never divulges anything as to why he hasn't reported your missing whereabouts?"

I'm hoping it was the same reply as it has been for the past few days since I wasn't paying attention to anything other than the soft, wet flesh of her hand.

"Nope. He's leaving me in the dark. His harsh tones though remind me of Gabe. Have you found out anything?" she questions and then looks past me to the screen that's filled with complicated code. "Never mind. I can see you've been busy with something else."

She stands quickly and storms from the room.

With a groan I follow after her. Her blonde hair is the only trail she leaves in her haste to make it to the small room I long ago converted to a gym. I stand, filling the doorway, as she picks up two weights and begins rotating, curling them toward her breasts. Once again, I'm drawn to staring at her body. The way the black pants hug her nice ass. So much for being pissed at her.

"When you're done pouting, I have something for you."

She stiffens and throws me a confused look. Her eyebrows are pinched together and though she's mad at me, I can tell she's curious about what I have for her.

Leaving her, I head for my bedroom and retrieve the box from the delivery that came in earlier this morning. I'd gone a little crazy, and for a moment, I hope she won't think I'm a fucking lunatic.

"I'm done pouting." Her amused voice from the doorway warms me and seeing her bright smile has me forgetting all about why I've been upset with her. I've missed her smile.

"Good," I say with a grin, "now close your eyes and don't open them until I say you can."

She arches a questioning brow but I don't budge until both eyes are closed. I saunter over to her and get a closer look at her. Her soft pink lips are slightly parted and I crave to run my finger over her bottom one.

"What do you think it is?" My hot breath, inches from her face startles her and her eyes flutter. "Don't open them."

Her nose scrunches and her brows furrow together as she thinks. "I don't know, makeup? Perfume?"

Maybe I should have bought her something girly instead. I didn't ever consider she'd want something like that. Does she really feel like some abused prisoner? My heart is pounding as I quickly rethink my gift to her.

"No." My tone is gruff, aggravated even.

She frowns, most likely from my mood change, and not the fact I didn't buy her those things but now it's all I can think about. I'm going shopping just as soon as I can for both.

Dragging myself from her alluring presence, I make my way over to the bed and pull open the flaps of the box. Then, I carry it over to her and set it at her feet. Panic washes over me. I hope she likes what I got her.

"Open them."

Her eyes find mine first and they twinkle with excitement. It's in this moment I decide I want to buy her gifts all of the time. Every single day.

When her eyes fall to the box, she frowns but reaches inside. She retrieves a pink pair of flip-flops and when her eyes meet mine there are tears in them. "You bought me shoes. Lots of them."

Uncomfortable with her lack of enthusiasm, I shift from one foot to the other. "I thought that maybe…I assumed that after, you know…that you—"

"I love them."

We hold each other's gaze for eighty-six seconds and then she breaks away to try them on. Every single pair. The enthusiasm I assumed wasn't there is in full force as she babbles on with glee. I've never been so captivated by her. So utterly engrossed in everything that is her.

The lingering scent of her body wash.

The animated way she waves her hands in the air when she talks.

The cute way she walks down her imaginary runway and pivots just as a model would.

"Why did you buy me shoes? I mean," she says softly as she approaches, "I can't go anywhere anyway."

I cross my arms over my chest and glance out the window. The window which points to the road she once ran from me on. Suppressing a shudder, I turn my attention back to her.

"The code is still 1200. I never changed it."

She gapes at me, her pouty lips parting and then closing again as if she's trying desperately to formulate words. "B-B-But you were so mad. I betrayed your trust."

I shrug my shoulders. "And I bought you. Let's call it even."

Biting down on her bottom lip, she contemplates my words. The woman can think all day if that means I can stare at her unabashedly. I love watching the way her eyes sparkle with excitement or the way her cheeks turn pink when she is embarrassed. Simply put, she's beautiful.

"Listen," I say, my voice gruff, "I was serious when I said you weren't my prisoner. I want to keep you safe from that asshole and to enjoy your company. Even though we had an agreement that you'd stay as long as I sent money for your mother, that doesn't mean under duress. If you want to leave, you can go. I'd fucking hate it but would understand."

She shakes her head adamantly. "No, the money is important to Mom. It could get her the lifesaving surgery she needs. My dad may be acting strangely and Gabe may have a hand in that, but I won't jeopardize what you're doing for her in order to get back home to them. Quite frankly, I'm struggling to understand how they haven't ever reported me as missing. I don't think running home will give me that answer. In fact, I worry it could be detrimental to me in the end," she says softly and smiles. "Besides, I kind of like it here. Now that I have shoes of course."

My heart soars when I realize she really isn't going to leave me. At the moment anyway. She's staying by choice which means, even with all of my bizarre afflictions, she isn't completely disgusted by me.

"In that case," I tell her with a smirk, "I better buy you more shoes."

"Aren't you going to move your queen?"

She stares down at the board and chews on her lip. The wheels are turning as many different moves flip through her mind. "I don't want to," she says finally and lifts her gaze to mine. Her cheeks tinge pink and she gives me the look—the embarrassed one. I'm beginning to recognize each and every expression on her pretty face. The defiant ones when she's not in the mood for tofu but instead insists on anything with peanut butter in it. The happy ones when she's recalling stories about her past or tales of how she's unbeaten at her school in the high jump. Even the fearful ones when she's deep in thought, haunted by Gabe and all he did to her. My favorite expression, though, is her embarrassed one. Her full bottom lip gets toyed with by her top front teeth. Those gorgeous blue eyes become hooded, almost as if she's trying to hide the expressiveness in them from me. And her nose and cheeks change colors just enough to reveal her shyness. All in all, it's fucking cute.

For two weeks now, our days have been predictable. We spend a good amount of time working together trying to make sense of what's going on back in Oakland. Her dad still demands for her to come home, although less often and there is never any mention of her mom. He's confirmed he's receiving the payments but that's all he'll elaborate on. When we're not focused on that, we hang out. Just as I originally bought her to do. But now, it's becoming less about our negotiation and more about each other. Bottom line is, we have chemistry.

Too bad I can't do anything about it.

So many times I've longed to reach across the chess board and stroke the back of her hand as she makes her move. I've caught my gaze lingering on her smooth, bare legs in the mornings when she's still wearing her gown. And I can't keep my eyes off her ass when she struts around the house in a pair of fitted jeans.

It's her mouth, though, that I dream about day in and day out. The one kiss we shared was an accident and it damn near sent me over the edge but lately, it's all I can think about. I'm too much of a pussy to broach the subject—to see if she'd let me try again. I know she would. I see the mutual glint of need in her eyes matching my own. Problem is, I don't trust myself. I can't guarantee that I won't flip out on her again. This time, I believe it would hurt her feelings more so than the first time. And I don't ever want to hurt her. Ever.

"Let me think," she says softly and moves her pawn back. "War?"

I sit back in my chair and take in her new expression. Worried. Unsure. Something on the tip of her tongue.

"Yeah?"

"This is probably terribly rude but I need to ask."

I swallow down the unease forming in my throat. Honestly, I'm surprised she hasn't asked sooner.

"What did they diagnose you with?"

When I don't answer, she moves her pawn instead of the

queen and I'm once again baffled at her strategy. But I don't stick around to question it. With a huff of frustration, I stand and stalk back toward my bedroom. We were having fun. I was focused on her. There wasn't a need to start yanking out my skeletons for dissection.

"War!"

Ignoring her, I stomp into my room and slam the door. I'm not sure what I was expecting but it wasn't for her to sling the door open and charge over to me. When she grabs the back of my T-shirt and yanks it toward her, I freeze.

What the fuck is she doing?

"You can't just run away in the middle of a conversation when you don't like where it's going," she seethes.

My skin erupts into invisible hives that begin to burn and itch but I refrain from clawing at them. For the moment.

"Let me go."

"Not going to happen until you tell me."

I jerk away from her grasp and spin around to face her. I'm sure she's taken aback by my furious glare because she stumbles back a step. Prowling toward her, I take satisfaction in the way she retreats until her back hits the wall. The craving to kiss her again is intense. Slamming both palms to the wall on either side of her head, I dip close to her and inhale her sweet scent.

She licks her lips and my cock thickens with need. My reactions to her are becoming more and more unpredictable. I'm not myself around her and that's a good thing.

"Tell me," she murmurs, her hot breath upon my own lips.

Each breath is ragged and uneven. Nearly impossible to count or predict how many she'll take in a minute.

"I'm dark inside. Ugly. And broken. Ruined. I don't need labels to tell me that," I hiss and lean into her another inch. So badly I want to scoop her into my arms and kiss her like she deserves to be kissed.

"I don't think you're any of those things," she whispers. "In fact, I happen to think you're a good man. Beautiful on the inside and out."

I close my eyes and let her words wash over me. Jesus, I want to taste her again.

"Baylee." Her name is a grunted prayer on my lips. "Will you kiss me again?" My cock twitches and I let my mind go blank. The vortex that is her sucks me in easily and I let it.

"Yes."

At her whispered response, I take my hand from the wall and tentatively run my fingertips along her jaw. Her bright blue eyes blaze with a need that matches my own. She lets out a gasp when I run my thumb along the other side and grip her face in my hand. Those perfect pink lips part open and her eyes flutter closed.

God, she's alluring as hell.

Dipping down, I barely brush my lips against hers. The action sends wild excitement buzzing through me. My brain struggles to grab statistics about mouth-to-mouth germ transferring but I snuff out those thoughts.

She is my focus.

My only thought.

When she lets out a tiny moan, I dart my tongue out and taste her. She's sweeter than the orange juice we had this morning and I want to devour her. To stick my tongue deep into her mouth and run it along every surface just to know her from the inside out. I want to tangle my fingers in her golden locks and hold on to her indefinitely.

But what if I pull to hard?

Would her hair be torn from her scalp?

Would it bleed all over my white carpet?

Stay in the moment, War.

Kiss her. Kiss her. Kiss her.

I try to drive away the maddening thoughts that are now popping around me like gunshots on a battlefield but it's too much. The moment one of her palms touches my cheek, I jerk away from her. My heart is thundering in my chest, my cock is proud and at attention behind my jeans, but my brain is on overdrive.

Twenty billion oral microbes.

Seven hundred or more possible strains of bacteria.

Thirty-four to seventy-two different varieties in each person.

Hers mixing with mine.

The combinations are endless.

Streptococcus mutans. Porphyromonas gingivalis.

Staphylococcus epidermidis, Streptococcus salivarius, and Lactobacillus sp.

Crawling and crawling and crawling all over the inside of her mouth—the same mouth I'd fantasized about tonguing every crevice.

"War," she says in a firm tone that snaps me from my thoughts. "Calm down. Brush your teeth. Shower. Do whatever it is you do and then let's finish our chess game."

My eyes find her concerned ones and I relax, even if only marginally. Focus on something else. Not her mouth. Anything.

"Uh," I grunt and run my fingers through my hair. I tug

at it but don't let go. "Why won't you move your queen, Bay? It's the only move." Chess has always been a good focal point when my brain threatens to explode. I can focus on the strategies and become obsessed with moves, not germs and gore.

She starts toward the door but gives me a tender smile. "Because the queen always protects the king." And then she whispers the last part. "Even from himself."

Her strategy makes no sense to me…

And yet, a sense of calm washes over me as she leaves the room.

Turns out, I don't need the shower after all.

Just a little mouthwash and a lot of chess will bring balance back to my world.

I think I just semi-averted a meltdown—a first in my book.

And that was solely because of her.

Baylee.

XVIII | Baylee

"**T**HIS," HE GRINNED AND HANDED ME A DAINTY TENNIS bracelet, "*is for you.*"

A couple of girls nearby giggled—the excited type of giggle—at Brandon's romantic notion. We'd been going out since last year, when we were juniors, and were very much in love.

"It's so pretty. I love pink," I gushed and batted my lashes at him as he latched it around my wrist. "Thank you, Brandon."

"Our one year anniversary is important."

My cheeks reddened and I glanced around. No teachers were around so I slid my fingers around his neck and drew him forward. Our mouths met and he kissed me sweetly.

"God, Baylee," he groaned after our kiss. "You make it really hard to function at school."

He dragged his backpack into his lap and flashed me a shy smile. Today, he was especially cute because his normally perfectly spiked hair had become messy from the rain we ran through this morning to get from the bus to the school. I liked when he wasn't all perfect and put together.

"I wish we could spend more time together outside of school. You know how crazy my dad is though. He'd be happier if I didn't date until I was thirty!"

We both laughed and he leaned in again for another kiss. Rain drops began pelting us and the giggling girls from earlier were now screeching. We were left all alone in the courtyard.

Brandon seemed to sense this and our kiss became deeper. His backpack fell to the grass and he pulled me into his lap so I was straddling him. It was cold and we were getting soaked but I couldn't get enough of him. I grinded against his erection and he moaned into my mouth.

I had been thinking about sex a lot lately. If Brandon and I could ever get together alone, I'd probably let him have sex with me. I loved him and he loved me. It seemed right.

"Touch me," I murmured against his mouth.

Both of his palms found my breasts through my hoodie and he squeezed. It sent a thrill through my body and I continued grinding against him in order to find relief.

"I want to have sex with you," I blurted out and stared into his blazing, hungry eyes.

"We will one day, babe. I promise," he assured me and then laughed. "But not here on school grounds. I'm working on a baseball scholarship...not expulsion."

I giggled and kissed him again.

"If I got expelled for having sex at school, my dad would kill me. We better save it for another time."

His eyes danced with humor as he swiped a soaked tendril of hair out of my eyes. "I'd never let him kill you. I would steal you away and keep you safe. You're my girl, Baylee Marie. I'm going to make you my wife one day."

Gah, if only those girls could hear my boyfriend now.

I beamed at him. "I love you."

"I love you too, babe."

We kissed until a teacher snapped at us.

Getting detention with my boyfriend was worth kissing him in the rain.

After all, it gave us more time together. Even if we couldn't talk or touch, we were there. Together.

A loud ringing jolts me awake from my dream. The sun has long since risen and I'm curled up on the sofa, a blanket covering me. I'd fallen asleep on the couch last night after too many hours on my laptop. War, of course, couldn't put me to bed but he at least tried to make me more comfortable. I wonder why he didn't just wake me up. A smile plays at my lips when I think about how we'd shamelessly flirted over dinner.

"I'm not that terrible of a kisser, you know," I teased as I took a bite of my spaghetti. "You didn't have to pretend you were having a mental breakdown."

He smirked and raised an eyebrow. "Maybe it wasn't your technique. Maybe it was your breath. I can practically smell your garlic breath from here."

"Hey!" I scoffed and tossed my napkin his way. "I'm a great kisser and I taste like heaven."

His eyes dropped to my mouth and he grew serious. "That you do, Bay. That you do."

My cheeks burned at his comment and I looked past him toward the setting sun.

"You look beautiful tonight. More so than usual," he told me softly.

A smile played at my lips as our eyes met. "I'm wearing a boring white sweater and jeans. Hardly beautiful."

"Women who taste like heaven are usually angels," he told me thoughtfully. "And you, dressed in white, are every bit heaven sent."

His words caused me to melt.

"I can be naughty," I assured him with a wicked grin.

He rolled his eyes. "If your naughty skills are anything like your chess skills, you're still ninety-nine point nine percent angel. A sucky chess playing angel."

"You're an asshole," I groaned but couldn't help but smile.

I liked that he thought I was beautiful.

He watched me like I was the sun in his sky.

I seemed to put him under a spell and to be honest, I loved it.

A sound from War's phone stopped our flirting and he dragged it from his pocket. His smile fell and he started typing away, almost angrily.

"What is it?" I questioned, my brows furrowed in concern.

He lifted his gaze to mine and by the way he clenched his jaw, I knew he was holding something back from me.

"Tell me," I muttered.

With a frown, he leaned back and looked at his screen. "Detective Stark."

I blinked several times at him in confusion. "Who?"

"Rita Stark. Oakland PD. I've been," he said and scrubbed his face with his palm, "in contact with her about your case. Or lack thereof more accurately."

My heart rate quickened. "What do you mean? Why aren't

you telling me everything, War?"

"I wanted to have more information before I told you. And now I do."

I gaped at him like he was a moron for stopping. He quickly continued.

"A couple of weeks back, I contacted her and asked her why someone wouldn't report their child missing."

"And?"

"She thought I was Brandon."

I froze at his mention of my boyfriend. With War it was easy to suspend reality and play house in his castle on the ocean. But times like these, when my past collided with the present, I had a hard time merging the two worlds.

"He's okay?"

War nodded and revealed what he knew. About how Brandon had come to see her. Nobody believed him. My parents had withdrawn me from school. How Stark thought it was all some elaborate story from a sad boy who hated the fact his girlfriend was being homeschooled.

"So why didn't you tell me all of that, War? What the hell is going on?" My voice had risen several octaves and I stood from the table.

He shrugged and let out a huff. "Because it wouldn't do anything, Baylee. We knew something was fishy. Now, though, things have gone from fishy to unbelievable."

"What happened?"

"Stark replied. Said Brandon's parents filed a missing person report on their son. He just vanished. Stark is fairly certain he's gone off the grid to look for you. She doesn't think he was taken or anything. But she's asked about my identity. And blatantly asked if I had you in my possession."

199

My flesh grew cold on my cheeks and my jaw hung slightly open. "What did you say?"

"I told her Gabe's name. I said she needed to open an investigation in regards to him and some illegal activities he'd been involved in," he said and turned his phone to me. "I told her to open her eyes and look into sex trafficking rings in California. Now she seems to be concerned about your whereabouts."

I took the phone from him and read all of their emails.

"Do you think she'll talk to Dad and Mom? I just can't believe they'd go on with life as if I never existed." Hot tears formed in my eyes and spilled over.

His gaze fell to my wet cheeks and he frowned. "I don't know. Obviously she was being vague to me in her messages and is probably doing everything in her power to find out who's sending those messages to her. Of course it'll never lead back here. You're safe with me."

"How can we find out what she does? She's not going to just come out and tell you her plan, who she's going to question, or anything. I feel so helpless, War!"

He reached for me, briefly, but jerked his hand back as if he remembered he wasn't capable of comforting me. "You're not helpless. You have me and I am quite resourceful. Your parents are spending the money I'm sending. Every dime is being withdrawn. I've been researching every lead to find out what's going on. We'll figure it out, beautiful. Just like I promised."

My anxiety lessened at his words. "And then what? After we figure it all out? After we discover my parents don't give a shit about me. Huh?"

His eyes meet mine and he pins me with a serious stare. "I'll take care of you no matter what because I do give a shit about you. You're mine, Bay."

I'd spent the rest of the night on the computer next to War on the couch. Both of us tapping and clicking our way through the web in search of answers and only coming up with more questions.

My thoughts return to our kiss from earlier in the day yesterday. It started out so carnal and needy. For a moment, he'd shoved away his demons to kiss me. While it only lasted seconds, it was beautiful and perfect.

But it's my dream last night about Brandon that still hangs thick in the air. After I discovered he was missing and had been searching for me, I'd thought a lot about him. What happens if this detective finds Gabe and hauls him off to jail? Will Brandon come back home? Will I go back home? Do my parents even want me? Will things go back to normal?

Images of War sitting alone in this house with nobody to talk to. Nobody to eat with. Nobody to play chess with. It's all too much. He's grown on me too much to abandon him and run back home. Even if Gabe went to prison and all went back to normal, I don't think I could ever leave War on his own again.

It would crush him.

The doorbell rings again and I leap from the couch ignoring my stiff muscles. The memory of our kiss and my lingering dream of Brandon are momentarily put on hold as I make my way to the door. Hobbling over to the door, I question who could be here at this ungodly hour. Maybe another delivery of shoes. The notion has me reaching for the doorknob with a smile on my face.

But as I reach for it, a deep voice startles me.

"Don't answer it."

I turn and regard a sleepy War with furrowed brows.

"Why not? It's probably just a delivery."

He growls and storms over to me. "Because," he hisses, "what if it's him? Did you even look? I have the alarm on for a reason, Bay. To protect you. The deliverymen always leave the packages on my doorstep per my instructions. Whoever is here is not delivering anything to me."

Fear of Gabe assaults me and my knees buckle.

I could have just opened the door to him. I'd allowed myself to grow comfortable in War's home and forgotten what was truly at stake had that man found me again. He could have snatched me up and taken me to his stupid cabin before I even knew what hit me.

I'm frozen as memories assault me.

Frozen cucumbers.

Butt plugs.

His large fingers probing and stretching every hole in my body.

A shudder wracks through me. Mom would be screwed and I'd live the rest of my life getting tortured by that sadistic monster.

No thank you.

"I'm sorry," I tell him with tears in my eyes. "I didn't think."

He relaxes and I can see that he itches to comfort me in some way. Problem is, with War, there is no way. Only words, no embraces. "It's okay. Go get dressed. I'll figure out who it is."

Hurrying away from the door, I make my way into my room. I locate a pair of jeans and T-shirt and dress in record speed. By the time I finish, I can hear raised voices in the other room.

Oh, God.

He's here.

Snatching up a tall, metal candleholder from the bedside, I raise it and creep out of the room prepared to crack it over his head. War comes into view first, his features contorted into an angry scowl. I hold a finger to my lips to warn him. His face pales and he raises a hand.

"Bay, no!"

Charging from around the corner, I ready myself to kill Gabe. I'm furious for the horrors he put me through and am eager to break his skull. Then, this can all be over. I'm about to swing the candlestick when War snatches it from my grip and rips it away from me.

The man in the foyer is *not* Gabe.

He turns to regard me with a frown and I can see that this man is older and has greying hair mixed in with his dark hair. The man is almost an exact image of War.

"Baylee, this is my dad, Loveland McPherson." War's jaw is clenched in frustration as he sets the candlestick down on the entryway table.

I blink at the older man several times before responding. "I'm Baylee Winston, Mr. McPherson."

My words seem to drag the man out of his stupor and he reaches a hand out for me. "Call me Land. And I must say, I've never known War to have anyone over before. Ever. Are you two..." he trails off as if searching for the right words, "together?"

Glancing at War, I plead with my eyes for him to handle the explanation.

He nods and clears his throat. "Dad, Baylee is my, uh, girlfriend."

Land frowns at me before he flicks his gaze over to War. "And, son, how *old* is your girlfriend?"

XIX | War

FUCK.

I didn't expect Dad to show up for one of his random visits. I mean, I know it had been awhile since he'd last visited, so I knew I was due for another. But the timing is horrible. He won't understand about Baylee.

Her bottom lip trembles and I can almost feel her heartbeat in my ears. Thump, thump, thumping. I crave to hold her body that still quivers from the fear of thinking Gabe was here. The man is a fucking monster. I'm not sure I even want to know what all he's done to her. It might make me crazier than I already am. Or homicidal.

"She's seventeen."

I wince and then count the seconds until he explodes. With Dad, it's coming.

One, two, three, four...

"ARE YOU KIDDING ME RIGHT NOW, WARREN THOMAS MCPHERSON?"

In a natural move, I stand between her and him. My dad

wouldn't hurt her. Ever. But I still don't like him being near her while he's pissed. She's had enough bullshit lately to have to deal with my dad's tantrum too.

"Dad, listen—"

"No! You listen to me, son! This is un—"

"I'm here on my own free will!" Baylee shouts over us. "Land, I'm okay. I promise. And we haven't had sex, if that's what you're worrying about. I'm here to keep War company."

Dad's furious body that ripples with rage relaxes. "What about your parents? Do they know you're here?"

She lifts her chin bravely. "I'll be eighteen soon and I have been in contact with my dad. He knows I'm with your son. I promise, I'm not War's prisoner. He's helping me, too."

Dad flits his gaze from her to me. "How much did you pay her?"

"Can we talk about this later?" I question through gritted teeth.

He nods and I heave out a breath of relieved air. Turning around to face Baylee, I give her a smile. "Why don't you go and shower. I'll make you some breakfast."

She seems hesitant to leave but finally turns and bounces off toward her room. I stare at her perfect ass until she disappears around the corner.

"Tell me all of it. Now, Warren," Dad hisses out.

I sigh and motion for him to follow me. "I'm going to cook breakfast. We'll talk in the kitchen."

While I start pulling things out of the refrigerator, Dad respects my needs by spending a good ten minutes at the sink washing up past his elbows. It was a battle in the beginning but after passing out on several different occasions as he tested my will on the matter, he'd finally bent to my needs. And

I don't even have to look at him to know he's left his shoes by the door as well and is donning blue surgical booties.

"Start talking, son."

I begin chopping vegetables to make vegan omelets and sigh. "I'm lonely, Dad."

"I know this," he says softly and begins pulling glasses out to fill with orange juice. "But you've been lonely since Lilah. You haven't had one single female companion since her in fact. I'm not necessarily shocked that you've clearly paid a woman to entertain you but what I'm fuming about is her age. So I will ask you once again to tell me all of it."

My dad and I have always been close but when Mom died, we knew we only had each other after that. He expects the truth from me and I've never had a reason to lie. Now included.

"I stumbled across a site online. It seemed professional and legit. And it was fucking expensive," I say with a grumble. "I'd called ahead and spoke with the coordinator. They changed their event to a silent auction to accommodate my needs and even agreed to keep my participation anonymous. From the car, I watched them all prance across stage. But one stood out."

I've stopped chopping and I fixate on a small square tile on the backsplash. There are seven hundred and forty-six tiles on the backsplash. I've counted them. Five hundred and twelve are pure white and two hundred and thirty-two are slightly marred. And two have cracks near the sink. My gaze travels over to the two cracked ones. Perfect aside from the fissure that runs right down the middle. Most days, I crave to get a Dremel tool and grind them out of the backsplash. But other days, I focus on the imperfect ones as a reminder.

Maybe I can find another person, like me, and we can exist in a sea of perfection—broken but still beautiful and necessary.

"Son…"

I blink and continue. "She counted her steps across the stage. Seventeen steps, Dad. Her mouth moved as she counted and I became fixated on her. For a brief moment, I'd hoped she'd been like me. Different. When the man delivered her to my car and she spoke, I knew I wasn't going to let her go."

"Warren, I don't think this sounds legal. There's more to this isn't there? What did you pay for her?"

I groan and avoid his eye contact. "Five million."

"Jesus fucking Christ, son!" he hisses. "What were you thinking?"

"I wasn't. I was just tired of being alone."

"So, you paid a seventeen-year-old five million dollars to be your companion? Why is she still here?"

"Well, it's more complicated than that, Dad. I didn't understand what I was doing when I bought her. It was some sort of sex ring. I swear I didn't know," I tell him, shame causing my voice to go husky.

"Look at me."

I drag my gaze to his and frown. "I bought her from some asshole who did sadistic shit to her. Stuff that has twisted her head up. Evil bastard. And the shit he did to her against her will…" I trail off and shudder. "So incredibly sick."

"So you know all of this and you still kept her?"

"I'm fucking lonely!" I roar and slam the knife down on the countertop. "I wanted to die. Again. Those thoughts were swarming me, like they often do. I was drowning in them. But then Baylee came along. She makes me forget, Dad. I actually *want* to touch her."

My dad, after having had dealt with my issues for over a decade now, softens and his brows furrow together. "You want to touch her?"

I nod and smile sheepishly. "I kissed her. Twice."

His eyes widen and his brows fly to his hairline. "You kissed her? So you actually touched someone on your own free will? You didn't force her did you?"

"No, I didn't. In fact, she seemed upset the first time when I pulled away and had a fucking meltdown. I had to take a long ass shower to wash her off me. But…"

Dad is no longer angry. He seems hopeful.

"But then, as soon as I came back to her, I wanted her again. She's addicting. I want to hear her voice, see her smiles, and bask in her warmth. For the past few weeks, I've wondered if I have a chance at healing my fucked up head. That maybe she is my answer."

He nods thoughtfully. "If you have faith that she can, then it's most certainly possible. Promise me one thing though, War. Promise me you won't touch her until after her birthday. You're a good man and I don't want this underage thing weighing on your conscience or sending my only son to jail. You're not like the man who hurt her. You're my son and we've got morals."

I go back to chopping when he speaks again.

"So she's a millionaire at seventeen," he says, astonished.

"Well, not exactly."

He grunts. "But you just said—"

"Gabe has the money. The man I bought her from."

Risking a glance at my dad, my shoulders slump at his furious stare. "After all those things he did and…"

I huff. "I know. But what am I supposed to do about it?"

"I don't know, call the goddamned cops on him!"

"Dad, it's not that easy!" I snap and immediately feel guilty for yelling at him. "Besides," I soften my tone, "I'm in contact with a detective in Oakland. I've been giving her information that won't lead back to me in hopes they'll catch Gabe. Her parents never filed a missing person's report. Something is going on and I'm not about to send her back to the lion's den where that asshole will come back for her. She's safe here. Besides, we worked out another deal."

He waits expectantly.

"I've been sending money to help her mom. She's sick."

A groan rumbles from his chest and he turns away from me. His gaze falls to the windows that overlook the Pacific Ocean. I know he's thinking about Mom. Our thoughts always drag back to her. She's the reason I am who I am today.

"So you're dumping more money just to keep this girl? You do understand you'll be broke and heartbroken before it's all said and done." His voice cracks and I wish I could hug him. I've not been able to do that since I was a teenager.

"What else can I do? I was desperate. With Baylee, life is different. Less lonely. I know you may not understand all of my reasoning but trust that I'll be smart. I'm not going to hurt her but I'm also not going to let her go. I can't. Not now."

I hear someone clear their throat from behind me. "Am I interrupting?"

Whipping around, I smile at her. She's freshly showered, her blonde hair pulled into a messy wet bun on top of her head. The dark jeans she's wearing hug her figure and the baby blue sweater does nothing to hide her gorgeous tits. My cock reacts to seeing her, and I quickly turn back to my task of cooking to hide my erection. "No, we were just talking about how I came to acquire you."

"You told him?" she questions as if she's shocked.

My heart speeds up to see her from the corner of my eye beginning her hand washing ritual. She doesn't have to count. I'll count for her. But after today, neither of us will have to. Another gift for her should arrive at some point this afternoon. I ordered it not long after she arrived but it was being custom made to my specifications.

"Why wouldn't I tell him?" I say with a chuckle. "He's my father. I tell him everything. Didn't you tell your dad everything?"

Dad leans against the counter and watches our exchange with interest.

"Well," she says slowly and starts to turn off the water, "not everything."

Her cheeks blaze red with embarrassment and I laugh. But when she turns off the sink, my laughter dies in my throat.

"Not done. Forty-eight more seconds," I bark out a little more harshly than I intended. Dad grumbles behind me but doesn't say any more on the subject.

The water turns back on and she continues to scrub her hands. "Now?"

I start frying the vegan omelets and sigh. "Not yet."

The seconds pass by but I don't tell her when the time is up. A few more moments of washing never hurt anyone.

"Baylee," Dad says in a soft voice. "I'm sorry for what happened to you. You're a victim. And if you decide you want to leave, you call me. I'll drive you home myself."

She shuts off the water this time and I don't stop her. "I'm okay right now. Thank you, Mr. McPherson."

"Please, call me Land. You're strong and you're brave.

Thank you for attempting to help my son, no matter what your motives are for doing it. That means the entire world to me and I'll do whatever I can to return that favor."

In a surprising move, she hurries over to him and throws herself into his arms. He hugs her tight—*like I wish I could*—and strokes her back in a way that always comforted me as a child. I'm jealous of both of them. That they can hold each other and I can't hold either of them.

He murmurs whispered assurances and I finish the food up, careful to make each omelet the same size with equal portions of vegetables and tofu in them. Once I've added some sliced bananas to the side, I carry the plates to the table. She finally breaks away from his embrace and flashes me a shy smile.

"So tell me about yourself, Baylee. If you're someone special to my son, then you're someone special to me," Dad says after we settle at the table and begin eating.

She sighs and her eyes focus past him at the ocean as if she's recalling happy memories. "I run track and am pretty good at it. My parents Tony and Lynn are good to me, and we live in a modest home in Oakland. I plan on going to Berkley next fall. Well, I *did* plan to go there."

My father and I both frown. Guilt slices through me and I stuff another bite into my mouth as she continues.

"I love to read. Swimming is something I enjoy, especially in the ocean. Um, that's all I guess."

"Did you know War used to surf?"

Her eyes widen in surprise and she darts her gaze over to me. I grunt my confirmation and she smiles.

"I didn't know that. I don't know much about your son, I'm afraid. I mean," she says with hesitation, "besides the obvious. He doesn't tell me anything."

Dad glances at me, sadness and fatigue marring his features. "There's a lot to my boy. His sickness plagues him but he's still in there. I see him fighting to the surface sometimes. I'm glad that you're able to break through to him some."

"I'm right here," I complain and stab at a banana. "She's not my shrink."

He frowns and I wince. I shouldn't have said that. My father has only tried to help me ever since I lost my shit. It's not his fault I'm the way I am. He's only done everything he can to provide for me, accommodate my issues, and love me enough for two parents.

"What do you want to do when you, um," Dad says with a grunt, "grow up?"

I groan at his word choice but she doesn't seem to be affected.

"If you mean after high school," she says with a grin, "then I'd hoped to go to school on a track scholarship. I was always intrigued with medicine because of my mom. But now..."

I lift my gaze and meet her compassionate one.

"Now I'd like to get into psychology."

Her words are genuine and not meant to cut me. She's curious about my condition and it has sparked a desire to learn more. I should feel irritated that yet another person wants inside of my black brain.

But with Baylee?

I want her there.

"Have you been down to the ocean yet?" Dad asks as he stands and carries his plate to the sink.

She shakes her head. "It's the middle of winter. The water's probably cold..." she trails off, her sadness not letting her finish the argument.

He turns to me but speaks to her. "Nonsense. It's almost seventy degrees today. Sure, the water'll be a little chilly but you'd do well to get some sunshine. If it's okay with you," he says and his eyes meet mine, "I'd like to take her for a walk along the beach."

"Dad, I don't know if—"

"Really? I would love that. May I, War?" Her pretty blue eyes glitter with an excitement I've yet to witness. She's beautiful. And so deserving. How could I ever tell her no?

But the sand.

The salt from the water.

The wind blowing debris all around her, into her mouth and hair.

"Uh," I start and pinch the bridge of my nose.

She could bathe after.

Imagine how cute her nose would be with a little pink on the tip from the sun.

And she'd smell like memories that aren't tainted.

"Of course, Bay. I'll clean up while you two enjoy yourselves. But I can't promise I won't go fucking nuts if you track sand into my house. In fact, I'll have a broom waiting for you on the front porch. Make sure you hose off, too."

Her delighted squeal as she rises from her chair makes it all worth it and I find myself grinning.

XX | Baylee

I CAN'T BELIEVE HE LET ME OUT OF THE HOUSE, ESPECIALLY after my running away attempt. I'm nervous, fearing that Gabe could be lurking anywhere, but with Land within reach, I'm comforted. He makes me feel safe, like my dad always did.

"My son's a good man, you know."

Our feet squeak in the white sand as we trudge toward the crashing waves. I'd changed into a summer dress that billows in the wind and I realize this is the freest I've felt in weeks. I owe Land for that.

"Yeah," I say, probably not as convincing as he likes.

"There's a reason for the way he is, Baylee. And he's been," he chokes out, "so lonely for so long."

Tears well in my eyes. Despite having been stolen by Gabe and then sold to War, things feel different here. War doesn't hurt me. The only times my feelings get hurt are when I want him to touch me and he won't.

Well, he can't.

His mind won't allow him to.

But I don't miss the unmasked desire. Desire that ignites a flame inside of me. Shame courses over me as I consider what Mom and Dad would think about my sexual infatuation with a man I was sold to. What they would think of how I crave to make normal love with him.

And Brandon?

The boy I loved with my whole heart?

He's becoming more of a distant memory rather than a reality of someone I'll ever be with.

"It's pretty here," I say with a sigh, hoping to change the subject. Trotting off ahead of him, I grab the hem of my dress and run into the sudsy surf. The water is like ice but I welcome the way it envelops my ankles. Feeling braver, I wade out to my knees.

"Shit," Land curses, "that's cold!"

I laugh and turn to see him tip toeing toward me. "Big baby," I tease.

His chuckle warms me and he wraps an arm around me. Land is affectionate and it slices my heart thinking about how he'll never have that with his son again. I lean into his hug and let him hold me for a while.

"He had a girlfriend once," he says slowly, almost wistfully. "Of course, I didn't care too much for her. Lilah was rough around the edges. I suppose it wasn't her fault. Her dad was a damn idiot, but still. It grated on my nerves that they were together. Warren had potential. He was extremely smart and technical. But around her, he sort of walked around with hearts in his eyes."

I try to imagine a younger War. A War who was in love with a girl from the wrong side of the tracks.

"At the time, I'd been selfish. Tried to subtly push him in other directions—directions that she could be no part of. My Paula was not impressed with my actions. She'd reminded me of a time we'd been young, dumb, and in love."

"She sounds like a lovely lady. You speak fondly of her."

His grip around my waist tightens and his voice becomes hoarse as if he might cry. "She got pregnant, my Paula. At forty-four years of age. It was a miracle and a blessing."

I smile at his words.

But then he goes on to tell a horrifying story that roils my breakfast in my belly. A story that paints a vivid image of how War became the man he is today. The story of the loss of his pregnant wife causes Land to choke on his emotion.

A huge wave crashes toward us and if Land hadn't have gripped on to me at the right time, it would have knocked me over. My dress, now wet, clings to my thighs and I shiver.

"Come on," Land says gruffly and guides me out of the water and onto the warm sand. Together we sit and stretch our legs in the sun.

"What did you have?" I shouldn't ask but I'm curious.

He swallows and doesn't speak for a few moments. "A little girl. Constance was her name."

Was.

Tears brim in my eyes and I drop my gaze to my toes that are dusted with white sand and still dripping with ocean water.

A tear rolls out and I sniffle. He seems to sense my sadness for him and his wife because he pulls me against him again in a side hug. I like Land and am grateful for his presence.

"Poor War. My boy, my sweet boy."

His words are hollow and sad as he replays scenes so horrific involving War that I'm not sure I'll ever get them out of my brain. I try to quiet my sobs after hearing the details but they won't quit.

"After...after we lost them," he chokes out finally, the worst part of his words over, and I reach for his hand to grip it. "I lost War too. Not like I'd lost them but he'd become a shell of himself. And then, he turned into this person I was unsure how to help."

Something tells me he doesn't tell this story often—if at all. We both grow silent aside from our sniffling.

"Why couldn't the doctors help him?" My question is almost a whisper getting lost in the wind. I shiver and he hugs me tighter, rubbing his arm up and down my bicep that's covered in goosebumps.

"They tried. Believe me, they tried. But my son," he says with a teary chuckle, "is a stubborn one."

A smile plays at my lips. That he is. "I'm familiar," I tease.

"He spent five weeks in the psych ward after the accident, his obsessions grew and grew despite the constant psychiatric evaluations and therapies. The psychiatrist explained to me that he had PTSD, anxiety, depression, and OCD issues among other new problems including a delusional disorder. He seemed miserable there, so finally, I took him home where we struggled for months trying to learn how to cope. Together. Eventually, when his obsessiveness over blood and germs became too much, I'd asked if he'd feel more comfortable in his own place. A place where he could control the environment. I'd bought him this house in an effort to make him feel close to his mother and to give himself space. As time went on, I became angry at him for his behavior—as if he had some way to change it. We fought but eventually I decided having my son was more important than trying to make him heal when he wasn't ready."

I turn my head over my shoulder and look back up at the house. A dark shadow stands at the window.

War.

That poor, beautiful, tortured soul.

"What about his girlfriend?"

He groans. "Lilah? She only made things worse. Out of desperation for him to return to his normal self and either reconnect or break up with her, I'd invited her over while he was staying with me. I'd already learned to respect his no touching rules, but she'd barged in and had thrown herself at him. What she didn't know or understand was that War was no longer the boy she knew. When he pushed her away and roared at her to not touch him, she burst into tears and spewed nasty words at him that don't need repeating. Needless to say, I ended up dragging her out of my home and that was the last we'd seen of her. War tells me she's married now with three kids."

Turning back to look at the ocean, I sigh. "I feel so bad for him. For you. I'm so sorry. You both must have been so devastated."

He climbs to his feet and then tugs me up too. We embrace and I bury my face into the warmth of his chest. I wish I could do more to help them.

"Come on," he says finally, "let's get you back inside before you freeze. Besides, War looks like he's about three seconds from breaking from his cage to come fetch you himself. That boy likes you."

The fondness that he speaks of his son with warms me.

It's easy to forget my problems after hearing Land's story.

"What am I going to do?" I ask as we walk to the house. "I can't stay here forever. Once my mom gets the help she needs, I'll need to leave to be with her. Or worse yet, if Gabe figures out where War lives, he'll come for me. Either way, War will be hurt."

Land remains calm for a short while. "Just give him a chance to love you. Even if it is only for a short while. Then, when it comes time for you to leave on your own free will, I will be here for him to pick up the pieces once again. He deserves a sliver of, albeit brief, happiness in his dark world. And you're just the right person to give him that."

"What happens if my choice is taken from me? If Gabe finds me?" I shiver as I remember the terror of being chased in his woods and the things he did to me after.

"War and I will protect you. I swear it on every penny I own in this world."

A beeping wakes me up and I stretch. It's been over a week and a half since Land came to visit and my feelings for War have intensified. I can no longer hardly keep my hands to myself. On more than one occasion, I've had to physically refrain from touching him. After learning about what happened to his mother and sister, I crave to comfort him. To understand him. Land had given me insight into the issues that plagued War.

PTSD.

Depression.

Anxiety.

OCD.

A delusional disorder.

I've been a witness to his issues for over a month now. When I'm not trying to make contact with my dad, I'm researching all of his conditions until the late hours of the night. I want to understand him. I need to fix him.

Now that I'm getting to know him well, I watch for his non-verbal cues to better understand what he won't tell me. Sometimes I ask him to tell me stories of his childhood or the beach—times I knew he'd been happier. We've played chess every night, and every day we laugh until it hurts. He's funny, flirty, and incredibly good looking. I'm completely crushing over this flawed man.

And I know the feeling is mutual.

The intense desire he feels for me is evident every time our eyes meet and it thrills me to no end knowing he wants me. I just wish there was a way we could break through his mental barrier so it could happen.

Dad went silent which has upset me. No more replies. No more scathing demands for me to come home. Nothing. Despite my attempts to reach out to him or Mom, I'm met with silence. Thankfully, as promised, War has continued to wire money to them each day. Dad may have his reasons for cutting off contact with me but Mom deserves all the help she can get. And I know my parents, my father would die if anything ever happened to her. He will do everything in his power to save her.

I push the button on my watch to silence the beeping and can't help the smile that plays at my lips. After that day Land took me to the beach, War surprised me with a watch.

He'd told me he wanted rose gold because it reminded him of me—a sweet notion in itself—but then decided it should be bold, pink, and waterproof. He revealed that it fit me better because I was brave and indestructible. A shiver runs through me again at the memory of his sweet words.

"Bay," he says softly and enters my bedroom, interrupting my thoughts that are all over the place this morning. "I have something I want to give you."

I sit up in bed and push the hair out of my eyes. His gaze falls to the T-shirt I'd slept in for a brief moment before he smiles at me.

"I have fresh coffee waiting for you at your spot," he assures in a playful tone that has me crawling out of bed after him. His eyes flicker with a hunger that can frequently be seen in his stare. I walk past him, inhaling his fresh, manly scent on the way to the sofa that has a great view of the ocean.

"What's this?" I ask, seeing a black hatbox sitting on the table. It's tied with a pretty, hot pink ribbon. I sit down on the sofa and give him a confused look.

He smiles, almost as if he's embarrassed, and sits surprisingly close to me. "I got you a gift."

"My birthday isn't until tomorrow," I chide but can't help the excitement bubbling to the surface.

"Well, in that case, I suppose I'll take it back to my closet and hold onto it until—"

"Not so fast, mister!" I say with a laugh and playfully swat at him.

He beams at me and I adore the twinkle in his eyes.

Turning, unwillingly, from his handsome face, I grab hold of the ribbon and tug. After I lift the lid, I gasp.

"You hate it."

Ignoring his words, I lift the pair of pink Nike's from the box and stare at them. Underneath the shoes are some running shorts and a sports bra. At the very bottom is a pink iPod.

"What is all this?" My voice is breathless and I don't let go of the tennis shoes.

"I thought perhaps you'd enjoy running along the beach for exercise. You know, since it means so much to you. From my perspective, I can watch you all the way to the restaurant, a mile to the left, and the big dock about a mile to the right. It'd be a great length to—"

Without thinking, I launch myself at him. I'm thrilled and wrap my arms around him in a gracious hug. It isn't until a few heartbeats later that I realize what I've done. Tearing from him, I stand and look down at him.

"I'm so sorry! Oh my God!" I let out a ragged breath of air upon the realization that I touched him in ways he'd flip out over.

His jaw clenches and his hands fist at his sides. The internal battle that wages in his head is in full force. I have to do something.

"Warren, look at me."

Eyes remain fixed on the coffee table and he doesn't respond.

Doing the only thing I can think of, I grab the hem of my shirt and tug it from my body. My tiny scrap of black panties are the only thing keeping me from being completely nude.

"Warren, look at me."

It takes everything in him to drag his gaze to my body but when he does, the relaxing of his muscles is almost instant. His hands are no longer in fists and he rakes them through his chocolate-colored hair in a way that makes me think he's controlling himself from touching me.

"Follow me," I instruct.

He blinks a couple of times but stands on shaky legs.

"I won't touch you but you need to shower so you'll feel better. Come on."

I walk off toward his bedroom and am thankful to hear him padding behind me. Once I make it to his bathroom, I push my panties down and start the shower. His shower is a nice walk-in, tiled shower with plenty of space for the two of us. When steam starts to fill the bathroom, I turn to see his hulking frame taking up the doorway.

"Take off your clothes, Warren. I'm not going to hurt you."

He swallows but heeds my direction. With a quick grip of the bottom of his shirt, he tugs it off his body and up over his head in one swift movement. I chew on my lip when his muscular chest is bared to me. What I wouldn't do to touch that chest.

"I'll be waiting," I say, a hint of sauciness in my voice, and step into the warm spray.

My hope is that he won't leave me hanging. I want him in more ways than I should. And helping him is my priority.

"I used to be able to run a mile in six minutes. Do you think I can beat that with those shoes? They look awfully fast." My hope is to distract him with numbers. It must work because he steps into the shower and my mouth hangs open. The man's body is a beautiful sight to behold. His height combined with his lean physique is a turn on, and my pelvis begins to ache with need.

"I think you could beat that time. Easily." His response is

more than I could have expected and I sigh in relief.

I grab the bar of soap and lather up my body in a slow, teasing way. His eyes never leave where my hand travels. It's as if he's fixated on what it'll do next.

"Your turn." I hold out the bar by one end and he carefully takes it from me.

With the same level of excitement, I watch him cleanse himself. His cock, thick and long, points at me as if to accuse me for being some seductress.

"Why are we showering together?" he questions as he sets the bar down on the ledge.

I pout at his words, wondering if maybe he doesn't feel the same desire for me as I do for him. "I thought that maybe…"

His dark brow raises in an amused way that has heat creeping over my flesh.

"Since this is a safe place for you," I try again, "that maybe I could touch you or you could touch me. We're clean."

Dark blue eyes find mine and hope flickers in them. My body craves to climb up his firm chest and sink myself on his hardened cock but I know better. Instead, I wait for his next move.

XXI | War

HE WATCHES ME WITH NARROWED EYES, THE SAME competitive look she gives me when we play chess. In her eyes, she's calculated all of the moves and she's certain she will win. But for me, I've counted thousands of other variations. Move upon move upon move of how things could and should go.

This time, she might win.

Chess may be my game that I dominate.

But this?

This is clearly her territory.

My heart thumps in my chest as I contemplate whether or not I have the strength to do what she wants. Is it really that simple?

Suds run down her pert tits and my cock feels like it may explode with a long overdue release. I want to do so many things to her but I don't know that I can.

"Can I touch you? All you have to do is tell me to stop and I'll let go, War. Trust me."

Her smile is kind but her eyes are hungry. I do trust her. Problem is, I don't trust myself. What if I push her away from me in a moment of mental breakdown? Would she crack her head on the tile? Would blood run down and mix with the water at our feet?

I clamp my eyes closed.

I can't do this.

What if—

"Warren, look at me."

It's almost painful having to open my eyes, but I do. Staring back at me is the most decadent woman on this earth.

"Let me feel you," she says firmly and my dick twitches at her words.

Her arm stretches for me and I flinch when her fingertips tickle the flesh over my heart. Our eyes meet and I nod. She's right, I do want her to touch me. It feels safe in here. When they start to move down, I groan. My dick bobs up and down as if it begs to be caressed next. But she ignores my eager cock and pokes a finger into my belly button. Her smile is wicked and I chuckle.

"Okay so far?" she purrs.

That voice, low and seductive kills me.

"More than okay."

Her eyes shine with pride and her other hand begins to explore me. I should be obsessing over all sorts of chaos that normally plagues me but all I can think about is each cell in my body coming alive at her tender touch.

She revives dead parts of me.

She's the sun, water, and earth. And I'm a seed that has hope to grow into something strong and beautiful. Because of her.

One of her hands slides up my shoulder and cups the side of my neck. Her eyes darken and her other hand moves purposefully downwards.

"Jesus, Baylee," I say with a growl.

A choked gasp is the only sound I make as she softly grips my erection. Bliss explodes from where her small fingers touch me there. I'd expected the crawling, itchy sensation to overtake me at any second. The burning and the flood of awful thoughts.

But they never come. All of my focus is on the millions of nerve endings in my shaft all eager for her to stroke me to heaven.

"My God," I hiss out when she begins moving up and down along my length. My eyes start to close but I force them back open. Right now, I'm safe. With her. If I close my eyes, the demons will suck me under and it will all be ruined.

"Does that feel good? Am I doing it okay?"

I grit my teeth and nod at her. Every other stroke, her fingernails graze my testicles and I nearly lose it.

"I won't last long. It's been so long and—"

"Shhh," she murmurs and pulls her hand from my neck so she can knead her breast with it. "Come for me, Warren. I want you to let go and feel how much I want you."

Her thumb and finger pinch her pebbled pink nipple and I groan. So close. The sight arouses me even further, like nothing I've ever seen before, and I can't control myself any longer. A burn deep in my lower abdomen seizes me and I come without warning.

"Baylee!" I snarl out, but never take my gaze from hers.

She intensifies her actions as I throb out my release. It splatters her soapy belly before running down toward the drain. When I'm no longer twitching, she slides her hand off and sets to cleaning herself off. As if she knew I'd lose my shit about having my cum all over her.

What she doesn't know is that a fire has begun to burn inside of me.

Seeing my cum spurting all over her body awoke some carnal part of me.

A part that needs to possess and take what's mine.

Baylee *is* mine.

But can I do it? Can I actually make love to her?

"I want to touch you," I mutter. I wonder if the words were even spoken aloud. My gaze falls to her breasts, not because they're beautiful because they are, but I can't look at her. What if I fail? What if I pussy out and can't offer her the same pleasure in return?

Her even, melodic breathing calms me and I count five of her breaths before I have the courage to look back up at her.

"Is that okay?"

Pink, perfect lips turn up in a sweet smile and it spurs me on. I'll push through whatever mental barriers I can in order to have her. I will do whatever it takes. I can do this.

"More than okay."

I push a palm against the tile beside her and lean in. She gasps at my proximity but doesn't move.

"Spread your legs," I instruct with false bravado. I want to behave like a normal man, not some scared as hell boy. "I don't know if I can do this but I really want to fucking try."

She flashes me a naughty grin and does as she's told. Then, she gathers her half wet hair up in her fingers and piles it on top of her head. My girl is smart. She's keeping her fingers occupied so she doesn't accidentally touch me and ruin the moment.

Leaning in close to her, hovering just above her mouth, I make my move. With a shaking, unsteady hand, I lower it to cup her pussy. She flinches from my touch and lets out a tiny, pleased sigh.

"Want me to touch you?"

She nods and chews on her bottom pink lip. It drives me wild and my cock is already thickening again, ready to play once more. Slipping my finger between the lips of her sex, I locate her throbbing clit and massage her. It's been ages since I touched a girl—Lilah had been the last—so it takes a minute to figure out the right pattern.

"Oh, God," she whimpers and her eyes flutter closed. "Yes, that feels good, War."

My name on her lips makes me want to beat my fists on my chest. I love how it sounds. I don't want her to murmur it, but to scream it. Intensifying my movements, I draw her closer to the edge of ecstasy. I've never seen her look more beautiful than she does now with her mouth parted open and her eyes closed. A pinkness tinges her nose and cheeks as she grows closer to climaxing.

"Can you touch me inside, too?" she murmurs and jolts against my touch.

I grunt, unsure on whether or not I'll lose my mind and decide to at least try. Slipping my thumb to her clit, I then plunge my middle finger into her hot, tight center.

Jesus fucking Christ.

I can't think about anything aside from the way her body clenches around my finger, almost brutally. Images of how my cock would feel buried inside of her are the only ones in my diseased head at the moment.

"Yes," she moans, "deeper!"

Without thinking, I slip my free hand from the wall to grip under her thigh. I lift it up and it allows me better access inside of her. My finger grazes the pea-sized nub inside of her and she shudders wildly at my touch.

"Ahhhh!"

I massage that spot inside of her harder and force her into another orgasm before she even comes down from the first. When she lets out a pained sob, I slip my hand out of her and catch her before she collapses in the shower. Ignoring awful images, I delay those thoughts and stay in the moment with her. Gathering her soapy, languid body in my arms, I pull her to me—against my firm chest and hard cock.

Our heartbeats are now in competition on which can make it to the finish line first. The moment isn't ruined by talking or acknowledging that this hasn't happened to me in over a decade. Instead, we bask in the frozen moment of time.

"Are you okay?" she questions after some time. "I'm afraid to move. I can't tell you how good it feels for you to hold me."

I close my eyes but images of me holding her until I crush her ribs and puncture her lungs terrorize me. Quickly, I jerk them back open.

"I'm better than fine. I'm afraid to let you go."

But the water starts to cool and I'm forced to break from her so we can rinse off before the water turns to ice.

After we're both wrapped in our own towels and are standing in the bathroom, she speaks again. "What are those for? Do you take all of them?"

"Fluoxetine, fluvoxamine, sertraline, clomipramine. All antidepressants prescribed to help with OCD," I say softly. Then, I point to another group on the countertop. "Zoloft,

Prozac, Paxil, Klonopin, Valium. I've tried them all at least once. They never work."

She frowns and picks up the clomipramine. "I read good things about this one. A lot of studies had said it helped."

"That's the one that I tried to pick non-existent scabs from my belly. Apparently in some people, the anxiety worsens. Besides, I feel better when I don't take anything at all."

"Oh," she says, a hint of disappointment in her voice, and sets it on the countertop. "I see."

Needing to change the mood, I stalk out of the bathroom and into the bedroom. "Why don't you put on your new outfit? I'll make us some breakfast before your run."

I turn just in time to see her reaction. Her breathtaking smile lights up not only her soul but mine as well. It's a sight to behold. A sight I'll never tire of seeing.

My hot breath against the glass revives her smudges from when she first got here. The B encircling the heart warms me. I'll never grow tired of seeing it here. My housekeeper was informed to leave it be when washing the windows.

She's been running for two hours now back and forth up the beach. I miss her voice and her smell but I love how happy she seems. A couple of times she stops to suck down one of the three water bottles she took down with her in her bag. Other times she stops to stretch. And every so often, she turns toward the house and waves. I know she can't see me from where she's at but I always wave back.

The things she does to my heart are wicked.

Ever since she gave me the world's best hand-job known to man, I've been unable to force her from my mind. Not that I'd want to anyway. For the first time in a long time, I'm able to get lost in something that doesn't bring pain or heartache my way. She gives me something to look forward to. Baylee gives me hope.

Which is why...

I took the fucking Klonopin.

If it helps, even a little, I could touch her more. Kiss her maybe. Taste her. The thought isn't as abhorrent as it would have been a week ago. In fact, it's all I can think about. My mouth waters and I practically drool for a taste of her.

Perhaps tonight, I can dull my senses enough to get lost inside of her. What I wouldn't give to be able to thrust into her tight pussy and rain worshipful kisses all over her neck and face. To let my fingers dance all over her flesh in an effort to bring her multiple orgasms.

I can do this.

At least I fucking hope so.

The timer dings and I rush to turn the heat off of the mushroom bourgignon I'd been cooking for the past two hours. Only another ten minutes left on the mashed cauliflower with garlic and chive. I hurry back to the window and look up and down the beach for her.

No blonde ponytail swishing back and forth as she runs.

No perfect ass in black spandex shorts.

No long legs striding down the beach effortlessly.

"Shit!" I hiss and my panic rises, threatening to suffocate me.

What if he took her?

Did that motherfucker come onto *my* beach and take *my*

beautiful Baylee?

With a growl, I storm toward the front door. I sling it open, ignoring my fears and prepare myself to run after them. Instead of running for her, she nearly runs into me.

"Jesus, I turned my head for one second and thought he'd taken you. You scared me," I tell her with a relieved growl.

Sweat trickles down her bright red cheeks and she grins at me. "I was tired and hungry."

I swallow down my unease and let the joy of having her back in my presence overtake me. A week ago I'd be having a shit fit about all the toxins she's bringing into my home. But today, I just want her home.

"Why don't you run and shower. Dinner is almost done."

She flashes me another cute smile and bounces off. After I reactivate the alarm, I try to still my racing heart. Will it always be this way? Me worrying over her to the point of unhealthy obsession. I already can't work or sleep. And the only reason I eat is because she spends her meals with me. It's like if I have to have a moment without her, I'm fucking depressed about it.

Another timer sounds and I stalk back into the kitchen. While she showers, I set the table, careful to present each plate in a perfect, even way. Our wine glasses are both filled three quarters of the way full. Exactly the same amount.

I'm not one to drink but I keep it on hand for the rare times when I can't cope and want to drink away my insanity. I don't let it happen often but it does happen. Tonight, if I can manage to drink a little wine on top of the Klonopin, maybe I can calm the fuck down enough to make love to her.

I wait, watching the doorway, for what seems like ages before she finally appears. She's freshly clean but her cheeks are still a little red from her run. Her hair has been pulled into one of those neat buns she knows I love and she's put on a sleeveless black wrap dress which ties on one side. It's kind of short and distracts me momentarily. Her feet are bare—just the way I like them.

"You look incredible," I rush out, craving to pull her into my arms.

She blushes at my words and takes her seat at the table. "This looks amazing, War."

I turn on some music that calms me before sitting down with her. If we tried hard enough, we could almost imagine we were on a real date at a nice restaurant like normal people.

The evening goes off without a hitch and as we drink more wine, I feel a calm like never before settle over me. I'm not sure if it's the Klonopin, the wine, or just Baylee that's got me so relaxed but whichever it is, I am thrilled.

After dishes are done and put away, we retire into the living room. This time, she wins at chess and I don't care. I'm buzzed and happy.

"Checkmate!"

Her scream is loud and I start laughing so hard I cry.

"It's not funny!" she complains. "I win!"

"I let you win," I try to tell her through my tears.

She snatches a pillow cushion and heaves it at me. "Asshole."

I flash her a flirty grin that has her blushing. "You should take off that dress."

Her mouth pops open in shock and then she narrows her eyes at me. "Are you drunk, Warren McPherson?"

Smirking, I shrug my shoulders. "Maybe I just want to see your amazing tits again."

My cock has been at half-mast all during our chess game but now as she stands, her heated gaze never leaving mine, it practically rips through my slacks in an effort to be set free.

"You want me to strip for you?" she purrs, batting her eyelashes as she sashays over to the stereo. She bends over and my eyes fall to her perfect ass then along the backs of her creamy thighs and muscular calves.

"Depends."

She scoffs and puts her hands on her hips tossing me an annoyed glare. "Wrong answer. The answer is always yes when a woman asks if you want her to strip for you."

I chuckle and boldly rub my cock through my pants. Her eyes follow my action and she bites her lip. "Baylee, if you're going to be one of those strippers who teases me and leaves her underwear on, then I'm not interested. I want to see that pretty pussy and that fine ass."

She gasps, clearly embarrassed by my words, and turns away to find a song. Soon, the thump of a bass has her swaying to the beat. Her body begins moving along with Justin Timberlake as she "brings sexy back."

The music seems to be able to filter in through my ears and flow along my veins with my blood. Within seconds, I feel alive like never before. My cock aches to be inside her. My tongue waters to taste hers. My heart thumps with the beat in an effort to gallop right out of my chest and into her waiting arms.

She finds my gaze and holds my stare as she tugs at the ties on her dress. It falls open revealing nothing but skin from her collarbone to her now smooth pussy. I blink several times before attempting to speak.

"Oops, I forgot to wear them. You still interested? If not,

I can tie this back up and—"

"Drop the dress and come here so I can look at you properly," I order in a low, seductive tone. My skin buzzes and I think my cock might rip through my pants at any moment.

She lets the dress fall to the floor as she slowly moves toward me. Her body is all smooth curves. I have never wanted something so much in my entire life. For so long I've been shut off from the world and now it's as if the very best thing out there is presented to me on the shiniest fucking platter.

I'd be a fool not to at least try and take it.

I will have my Baylee tonight.

Even if it kills me.

XXII | Baylee

A HUNGER LIKE NEVER BEFORE BURNS BEHIND HIS EYES and all I want to do is add fuel to that flame. With War, he's always holding back, always living inside of that head of his, always afraid. But now, maybe the wine has gotten into him because he's hungry.

For me.

His tongue darts out and he licks his lips as if he wants to wet them before he puts them on my body. I'm slick between my legs with desire for him to lose control and take me. With Gabe, he'd been in control and I was a victim. Sure, I enjoyed a lot of what he did to me. But with War, I want whatever he has to offer. This morning, in the shower, it'd been heaven. Touching him and him touching me was erotic and addicting.

I want more.

"Do you like what you see?" I taunt and feign shyness as I approach.

His eyes darken and his gaze is smoldering. "You're the

most beautiful thing I've ever seen."

My first instinct is to be embarrassed by his words but his breathtaking smile is convincing enough to make me believe him. Tugging at my hair tie, I let my damp hair fall around me in loose waves in front of my shoulder. His eyes watch my every move.

"What now?"

He rises and takes slow steps toward me as if either he's afraid of me or he's stalking me, it's hard to tell. But by the ravenous glint in his eyes, I'd say the latter. When he makes it close enough for our chests to barely touch, he lifts a hand and brushes some hair from my eyes.

"You make me feel again, Bay." His eyes are narrowed as he inspects my features closely. I love looking at him closely because I can see flecks of green in his blue eyes. I can see the long silver scar along the side of his face more clearly and now understand he came to get it from the accident after what happened to his mother. I also like that I can see his full lips twitching at the corners as if he might break into another smile at any moment.

"You make me feel like we're the only two people in the world," I murmur back.

He lifts his hand and I close my eyes as he runs his thumb along my bottom lip. "So perfect," he says in a breathy whisper that tickles my face. "I want to kiss you."

I flutter my eyes back open and lean toward him. His scent is always so clean yet distinctly man. If I knew it wouldn't freak him out, I'd lick his neck to see if he tastes like a man too.

"So kiss me, Warren McPherson. And mean it this time."

His eyes darken, no doubt remembering our first kiss

not long after I'd arrived and the second one much later. He'd zoned out that first time, as if he were recalling his past, and kissed me like he wanted to fuck me against the kitchen counter. The second time, he'd seemed disgusted as the demons took over his mind. But tonight, I want him to kiss me like he wants to make love to me in his bed.

"So bossy," he says with a wicked smirk. He tangles both hands into my wild hair and draws me to his lips. The moment he grazes his across mine, a fire ignites between us. His tongue darts out, tentatively tasting my lips before pushing through and gaining access to me. I let out a pleased moan and happily meet his tongue with mine.

While he kisses me as if he'd love to devour my soul, I start undoing the buttons on his dress shirt as quickly as I can. I want him naked like me. I want him inside of me.

"Is this okay?" I murmur as I start pushing his shirt off his broad shoulders.

He groans and nips at my lip. "Better than okay."

I smile against his lips before pulling away to focus on his pants. He sheds the shirt and tank underneath as I attempt to free his thick cock from its prison. When he's finally standing naked in all his glory before me, I grin.

"Does the wine really help?" I question, my eyes landing on his proud cock.

He growls and scoops me into his arms. Never breaking stride toward his room, he flashes me a naughty smile. "It seems to be helping just fine. Let's make love before it wears off." His voice is tight when he says the words, no doubt fearing when the monster in his head will take back over.

Tomorrow, I'll pressure him to drink more wine. Clearly, he loosens up enough to lose his afflictions, even if only temporarily. I'll take what I can get.

When we arrive at his bed, he gently sets me down and a flash of apprehension crosses his features. I recognize the look.

What if?

What if?

What if?

"Shhh, quiet that head of yours, War. Grab a couple of towels, I'll lie on them so we don't mess up your blankets," I tell him.

Relief washes over him and he nods. I get a lovely view of his butt as he strides off to get towels. Moving out of his way, I let him obsessively cover his bed in not two but six towels. I suppose he's expecting a big mess.

I crawl back onto the bed and lie down on my back. With my best come hither stare, I non-verbally beg him to come make love to me.

"Bay," he says with a groan and runs his fingers through his hair. "There are certain things I don't think I can do—certain things I don't think I can let you do."

I frown and sit up on my elbows. "Are you going to make love to me?"

He nods but once again the demons fight for him. "I just…I just can't put my mouth there knowing…knowing…" His horrified expression knifes at my heart. In his mind, he won't be the lover I need him to be.

What he doesn't understand is…I just need him.

"Warren, come here and put your cock inside of my tight pussy," I taunt in a low, seductive voice. "I'm practically quivering with the need to have you inside of me. I don't care about that other stuff. I just want you."

He lets out a rush of air and nearly pounces on me. "Thank you, Bay. Thank you so much for being you."

His mouth covers mine as he settles his massive, warm body over mine. I hook my ankles around his waist and urge him closer. Each time his thick erection slides between the lips of my sex, I cry out with desire.

"Please," I beg against his wet mouth.

He reaches a hand between us and positions it at my entrance. "Our juices will mix," he says with a shudder and withdraws slightly, "the probability of—"

"We'll clean ourselves right after," I interrupt in a firm tone. "I promise. Don't make me beg for your big cock because I will. All night long."

His brows furrow in determination, hunger flashing in his eyes, and he nods. Slowly, almost painfully so, he pushes into me. I want to scream and beg and cry for him to slam into me, but I know this has to be on his terms.

"Jesus!" he hisses when he is seated completely inside of me. I can feel his cock throbbing and my pussy contracts with each pulse. We almost don't even have to move, our bodies knowing what to do without us.

"You've been missing out, huh?" I mutter and wriggle my hips.

He groans and begins a slow thrust into me. "Maybe I've just been waiting for the perfect woman. Happy birthday, Baylee."

My watch beeps indicating that it's midnight and I smile. Of course my obsessive man would know a second before midnight. My sweet, perfect, counting man.

"Go faster, mister, or you won't live to see yours," I say with a grin.

It's just the encouragement he needs. His hips buck against me, each thrust getting harder and harder. I try to kiss at him but he lifts up so he can watch me as he makes love to me.

"You're so tight and fucking perfect," he says with a grunt. "It's never felt this good."

I smile and then moan when he hits me deep. Curls of pleasure in my lower abdomen start their dance and I know it won't be long before I climax with him deep inside me.

"I like it too, War."

War satisfies a part of me that I never knew existed. He seems to own parts of my soul that I never knew were available for others to take. But he doesn't just take from me. In its place, he gives me parts of him that I will treasure forever.

"I won't last long, Bay. It's been so long."

"Shhh, just come. I want it."

I'm close but I don't care about my release. I want him to let go of ten years' worth of stress and sadness and despair. I want him to pour it all from him and never let it back inside.

"Bay!" he grunts out my name seconds before his heat explodes inside me. He doesn't quit his thrusting and I'm soon following.

Stars dance before me. Millions of them. I want to count them for him. Tell him exactly how happy he makes me in a numerical form he can understand.

"Oh God," he murmurs and buries his face into my neck. "You're so fucking beautiful when you come. I want to make you orgasm over and over again just to see the look on your face."

I run my fingertips along the bare, contoured flesh on his

back. I'm not sure how long he'll let me inside of his heart and head, but I'll be selfish and enjoy it while I can. After some time, he begins to tense up.

"Baylee, can we…"

"Shower?"

A huff of hair tickles my neck. "Please."

I nod and smile. "That's normal you know. So don't start thinking you're some weirdo because you want to clean up. Can I sleep in your bed after?"

He lifts up and gives me a look of sadness that overwhelms me nearly to the point of tears. "I want you in my bed every night. I want you in my arms every second of every day. And tonight, I will take you as long as I can have you."

I let the tears well in my eyes. When one races down my cheek, he swipes it away.

"But forgive me if my mind takes over and makes me its fucking hostage again. Promise me, beautiful."

As if I'd do anything else.

"I promise. I'm still yours even when you don't want me."

His face darkens. "You're always mine and I'll never stop wanting you."

As he sleeps, I stare at his handsome face. The bathroom light is on so his features are shadowed. Even in the dark. In the shadows. He's still innocent and pure. Warren has led a sheltered life from his own volition. His mother made a choice that ruined her son for life.

My thoughts drift to my own mother. I miss her so much.

There have been times I thought about calling Land to ask him to take me home. Not that I plan on staying there but so that I could check on Mom.

But once I was home?

I'd be right in the clutches of Gabe.

What would he do this time?

I shiver at the thoughts of him finding more objects to use on me. More chases through the woods. More pain. More mental head games.

No, I can never go back to that again.

I belong here with War.

A smile plays at my lips and I stroke his hair. His dark lashes jut out over his cheeks and his lids twitch every so often as he dreams. I could get used to staring at him every night while he sleeps.

My heart feels intertwined with his in a way Brandon's never had a chance to be. War and I've made love. Our connection is on a cellular level that I'm afraid can never be severed. Not that I want it to be. I'm afraid I'll feel lost and alone without him. The idea of leaving him is no longer an option I want to consider. I want to see my parents, sure. I miss Mom and Dad, incredibly so. But with Gabe in the picture, I know I'll live with that fear always hanging over me.

With War, I'm not afraid.

I feel powerful and cherished.

I feel cared for.

I even feel loved.

Leaning forward, I press a kiss on his cheek. His breath quickens and he frowns in his sleep. I hold in a chuckle and snuggle closer to him. My thoughts drift to earlier in the shower when he'd shown the first signs of coming down from the wine.

His eyes darted back and forth as if he were trying to listen to all the voices in his head at once. He raked his fingers through his wet hair and shuddered before meeting my gaze with an intense one.

"Let me clean you. I need to rid you of that bacteria. If you got a urinary tract infection or vaginal infection, I'd feel horrible."

My eyes widened as he dropped to his knees and I palmed the cold tile behind me to brace myself. He lathered up a rag with soap and then began an extremely thorough cleansing of my inner thighs, lips of my pussy, and even my ass. It was nothing like the time Gabe cleaned me. This was done out of pure obsession for my health and wellbeing. Instead of taking offense to his actions, I ran my fingers through his hair and massaged his scalp.

Once my skin was rubbed raw but squeaky clean, he rose to his feet.

"My turn," I told him with a smile.

I could tell he wanted to do it—to get every microbe off his body but he clenched his jaw and conceded by handing me the rag. With vigor, I soaped down the rag and then knelt down like he'd done moments before.

Taking my time, I scrubbed his cock and balls like he'd done for me. His hand stroked along the side of my wet hair and he groaned. The soft cock in my hands was growing harder by the second.

"Maybe you cleaning me was a bad idea."

I looked up at him and grinned. "Or a good idea. Depends on who you ask."

He tugged me to my feet and then pushed me against the

tiled wall. "I'm all clean but I want to make love to you again," he murmurs against my lips, "before all this slips away from me. I can feel it slipping, Bay."

I linked my fingers around the back of his neck and let him lift me. A moment later, he was deep inside of me. The burn from his obsessive cleansing was overshadowed by the intense bliss at having him stretch me with his thickness.

Our leap into oblivion was quick and after another careful cleansing, we turned off the shower and got out. I wasn't in any hurry to let his demons come rushing back in to steal him away from me which is why I took the eighteen-minute shower with him. I knew this because he timed us.

When we'd finished, I was worried he would push me away and want to sleep alone. Instead, he made no moves to send me away. I stood beside the bed and watched as his muscled frame flexed and tightened with each towel he picked up. Then, he discarded them in a hamper and climbed into his bed.

"I need to feel you," he murmured as he pulled back the covers and motioned to the bed beside him.

With a huge grin on my face, I scrambled into the bed and molded my body against his hot one. His fingers found my hair as he gazed at me with an emotion that nearly brought me to tears. War has eyes that sometimes let you glimpse into his soul. And right now, I had full access.

"Did you know you have between 120,000 and 150,000 hairs on your head?" he questioned and twisted a wet lock around his finger.

I smiled at him. "You told me a time or two."

He continued to regale me, despite having told me before, on how many hairs an average human loses all the while playing with mine. Even though I'd heard it before, it was still fas-

cinating and necessary for him to share that information with me.

"Up to a hundred strands a day in rare cases," I said, remembering a conversation before. "That's a lot."

He groaned but flashed me a sweet smile. "Tell me about it. If I let myself think about it, I'd go mad wondering how many you've shed since you've been here."

His eyes began their darting and I knew he was calculating. He thrives on details. The forces that normally possess him seemed to be in control when he could explain them to me. I also got a run down on my average breaths, heartbeats, and blinks per minute. But what got me was my smiles.

"Sometimes, your smiles run together," he said thoughtfully and ran his thumb along my bottom lip. "For someone who likes to count, this is difficult to calculate. When we play chess, you smile once. And it lasts the entire game. I live for that long precious smile."

I smile again recalling his words as I stare at the handsome sleeping man. His obsessions and compulsions may horrify others, including him. But I like learning about them because they're a part of who he is. As much as running is a part of my life, his quirks are a part of his.

"Momma," he mutters in his sleep. "Momma, no."

Frowning, I inspect his features. He's upset about something he's dreaming about. A part of me wants to wake him. But the selfish part worries he'll be back to his old self when he does wake. I'm worried he'll have a fit and kick me out of his room where I won't be able to touch and smell him. Where I won't be able to pepper kisses all over his face when the mood strikes.

I reach between us and grip his flaccid cock in an attempt

to draw him from bad dreams to a pleasant reality. With each stroke, he hardens and soon his hips are bucking against my hand.

"Shhhh," I whisper as I roll him onto his back. "I'll take care of you."

He cracks his eyes open and they widen. I recognize the fear in them—the fear of germs and catastrophes and touch and me. But I don't let him recoil. Instead, I straddle him and sink my body on his thick cock.

A pleased groan rips through him and his hands find my hips. His eyes have slammed shut and I smile, realizing I've won over his mind, even if for a short while. I've never been on top before with him so I'm unsure what to do at first. He seems pretty content to simply have me there. But soon, his fingers dig into my hips and he urges me to move. It takes a minute to get the hang of it, adjusting to his thickness, but I eventually start bouncing on him with vigor.

From this position, he's deep inside of me and reaching me in places that make me crazy. My breasts bounce and the slapping sound of my skin against his only serves to make me wetter for him. His hands slide up and begin kneading my breasts. When he pinches my nipples, my vision goes black with pleasure and I lose myself to an orgasm.

"Oh God!" I shriek and spasm around him.

It must send him over the edge because he hisses and throbs out his release inside of me.

"My Baylee. My sweet, sweet Baylee."

I don't climb off of him but instead rest on his chest and bury my face in his neck. His palms stroke my back. He doesn't urge me to get off of him. I'm relaxed and sated.

Warren is my whole world.

And I think I'm his too.

For now.

XXIII | War

"WHEN WE GET MARRIED, I WANT TO MOVE TO NEW York," Lilah mused as she took a hit of her joint. She attempted to pass it to me but I waved her off. It's something we didn't agree on, but I didn't press her to quit despite her many attempts to talk me into trying it.

"Our family is here in San Diego," I said with a frown. "Mom is pregnant. I can't leave my little sister or brother to move to New York on a whim, Li."

She pouted and I instantly felt guilty. "Warren, I can't stand my family. You know that. If we marry and move there, it won't matter about my age anymore. We can be free to make love all day and do whatever the fuck we want."

What I wanted was to get a degree in computer engineering and go into business with Dad like we'd talked about on numerous occasions. He had a business plan and everything. All he needed was my techy brain to learn more and we'd be in business. His plan was solid for where he wanted to take his company. And I was supposed to be a part of that. Running off *to New York with Lilah was not a part of that plan.*

"We can make love all day here," I said, my voice faltering.

She narrowed her eyes at me, understanding my hesitation, and slid off the bed to sit on the floor in front of me. Her glare stayed on me as she began unzipping my jeans and pulled my dick out. This was her thing. The girl would give me blow-jobs all day long as long as it meant she got her way.

As soon as her mouth wrapped around my dick, I snapped my eyes closed in pleasure. I hated that she could control me so easily with her mouth. While she bobbed her head up and down, taking me deep in her throat, I wondered if Dad would be okay with us leaving. I'd need his support for a move like that and—

My phone started beeping over and over again with texts, to the point I couldn't ignore it, despite needing to come so desperately. Lilah didn't quit as I read Dad's text.

Dad: GET HOME NOW! MOM LOST THE BABY! I'M ON THE PHONE WITH HER NOW—CAN'T TALK!

I shoved Lilah off my cock and was already yanking my pants up as I ran for the door, texting him back that I was on my way.

"What the fuck, War?!"

Ignoring her, I zipped my jeans up and snatched my keys. "I have to go. Love you," I blurted out as I ran for the door.

She cussed me out and called me a pussy. Her words stung but I didn't have time for explanations. I needed to get to Mom. The drive was a blur and all I could feel was the sticky saliva that had now dried on my dick. If I had the time, I'd have washed her off of me. Lilah was fucking insane. There was no way I could ever leave Mom and Dad. Especially now. Lilah would get over it and we'd stay in San Diego.

Slamming my car into park, I jumped out and bolted into the house. I could hear wails upstairs in her bedroom so I took the steps two at a time in an effort to get to her quicker.

"Mom!"

Her back was to me, but all I could focus on was the blood. So much fucking blood. And she was sitting right in the middle of a darkening, growing pool of it.

"I love you, Warren," she sobbed. "Please forgive me."

I peered over her shoulder and my jaw dropped to see the tiniest baby in her grasp. So bloody. So innocent. Not breathing. My heart lurched into my throat and I swayed with dizziness when I saw Mom bring the handgun up to her mouth. I didn't have time to stop her when a blast roared through the bathroom.

Time stopped. My eyes clamp closed. The bang echoed over and over and over again as I tried to find the nerve to reopen my eyes. It wasn't until I felt something trickle down past my nose and over my lips that my senses forced me to face my fears.

Popping my eyes back open, I stared in horror at the scene. Blood was everywhere. It coated the entire front of my body. Chunks of flesh were stuck to my throat and cheek. I scraped them off quickly. Dark hair hung from part of the fleshy pieces and I gagged at the sight.

This was my mother.

This was my mother.

Holy fucking shit I had to get her to a hospital!

Without hesitation, I began gathering all of the larger pieces of her skull and brain and collected them in a towel. I could have sworn I heard my dad calling for me but it had to be a hallucination. He was in LA. I was the man of the house while he was gone and it was my job to fix this. To save my mother. When I went to take the baby from her lap, I realized I had a sister. Her umbilical cord was still attached inside Mom. I'd seen on TV how they could save the baby sometimes as long as it was still connected.

With newfound determination, I scooped Mom, my sister, and the towel full of pieces the doctors would need into my arms. I slipped in her blood but managed not to drop her. The trip down the stairs and out of the house would later become complete black memories. I didn't recall how I got to the car, yet there I was, buckling my mother in, so she would be safe.

I climbed into the driver's seat and tore out of the driveway. Miles and miles, I drove at full speed trying to get to the hospital in time. I could save her. I could save my mother and sister. She'd become one of those famous stories the whole world found out about. A medical miracle. And I would be her hero. There was no reason for her to ask for forgiveness for anything. Everything was going to be fine.

"Momma," I choked out, "hang in there. Please. I need you. The baby needs you."

She was quiet and wouldn't respond. I risked a glance at her and my world ripped apart.

This was a fucking nightmare.

A replay of some horror story I watched as a kid.

The gore isn't real.

The blood is fake.

I would wake up soon.

My stomach heaved as I realize the half blown out skull belonged to my mother. It wasn't a small wound. Half her head was gone. There was no way anyone could survive such a blast.

She was dead. My sister was dead too.

What the fuck!

My skin began burning and itching where her blood and brain matter clung to me. I started to panic trying to wipe it away.

"Get it off of me!" I screeched and released the steering wheel to scratch at my flesh.

But in a matter of seconds, we hit a bump. The car jerked. I tried to grasp the steering wheel. But for the second time that evening, I was too late. We were airborne. A half-second later, we crashed head first off the side of the road.

The car was flipping one, two, three, four, five, six times.

Or twenty.

Or once.

Everything was a dizzy, painful blur.

When we finally came to a stop, all that could be heard was the hissing of the engine and my ragged breaths. And as I began to black out, I counted them.

One.

Two.

Three...

"War!"

I blink my eyes open and find that I am staring into the prettiest blue ones I've ever seen. I plead with my mind to allow me to stay there. With her. With an angel.

But I have to get this shit off of me.

"Get away from me!" I bellow. "I have to get it off me!"

Shoving her away from me, I stumble out of the bed and toward my shower. With shaking hands, I turn on the shower as hot as it will go. I need the soap and the water and the rag. I need to get this fucking shit off my skin.

Oh God.

Is it in my mouth?

I start scraping my fingernails on my tongue until I'm gagging. From behind me, I hear crying and I can't tell if it belongs to me or my sister or an angel.

"T-T-The water is too hot, War!"

A slender arm reaches past me to change the temperature. I reflexively slap the hand away. "Don't touch it!"

A shriek followed by sobs is all I hear as I start to step into the scalding rain. I need it gone. I need the blood down the drain and away from my orifices.

"Warren, please!"

Hands clutch on to my bicep and I go black with crazed rage. Spinning to face my attacker, I shove as hard as I can until they are out of the bathroom. My trembling hands slam and lock the door.

The heat is my salvation.

I will burn away the blood.

Stepping into the shower, I wince as the water scorches my flesh. I cry out and slam my fists into the tile. Pain explodes all over my knuckles and I gape in horror to see blood streaming from them.

Her blood.

Her blood.

Her motherfucking blood!

Snatching up a rag, I start scrubbing at my knuckles. I must wash every trace of her from my flesh. It stings and the blood only seems to run heavier.

I scrub and scrub and scrub.

Until…

A crash startles me.

"Warren." A deep voice.

I blink and shiver. The scalding water has somehow turned to ice. I'm confused and disoriented. I could swear it was just hot.

"Time to get out, son."

My dad.

I turn to the voice and shudder. My body aches and my heart feels empty. I'm missing a part of it. I start to claw at my chest in an effort to piece it back together when Dad grabs hold of my jaw. I've barely had time to process that he's touching me and to fight him off when he shoves something down my throat.

"D-D-Dad," I choke out, gagging on the acrid taste of the pill. "What's happening to me?"

"You're just having a panic attack. I gave you something to calm down. Get back into bed and sleep." His voice is calm and soothes my pounding heart as he wraps a towel around my shoulders.

But the ache in my chest…

It's unbearable.

"Dad, it hurts," I tell him, a sob hanging in my throat. "Something's gone."

His eyes search mine and he nods. "Baylee's safe. Go to sleep and I'll have her visit you when you're feeling better."

Baylee. Blue eyes. Blonde hair. Breathtaking smile. An angel.

Nodding, I stumble over to my bed and climb in under the covers. It's warm and smells good. Like her. Like the missing piece of my heart.

She's safe, he'd said.

I let out a sigh of relief and with it hope to push the confusion out, too. Three long breaths later and I'm losing my hold on consciousness.

The pounding in my head is intense. And the sun shining in on me is practically blinding me. I squint and try to recall the night before.

Why the fuck do I feel like death warmed over?

Why do my muscles ache as if I ran a fucking marathon?

And why in the hell do I feel like I could sleep for a week?

I sit up and take in my surroundings. The bathroom door is wide open with the light on. A towel is on the floor halfway between here and the bed. And voices.

A rich, deep, loving one.

A sweet, soft, beautiful one.

I love these voices and want to hear more of them. As if on cue, I hear heavy footsteps thundering my way. When they stop, Dad stands in the doorway. He's dressed casual today in a pair of jeans and T-shirt. His hair is messy and he has dark circles under his eyes.

"Hey, Dad. What're you doing here?"

He frowns and casts a glance over his shoulder before stepping over to the bed. "You had another delusional episode. I'm here to make sure you don't hurt yourself and…"

I squint at him, not understanding his words.

"Baylee. I don't want you to hurt Baylee either."

My heart flutters to life and begins galloping out the door past him. "I need to see her." I'm already stumbling out of bed and heading my naked ass to my closet. He starts making my bed knowing I won't leave this room until it's done.

"Warren, do you remember much from last night?"

I remember dinner. I remember the dress. Baylee's amazing fucking body. I remember making love to her and holding her tight. It was heaven.

"We made love," I admit as I dress.

He remains silent until I come out. I button my shirt and regard him with a raised brow.

"What, Dad? You said to wait until she was eighteen. She's eighteen now. And," I say almost shyly, "I think I love her."

His gaze falls to the floor and he clenches his jaw. "Do you remember hurting her?"

I gape at him. "What?"

"Last night," he reveals, "you became severely paranoid and delusional. You struck her, Warren. And then you shoved her."

The blood drains from my head and dizziness washes over me. "N-No. You're mistaken. I would never hurt her."

He walks over to me and frowns. "Son, she's bruised on her arm and winces when she walks. She's trying to play it off but she's hurt. Whatever you did to her, hurt her."

I struck my Baylee.

The woman I made love to not once but three times.

This can't be.

"I need to see her," I snap and storm barefoot down the hallway. When I reach the living room, she's curled up on the couch sipping coffee. Her eyes are red and she looks like she's been crying. The devastated look she regards me with crushes my soul.

"Baylee." I stalk over to her but stop just before I reach her. I want to touch her and hold her and kiss her. But as I reach my hand toward her, I know I won't be able to. "I'm so sorry. What have I done?"

Tears well in her eyes and she looks past me to my dad. "Are you hungry?"

Her weak attempt to change the subject unnerves me. Of course I'm not fucking hungry. I'm worried sick that I abused the only woman who heals me.

"No. Jesus, Bay. What happened? Whatever it is, I am so sorry."

A tear trickles down her cheek and she nods. "I know. I'm not upset with you, War. You weren't really yourself."

Running my fingers through my hair, I suppress a rage-filled scream. "Are you afraid of me?" If she is, I'll pack her bag now and send her back home to the safety of her parents.

She shakes her head and the tears continue to spill. "I'm afraid *for* you. Things were perfect and then…" she trails off and lets out a ragged sigh, "you were gone."

I clamp my eyes closed and try to remember what happened.

Flashbacks of my dream of Mom and Constance.

Flashbacks of the scalding shower.

Of Baylee trying to help me. I did hit her. I did push her away from me. I'm worse than Gabe. I'm the rotten filth of the earth. I am sick and undeserving of someone as perfect as her.

All it would take was one bullet.

That's all it took for Mom.

No pain of having miscarried. No depression and grief at having lost a child. Nothing.

Click and boom.

Her life ended and she was nothing but sticky blood

painted on my shirt.

I shudder. Could I do that to my father again? Spray my brain all over the walls and leave him to clean it up. What would that do to Baylee? Somehow, I don't think it would make her happy. In fact, I think, perhaps she'd be crushed and ruined. The thought of ruining her steals my breath.

She's a perfect, pure, sweet smelling gardenia.

And all I do is crush her in my fist.

"Warren, I'm hungry."

Her voice snaps me from my dark thoughts and I stare at her. She's standing now and the sun surrounds her from the windows giving her an angelic aura. Such a vision.

"I'm hungry for pizza," she says in a firm tone. "And either you can make me some of your vegan crap or I'll call Pizza Palace. Since it's my birthday, I think you owe me." Her lips curve up into a sweet smile and I can't help but reciprocate.

Of course I'll cook her something.

I'll give her anything she wants.

XXIV | Baylee

I LIFT MY HAND FROM THE WARM WATER AND SIGH. TODAY started off terribly but it ended well. When War woke up in the wee hours of the morning flipping out, I hadn't known what to do. His eyes were crazed and he spoke like a madman. All I wanted was to calm him.

But he was far from calm.

He'd hit me when I tried to turn the water cooler but it didn't deter me, despite the strength with which he'd struck. Now I'm sporting a big purple bruise. When he shoved me though, I was frightened. I'd landed hard on my butt and my breath was knocked from me. All I could think was to call Land and get his help. Turns out, he lives less than five minutes away, and was here before I could formulate what to do next. I was thankful when he'd gone in there, forced War to take a Xanax, and then put him to bed.

Land makes me feel safe. Not that I'm afraid of War. I'm afraid of that monster that lives inside of War's head. A monster that I don't really know or understand but would be glad to murder any day of the week. War is a victim of that beast which only managed to stay away for a little while before he came raging back with claws bared and a thirst for blood.

This is normal.

This is who he is.

This is War.

Land's words keep replaying over and over in my head. I selfishly wish I could fix my War. Help him heal and become human again.

This afternoon, he'd returned mostly to his normal self. He obsessed over the homemade pizza and even threw a conniption when Edison showed up with a store-bought chocolate cake. But, to make me happy, he suffered through and watched with a frown as I ate it up. It wasn't until I licked my lips and flashed him a seductive grin that he seemed to relax about the cake.

I'd actually enjoyed spending my birthday with War, Land, and Edison. It made me miss Mom and Dad more but Dad still won't respond to my e-mails. To say I'm hurt is an understatement.

The alarm sounds as it activates and I sigh. Land and Edison must have gone for the evening. That leaves me alone with War and I'm not sure how things are with us. I'd like to think that we could forget about his episode last night but I can't be certain. All I know is that I miss him.

I hear a timid knock followed by the sound of his voice. "Baylee? Can I come in?"

I shiver and turn to see his powerful presence standing in the doorway. His gaze falls to the water where my naked body is hidden beneath a sea of foamy bubbles and I can't help but smile. I like that he's distracted by thoughts of my body.

"Yeah."

He awkwardly makes his way into the small bathroom and sits on the edge of the tub. His jaw clenches as his eyes drag along my wet flesh. "I'm so sorry."

I lift my hand from the water and draw hearts in the suds. "What happened?"

A loud sigh escapes him and he pinches the bridge of his nose. "I have a delusional disorder. When my OCD gets severely out of control on occasion, I'm more prone to episodes sparked by paranoia and fear and my haunting past. The crash from the pill and the wine coupled with memories of my mom were too much. I spiraled out of control," he huffs out and meets me with a serious stare. "If I'd done something to you…"

I shake my head. "Don't even think about it. Yes, you hurt me. Will I heal? Quickly. But for me to be with you, I need to understand you. I want to help you, War. You have to open up to me."

His lips press into a firm line. "I know and I'm working on it. I hate not being in control of myself. It's embarrassing for you to know all the broken, wrong parts of me. I fucking hate the way this shit rules my life."

I scrunch my brows together and recall some of the things I'd learned while researching his conditions. "You know there are psychotherapies you could try. A therapist could help."

He grumbles but nods. "I think with time—with you—I could try them again. I want to get better for you, Baylee."

Sitting up in the water, I watch him as his gaze falls to my breasts. "We'll get through this. You know that right? I know we'll find a way to be together."

A breathtaking smile spreads across his face. The man is

handsome and when he smiles, the world tilts on its axis.

"You're beautiful. And I'm lucky you haven't run for the hills."

I laugh and splash at him, loving the now boyish grin I'm met with. "Who says I'm not planning to run tomorrow?" I tease but then regard him seriously. "I'm not going anywhere. I was actually hoping you could make love to me again." I'm not sure if he'll take my bait but am thankful when his eyes darken.

"You still want me? Even after..." he trails off, shame morphing his features into a frown.

"I can't help but want you. I mean look at you," I tell him playfully, "you're hot."

He flashes me a wicked smile that makes its way straight to my core. "You're an amazing woman, Baylee. Don't ever think for one second that you're anything less," he says softly. "When you get out, I have something for you."

As soon as he's gone, I'm already standing in the tub, eager to find out what he wants to give me. His gifts always make me happy. I dress in my robe sans underwear and smile to see him stretched out on my bed.

"That was quick," he says with a smirk. "You and your love for presents."

I laugh and bounce on the bed beside him, careful not to touch him. Once I'm settled, he opens his palm up to me. Inside are two rose gold earrings in the shape of a heart with a *B* inside.

"These are pretty," I say softly and open my palm to him so he can drop them into my hand.

He flashes me a shy smile as he gives them to me. "That first day when you longingly stared out at the ocean and wrote your initial with a heart around it on the foggy glass, I'd been a little fucked in the head about you marring my clean glass. But then…"

"I don't even remember doing that. It used to drive Dad crazy when I'd write on the windows of his car but Mom always said they were little Baylee notes left all over, and that he should appreciate them." My voice wobbles and I choke down the emotion of thinking about her.

"Well, I did appreciate it. For once, I didn't strive for perfection," he says, "I wanted something better than perfection. I wanted you."

"This is so thoughtful. Thank you, War."

He shrugs. "I took a picture of it so the jeweler would get it exact. It may seem obsessive but I really wanted it—"

"They're beautiful, War."

I take my time putting them in each ear and then beam at him.

"Listen, Baylee," he says slowly and brings his gaze from my ears to my eyes. "I'm not going to take that medicine anymore. The side effects always seem to be worse than the actual problem."

He'd confessed earlier today to taking Klonopin before the wine, hence the unusual reactions. My heart sinks and I wonder if that night would be the only night we'd ever spend together.

"But, that being said, I can't stop thinking about you. I can't stop thinking about the way it felt to be inside of you. To kiss you. To make love to you. Medicine or not. Wine or not. I want to try to be with you again." He sighs and scrubs his face with his palm. "I can't promise I'll never have another episode again, but as long as my mind is clear from the drugs,

I vow to never hurt you again. I may not be able to touch you, but I won't ever put my hands on you in anger for as long as you live."

"You know, those pills are meant to be taken each day and not sporadically. Most have a two week or more loading dose before noticeable changes. I've been reading up on ways to help you. You're not giving your body enough time to adjust to them I'm afraid," I tell him firmly.

His jaw clenches but he nods. "Maybe we can research it together. I'm willing to try if that's what you want."

I nod and will the tears away. I miss the man from last night but I also want the man in this bed with me. "So what now?"

He leans forward and tugs at the rope on my robe. It falls open and reveals my breasts. "We see what happens."

"See what happens," I murmur as I slip out of the robe and toss it away.

He climbs off the bed and undresses. I'm in awe of his sheer, masculine beauty. All contours and curves. Beautiful. He strides off and returns with a towel. "I'd feel more comfortable with this underneath us."

I smile and nod. My eyes never leaving his, I climb onto the bed and lie on his newly situated towel. His entire body trembles as he watches me with both fear and anticipation. The eagerness squashes his apprehension because he slowly slides between my spread legs.

"Focus on me, War. Focus on how good I make you feel. Kiss me. Don't think, just do."

He launches himself on me and our lips smash together. I let out a moan that has his erect cock pressing against my belly. Running my fingers up his ribs, I then rake them through his hair.

I need this man. Desperately so.

"Make love to me."

"God, Bay," he groans as he positions his cock against my entrance. "I can't think when I'm with you."

I cry out when he pushes into me. "Good. Don't think. Just be with me."

Our mouths tangle again and he bucks into me over and over again. The slapping of our flesh echoes in my room and with each pound into me, I grow closer to orgasm. My body thrums with desire for him to touch me all over, but right now, I'll take what I can get. His mouth on mine, his body connected inside of me—it's enough.

"So perfect," he chants over and over again.

My body writhes beneath his, growing closer with each breath to an incredible orgasm only he can give me. "I'm close."

He grunts and his finger finds my throat. His strong hand cradles my neck and he holds me as he loses himself to a body shuddering climax. My name is on his lips—a violent whisper as he releases more of his inner hell by means of pleasure.

The heat that pours into me stings but it signals my own climax. I cry out and give in to the bliss he saturates me with.

This has to be love.

Thirty minutes later, we're sufficiently cleansed—after an almost too hot shower—and are curled up in his bed this time.

"You're the sun on the horizon. I ache for you," he says in a soft, pained voice, his eyes falling to my lips. "I don't get it, Bay. If I think hard enough about it, I start obsessing over something crazy; tainted meat or airborne bacteria. It consumes me. But all it takes is looking at you and the storms that rage inside of me suddenly dissipate."

He runs a tender thumb along my cheek and I shiver with delight.

"All I care about is you, woman. You're my peace."

"Then make love to me again, Warren. Take me over and over again until we become one."

And he does.

Three times in fact.

Three more towels and three more showers later, I'm exhausted but happy. He holds me in his strong arms and I melt at his touch. Nothing else exists with War. Just us.

"Still no response?" War calls out from the kitchen.

I stretch my long legs out and wince in pain. Every muscle aches this morning. Yawning, I set my laptop on the table and turn to watch him. His back is turned as he cuts vegetables for breakfast. "Nothing. It's so weird. Dad can be a jerk sometimes but it's strange for Mom to not ever respond. She isn't one to get mad or hold grudges. It makes no sense. Do you think something happened to her? Do you think Gabe did something to them?" A shudder wracks through me at the possibility.

He walks from the kitchen into the living room and regards me with a frown. "The money keeps getting withdrawn according to my research. I don't understand why they aren't speaking to you." I wonder about his methods of research but seeing how he flies through screens on the computer, I can bet they're illegal means of obtaining information.

"How much have you been sending them? I'm not going to leave you no matter what, so you may as well tell me."

He lets out a rush of air and darts his gaze to the ocean. "Only fifty thousand a day."

I blink at him and wait for him to laugh. To tell me he's joking. But he doesn't.

"Wait," I say carefully, "you said you were sending them a little at a time."

He nods and heads back for the kitchen. "That is a little."

Considering Dad only made forty-seven thousand in a year, I'd say his wire transfers are more than a little. Jumping up from my seat, I hurry into the kitchen after him. "War, that is not a little. That is ridiculous. You let me scream and yell at you—bribe you with my body. All along you were sending outrageous sums. Mom should have been more than able to afford a liver transplant. Why aren't they responding to me?"

He stalks over to me and draws me to him. I'll never tire of his comforting presence. I inhale him and lean my forehead on his chest.

"I don't know. I didn't want to tell you but I've been all over the Internet searching for a trail on them. What they're doing. Everything seems normal. Debit card is being used. Bills are getting paid. And my transfers are being withdrawn. I'm not sure what's going on but everything appears to be business as usual there. I'll keep checking into it though."

I nod as he pulls away and continues making our food but my mind is still flitting through a million what-ifs. The worst what-if is…what if they're dead?

That thought is unbearable and I won't give voice to it. Instead, I'll focus on my time with War and together we'll figure out a way to expose Gabe. Then, I'll sort out making amends with my parents.

This will work.

War is my happily ever after.

XXV | War

Two months later...

THAT MOTHERFUCKER IS SMART. IT'S AS IF HE KNOWS I'M tracking his ass. Dad and I have been working to find evidence against the White Collar Trade I'd bought Baylee from and have even passed along the information to Detective Stark who asked me a billion more questions I didn't know the answers to. I still cringe thinking about my reasoning and stupidity for acquiring Baylee in the first place. But, I will never be sorry for rescuing her. Because, in the end, she's out of that bastard or any bastard's clutches. She's safe and I will never let her go.

I sigh as I sift through more land records in search for this cabin Baylee spoke of. Gabe no longer lives next door to her house. Records indicate a new family moved in not long after he abducted her. I just need to locate where he went.

"Do we have any crackers?"

I click off the land records and swivel in my desk chair to

look at my woman. It amazes me that she was able to drag me from the hellish depths of my mind back to reality. I still have difficult days from time to time. I still won't touch meat even if it is the only thing left on the planet to survive on. And of course I don't go to the beach with her, or anywhere else for that matter.

But I *can* touch her.

I even managed to give Dad the world's most awkward hug the other day.

Baylee spends all day long researching OCD psychotherapies and makes me try some of them since I refuse to be seen by a therapist just yet. I'm not ready but I keep assuring her I will be. Mostly the therapies she's found involve retraining my brain and talking through the pain of what happened to Mom. I might not be close to being completely healed, but I'm happier than I've been in my entire life. Dad practically lives over here because not only does he adore my girl, but he loves being able to spend time with his son free of afflictions for the most part.

"Did you look on the bottom shelf in the pantry? I think there still may be a sleeve," I tell her. Anxiety infects my chest and my heart begins to race once I really take in her appearance. "Are you okay? You look pale, Bay."

She makes a face and groans, crossing her arms over the T-shirt she's wearing. "I don't feel so hot. I'm going to call Land to see if he'll bring me some ginger ale."

I stand from my chair and walk over to her. "Do I need to call a doctor? Dad is friends with one who could come over."

"No," she mutters and accepts my hug. "I'll be fine. Just feeling a bit blah today. Maybe I've been running too hard lately."

I frown but slide my hands down to her ass. She's not wearing panties under the oversized shirt she stole from me and if she weren't feeling so sick, I'd already have dragged her back to our room to make love to her.

Now that I can more easily touch her, I find it hard keeping my hands off her. There are certain things I haven't yet been able to bridge—the idea of oral sex, for example, still seems abhorrent to me, giving or receiving—but we have sex more than most humans do, I'm sure. Recently we've done it doggie-style a few times too. I feel like, in time, I'll jump all the hurdles between us and nothing will stand in our way ever again.

"Go call Dad and put some pants on before I try to make you better with my cock," I tell her with a growl. "I'll finish up in here and then I'll make you something to eat."

She giggles. "Such a tease, Warren McPherson."

I grin crookedly at her. "I love you, Baylee. I just want you to know that. Through sickness and in health," I promise and my smile falls. "I know you don't believe that—that I'll run at the first sign of illness. But I won't. I'm here, beautiful. Always."

She sniffles and presses a kiss against my chest. "I love you too."

With a smile, I kiss her hair and release her. "Good, now go grab some crackers."

Once she's gone and I'm settled at the computer, I start perusing the records again. I toggle back and forth between screens looking at remote cabins outside or near the San Francisco area and cross-reference them to the land records.

Nothing.

With a sigh, I open a new search and go back to hunting

for the sex ring site. You can't just type in White Collar Trade and find it. Last time, it had been pure luck when I'd found it. Apparently these people create a new website each time and kill the previous after the event. I have to back track back to when I found the one Baylee was at from one of Dad's client's servers. There are no other sites on his computer and I want to scream.

Until…

I keep thinking back to the man who ran the event. Surely there is a lead there. He'd only referred to himself as "Buck" and we'd never met in the flesh, but he'd mentioned that proceeds from the event would go to his wife's pediatric association at the hospital. I do remember the hospital name he'd spoken of when we'd talked over the phone. A few searches later and I've found her hospital, name, and husband.

Forrester "Buck" Whitehead.

And the very first thing that shows up on his Facebook page is a link to his obituary.

My stomach flops as I follow the link dated last week.

Murdered.

In his office.

Items stolen from his files.

"Fuck!"

I'm out of my seat and stalking out of the office without a backward glance.

"Baylee!" I call as I stride down the hallway. "Baylee, we have a serious fucking problem!"

When I round the corner, I freeze.

My Baylee, my sweet fucking Baylee, is crying silent tears. Her eyes, which were happy ones just moments ago, are pleading for help now, as the monster I hoped to only meet again in hell stands there, in my foyer. He holds his hand over her mouth with one hand, his other bulky arm tight around her waist, a gun in its grip. Her back is against his chest and she breathes heavily.

"Let go of her," I snarl, fisting my hands at my sides. I briefly contemplate what I could use for a weapon. My quick assessment of my surroundings yields nothing and my heart sinks. "How did you get in here?"

He laughs, the sound dark and evil, and digs the gun into her ribs. "I knocked on the fucking door. My baby opened it right up for me."

She must've thought he was Dad.

Jesus.

Tears roll down her bright red cheeks and she apologizes with her eyes. My Baylee.

"Let go of her."

He shakes his head. "Actually, Warren *McPherson*, I will *not* let go of her. She's mine. Always was and always will be."

I start for him but he halts me with his words.

"Take another step and I'll put a bullet in her skull. Just like Mom. Isn't that right? Your mom blew her fucking brains out all over you. That's what made you into such a goddamned nut job?"

Bile rises in my throat and I can almost feel the sticky residue on my flesh. "Gabe, please. If you want money, I can give you fucking money. You can have it all. Just please don't hurt her. Leave us and we won't tell a soul."

He drags the barrel of his gun along her rib cage and then between her breasts toward her throat. She whimpers but he doesn't take his hand from her mouth. "I don't want your fucking money. I already have millions from you, asshole.

276

That shit doesn't compare to the tightness of this little one's ass. Some things, money can't buy. Time's up. Baylee's coming home with me."

I charge for him but he shoves the barrel inside of her mouth. Jesus Fucking Christ. If that gun goes off. My Baylee will be... She'll be...

Images of what damage the bullet could do to her horrify me. I claw at my head in an attempt to run them away from my mind. There'd be no way she'd survive. Her blood would splatter the wall behind them—like Mom's coated the front of me that day she delivered Constance too soon.

So.

Much.

Fucking.

Blood.

"D-Don't..." I clench my eyes closed. *I don't know what the fuck to do!*

"Open your eyes, asshole. You need to see this."

I open my eyes and glare at him. Her eyes stay on mine as she sobs. I've never seen her so terrified—so upset. It scares the shit out of me. I want her smiles back, goddammit!

"Suck on the barrel, Baylee. Let's show your boyfriend how you always obey me," he murmurs against her hair. "How you're *my* good girl."

She shakes her head, but he rams the gun deeper inside making her gag. The morning sun pours in through the windows and blankets them, causing her blonde hair to shimmer in the light. Every bit an angel in the devil's grip. I want to save her. Save my angel that saved me. I want to grab him by the throat and throw him off the balcony. To take his gun from him and paint the sand the color of his blood from his head.

The sound of Gabe's sinister growl fills the room, interrupting my desire to murder him. "You're going to suck on the goddamned gun or I'll fuck your ass with it instead. I know how you like your ass played with, baby."

She opens her mouth, fully accepting the gun, and once again shoots me an apologetic look. What the fuck does she have to apologize for? This bastard is shaming her by using her body for his own twisted enjoyment.

"Good girl. Keep sucking. But one false move, Baylee and I'll pull the trigger."

When he shoves the barrel deeper into her mouth, causing snot to drip down her lip and over her chin, I gag. I fucking gag like a pussy. The demons are revolting in my head, threatening to take over, and I'm trying desperately to keep them under control. He starts to slide the barrel in and out of her mouth to which she squirms.

Don't fucking squirm, Bay. Don't do it.

"Shhhh," Gabe says with a grunt and nips at her shoulder. "You're doing so well. I missed you, baby."

And I watch, unable to protect her, as he fucks her mouth with that gun. Each time he withdraws the gun, it glistens with her saliva mixed with snot and I fight to keep from gagging. Memories of my mother—of Constance—assault me and the room spins around me. Her sobs echo around me only making me feel like less of a man for not being able to help her. I wish I could fucking help her.

I could charge at him.

But he seems the type to pull the trigger because he's a psycho bastard.

He chuckles, the sound dark and revolting to my ears.

"Listen to her breathing picking up," he tells me with a smirk. "I know her better than you. She's enjoying every second of this. My girl is depraved."

I glare at him. "Fuck you."

He laughs but when she starts to wiggle, he snarls against her ear. "Don't fucking try it, baby." She lets out a sob—almost rage-filled as he nibbles at her ear. Her tears don't stop but she sags in his arms. My Baylee is so weak.

"Good girl, sweetheart," he says and drops a kiss to her temple. "And for the next act of our show," he says to me, ignoring her cries. "You get to watch *my* girl deep throat."

My skin grows cold and I start to grow dizzy.

Focus, War.

Don't let this asshole win.

When he's preoccupied, make your move. Charge for him.

"Go to hell," I snap at him before speaking to her. "Bay, hang in there. I love you."

Gabe grabs a handful of her hair and forces her to her knees in front of him. "Your lover boy wants you to hang in there. Can you hang, baby?" he taunts. "Suck on this gun like it's your last goddamned meal. Who knows, maybe it is. Or maybe you'd rather suck on my cock instead. Do you want your boyfriend to watch?"

I snarl and attempt to stay still. She shakes her head in vehemence and heeds his instruction. The moment she starts bobbing her head on the gun, my world tilts again.

Sucking and slurping.

Dark chuckles and whimpers.

My stomach churns at the thought of him accidentally pulling the trigger. Parts of her brain blowing all over my home, covering every white inch of it. I gag again.

Stop fucking thinking about it!

"How's your deep throat these days anyway, baby?"

He shoves his gun as far as it will go and this time, she's the one that gags. Loud, sloppy, wet. A croak echoes off the entryway walls before she sprays vomit all over it and the front of his jeans. Falling to my knees, I claw at my throat. Don't throw up, too. Don't fucking throw up. This shit will be everywhere.

The walls.

The floors.

Her clothes and mine.

FUCKING FOCUS!

He laughs and releases her. "Without further ado, the grand finale…"

I tear my gaze to his. "You're fucking sick."

His gun raises and he points it at me. "And you're fucking dead."

Pop!

Pain explodes in my chest.

Nooooo!

I clutch my chest and hiss when blood blooms out over my fingers. Just like Mom. Just like the day she died. So much blood. It won't stop.

My eyes blink.

One.

Four.

Or was it three.

Black and black and black.

"WAR!!!"

That voice. *Her* voice. It's my heavenly oasis although it sounds distant. I don't want to close my eyes but they're already shut and I'm spiraling into the darkness.

"War is over." The sick twisted voice knifes its way into my darkness.

War is over.

Gone, gone, gone.

Goodbye, my Baylee. You kept me happy from the very first time I laid eyes on you.

I blink them open and get a brief glimpse of her reaching for me as he drags her away.

Closed.

And you kept me happy the last time I laid eyes on you.

Wherever I go, I'll only think of you.

My Baylee.

My Peace.

TO BE CONTINUED...

This is Love, Baby – Coming 3.29.16

My War was over and all was lost. My captor reminded me I was nothing more than his pawn. His agenda never changed...it was always me.

In my War, I'd found not only peace but LOVE. I'd been through a battlefield with my War and LOVE was what brought us to the other side. Our LOVE was beautiful and pure. Undying.

My captor thinks he has won this war. That I will LOVE him. What he doesn't know is this time, I'm the one with the agenda. I'm several steps ahead of him, my War taught me that. I will outsmart him and find peace again.

I'm no pawn, as he underestimates me to be, and he'll soon learn that. A bishop, is no match for a queen. This queen lived to protect her king. There are some games my captor is no longer the best at. Some games he will not win because...

LOVE always wins.

My LOVE will conquer all.

The war has only begun and the winner will be me.

Pre-Order coming in early March!

PLAYLIST

Where is My Mind – Pixies

War Baby – Big Wreck

Fix You – Coldplay

Unsteady – X Ambassadors

Control – Big Wreck

What's Up? – 4 Non Blondes

Fire and the Flood – Vance Joy

Snuff – Slipknot

Stay With Me – Sam Smith

ACKNOWLEDGEMENTS

Thank you to my husband. My peace. Your support during the hard times make the good times that much sweeter. I love you more than life itself. You're my hunky hero and my whole heart.

A gigantic thanks to Nikki McCrae—your constant support, friendship, and assistance mean the world to me. You always go above and beyond the duty of friendship. Thank you for always doing what you can to be not only a great friend but an amazing assistant. Don't ever change because you're one in a million.

I want to thank the people that beta read on this book. Nikki McCrae, Wendy Colby, Elizabeth Clinton, Ella Stewart, Nicky Crawford, Jessica Hollyfield, Mandy Sawyer, Amy Bosica, Shannon Martin, Brooklyn Miller, Robin Martin, Amy Simms, and Sunny Borek. I hope I didn't forget anyone) you guys always provide AMAZING feedback. You all give me helpful ideas to make my stories better and give me incredible encouragement. I appreciate all of your comments and suggestions.

A big thank you to Pepper Winters for guiding me into the darkness. Without your words of encouragement about this book and advice, I'd never have gotten it here. You're an amazing friend and role model. Love you, girl!

Thank you to all of my blogger friends both big and small that go above and beyond to always share my stuff. You all rock! #AllBlogsMatter

I'm especially thankful for my Krazy for K reader group. You ladies are wonderful with your support and friendship.

Each and every single one of you is amazingly supportive and caring.

I am totally thankful for my author group, the COPA gals, for being there when I need to take a load off and whine. Y'all rock!

Vanessa Bridges, thanks again for kicking this book's butt into shape. The work you made me do was incredibly difficult but it made for a better story in the end. I can't thank you enough. Your beta, Manda Lee, rocks too! Love you ladies!

Thank you Stacey Blake for being a superstar. You make my books beautiful and I can't thank you enough.

Lastly but certainly not least of all, thank you to all of the wonderful readers out there that are willing to hear my story and enjoy my characters like I do. It means the world to me!

ABOUT THE AUTHOR

K Webster is the author of dozens of romance books in many different genres including contemporary romance, historical romance, paranormal romance, dark romance, romantic suspense, and erotic romance. When not spending time with her husband of nearly thirteen years and two adorable children, she's active on social media connecting with her readers.

Her other passions besides writing include reading and graphic design. K can always be found in front of her computer chasing her next idea and taking action. She looks forward to the day when she will see one of her titles on the big screen.

Join K Webster's newsletter to receive a couple of updates a month on new releases and exclusive content. To join, all you need to do is go here (http://authorkwebster.us10.list-manage.com/subscribe?u=36473e274a1bf-9597b508ea72&id=96366bb08e).

Facebook: www.facebook.com/authorkwebster

Blog: authorkwebster.wordpress.com/

Twitter:twitter.com/KristiWebster

Email: kristi@authorkwebster.com

Goodreads: www.goodreads.com/user/show/10439773-k-webster

Instagram: instagram.com/kristiwebster